GRAHAM MORT, poet lives in North Yorkshire. He Creative Writing and Transcultural Literature at Lancaster University and a visiting professor at the University of the Western Cape, South Africa. He specialises in literature development work and recent projects have taken him to South Africa, Kurdistan, Vietnam and China. His first book of stories, *Touch* (Seren), won the Edge Hill Prize in 2011; his latest book of stories, *Terroir* (Seren), was published in 2015 and long-listed for the same prize. A new book of poems, *Black Shiver Moss*, appeared from Seren in 2017.

Also by Graham Mort

SHORT STORIES
Touch
Terroir

POETRY
A Country on Fire
Into the Ashes
A Halifax Cider Jar
Sky Burial
Snow from the North
Circular Breathing
Visibility
A Night on the Lash
Cusp
Black Shiver Moss

LIKE FADO

AND OTHER STORIES

GRAHAM MORT

CROMER

PUBLISHED BY SALT PUBLISHING 2020

2 4 6 8 10 9 7 5 3 1

First published in Great Britain in 2020 by
Salt Publishing Ltd
12 Norwich Road, Cromer, Norfolk NR27 0AX United Kingdom

www.saltpublishing.com

Salt Publishing Limited Reg. No. 5293401

A CIP catalogue record for this book is available from the British Library

ISBN 978 1 78463 227 4 (Paperback edition)
ISBN 978 1 78463 228 1 (Electronic edition)

Typeset in Neacademia by Salt Publishing

Printed and bound in Great Britain by Clays Ltd, Elcograf S.p.A

for Maggie

CONTENTS

"The famous saudade of the Portuguese is a vague and constant desire for something that does not and probably cannot exist, for something other than the present, a turning towards the past or towards the future; not an active discontent or poignant sadness but an indolent dreaming wistfulness."

F. G. BELL, *In Portugal*, 1912

LIKE FADO

LIKE FADO

EMPORIUM

T HE WOMAN WAS leaning on the back of a Victorian chaise longue, beaming at him with those deep-set, dark eyes. Keith hesitated. Her daughters had the same eyes. Bright, but with an agate depth. And there he was, reflected in the window: his silver hair tousled, slim in his new coat. His image was superimposed on hers, like two spirits, neither quite real.

The coat was a size too small, really. He'd bought it in the spring sale from Vijay. Vijay Darvesh, nodding, smiling with approval as Keith tried on the coat he'd fetched from the window. He could sell you anything. *Take off your jumper, this is not a coat to wear with a jumper*. Then, *let me open the pockets*. And with a few strokes of the unpicker, he'd released the stitches that held them closed. Until, tilting his head. *It fits perfectly, just perfectly so*. And all with a tinge of regret as if he didn't really want to part with it. Then flashing that perfect smile as he took your credit card, a smile that held just a tincture of pity or triumph. *Enjoy the coat, enjoy, my friend*.

He'd got it home and then had to move the buttons to make it fit, threading them around a match-stalk as Meg had showed him, so that they didn't pluck the cloth. Bloody awkward manoeuvre, but he'd managed it. The fabric was twenty per cent wool and eighty per cent cashmere. Or was it the other way around? That was the problem with sales, wishful thinking took over. Chasing a bargain. Not that he needed to. But he could do with losing half a stone, maybe a bit more. Cycling might do that, a spell with the rambling club if he could face them again.

Keith raised his hand to wave or brush her away, the woman. *Eunice.* Then he changed his mind and was pushing open the door of the shop, the bell jangling over his head. He'd had lunch in The Saracen's. Game pie with a pint of bitter he didn't really want, sitting on his own at a side table, feeling conspicuous. Feeling old. He wasn't used to drinking at lunchtime and felt the flush of alcohol in the overheated shop. Sometimes you did things out of habit. You did things because you didn't know what else to do.

The shop was one of those self-conscious, shabby chic, cleverly old-fashioned affairs. It was fitted out in dark oak and they'd had the sense not to modernise – unlike the old chemist's, which had been gutted of all its beautiful hand-fitted mahogany shelves and cupboards. After all, this was a town that bishops retired to. A town that still had local shops, its supermarket discreetly hidden behind the Health Centre. A town that that sat above a salmon river and faced a line of hills across the valley. Stone walls divided them into chequered fields until half-way up, where they lost the battle with gravity. The rest was bracken and outcrops of gnarled limestone. It was early December and the gullies were striped with snow. Above the river was a churchyard that had been used in a few film shoots. Beyond that, a viewing point beloved of local artists and tourists. So it made sense to appeal to people's sense of nostalgia, some rosy folk-memory of the past. He liked it because everything was close at hand. And Meg liked it because it had an old-world charm. *Solidity.* They'd moved to an Edwardian town-house on the outskirts when they retired.

Keith smiled at the woman, feeling the coat a little tight under his arms, reproaching him. It'd be a crying shame to have to give it to Age Concern. Sod it. The kids could clear it out when he died, the way he'd bundled up Meg's clothes and taken them out in bin liners to the car. He wasn't sentimental, not if things could be of use to someone.

The other clever thing about the shop was that it was neither one thing nor the other: part haberdashers, part antique shop, supplier of fine bedding and tablecloths. You could buy old cotton nightdresses edged with lace, new pillow cases and sheets, hand-stitched quilts, re-upholstered chairs and settees, Welsh dressers, willow pattern plates, china tea sets, footrests, stools, linen chests and rugs from Afghanistan and Persia. Prayer rugs. He and Meg used to look for the deliberate mistake, the false stitch that allowed an evil spirit to escape, put there because only God was perfect. The shop was a real emporium and Meg had loved to linger there, marvelling at rich brocades, trying out cushions that were tastefully refurbished in antique patterns. And the three women were always there, quietly in attendance.

The shop was double fronted and there was a border terrier on a cane chair in the window, sleeping away its old age. The rooms ran back, three-deep, so it was like entering the shade of a bazaar, journeying deeper into its mystery. There was something Oriental about it, something of the cultural collision of empire. East meeting West. A sense of opulence. Keith let the brass sneck click behind him with the weight of the door. The shop smelled faintly of floor polish, lavender and joss sticks and something else you could never quite place. The older woman smiled her shrewd smile and met his eyes in that direct way they had.

- Good afternoon!

They all spoke with soft Northumbrian vowels. That seemed another quirk of the shop's special atmosphere. The mother's teeth were stained with lipstick. Keith had managed a dental practice in Newcastle for twenty years. Free check-ups were a perk. It was hard not to zone in.

- Good afternoon.

There was a slightly satirical acknowledgement of this formality on both sides, a playful ritual between old friends. Keith had hardly been out and about in months. Just quick visits to the supermarket and post office, the doctor's. Partly because he'd turned his ankle at the funeral when Meg's sister stumbled against him, waving her hanky, milking the occasion for all it was worth. The bruise had gone from blue to yellow, his puffy skin threaded by tiny purple veins. He'd dreaded going out. The awkward questions, the solicitude, the falsity of it all. He'd not been to this shop in over a year. Something in the woman's gaze had invited him in. Now here he was, not quite knowing how to carry it off.

Eunice. He could never call her that, it was too intimate somehow. She smiled and made way for him. And there were her daughters. Small-boned women who hardly came up to his shoulder. One with page-boy hair, and one who wore it shoulder length. Black hair, finely textured. And those eyes that seemed to glitter in the gloom at the back of the shop. Like the eyes of Turkish women they'd seen at the market in Istanbul. The older one with the short hair wore riding boots and a flared skirt, the younger one had close fitting slacks and an embroidered jacket. They both wore open-necked blouses. There was something about them. He couldn't think of the right word. *Ingenuous?* And that was unfair, because they

4

never exhibited the slightest curiosity about him. Why would they when he was almost as old as their mother? But it was uncanny the way the three of them had the same eyes. The way they glowed with inner darkness. The way they followed you around the room.

Keith took an interest in a half-glazed earthenware pot that doubled as an umbrella stand, almost tripping over the rug. Halifax-ware, probably a potato pot originally. But the lid had been broken and the base was chipped. The dog looked up at him, pointing its ears and making a low rumble in its throat.

– Sky, don't be silly.

Keith chuckled at the dog's readiness.

– I think I startled him.

– Go back to sleep, you daft thing.

The older woman shushed him and the dog lay back down, putting back its ears, yawning, mooning its eyes. The young women smiled indulgently, showing almost identical white teeth. Small and sharp and slightly backward slanting.

A middle-aged couple emerged from the middle room and pushed past Keith into the street, zipping up their Barbour jackets. You could smell the money on them, but they hadn't bought anything. He edged into the room where an elderly lady in a pale cream coat was testing some cushions on a settee. Her cheeks were rouged and her legs stuck out like sticks as she sat down and stood up again. She reminded him of a Punch and Judy puppet, her glasses bobbing to the front of her nose. Keith nodded to her and moved into the far room. There were some gilt-framed Victorian prints standing against the wall, a dressing table, a quartet of high-backed chairs and a large reproduction mahogany desk. They'd even spilled ink on the writing pad to make it look authentic. Then a flat-topped display case with silver earrings and brooches, some jet funeral pieces and others studded with garnets, malachite and onyx. Keith pushed up his spectacles and peered into the case, a silver brooch in the shape of a curled fern snaring his eye. It was delicately made with lots of fine detail. He saw his own face in the glass like a ghost in those fake photographs. Then the older of the two sisters was beside him.

– Would you like to see anything?

She wore the key to the cabinet around her neck. She smiled and her eyes were almost black in the dim room. Those neat, even teeth. For a second she reminded him of Meg. How stupid. Keith pointed into the case.

– That brooch, the silver one. It's unusual.

– The fern design? The Victorian loved them. They crop up everywhere. See?

The young woman pointed to the settee and the upholstery was a pattern of ferns curling into each other.

– Ferns were quite the vogue at one time. Would you like to see it?

Keith nodded and she bent down to unlock the case. There was the faint scent of her perfume. So close. He shut out the thought. She was holding the brooch out to him and he took it. It was beautifully made. Surprisingly heavy for its size. He checked the back for a hallmark.

– It's real silver.

Her voice was a little sharp, as if he doubted her.

– Yes, I can see. Just about . . .

He squinted at the markings, pushing up his varifocals, smiling apologetically.

– *Anno Domini*. Comes to us all . . .

– Pretty, eh? Your wife would love it.

6

- Yes, she would.

There it was. A lie? Almost. Though a lie was something you told on purpose to deceive. He was just being polite. He'd replied without thinking. But Meg *would* have loved the brooch. It was just her kind of thing. What was he supposed to say now? To add casually that it was a shame she'd been dead almost a year? What good would that do? He wondered what had drawn him back here. Memory? Habit? A way of stepping back into the past as if what followed had never happened? He'd avoided them so far, their old haunts. He handed the brooch back, his fingers touching the woman's palm. It felt hot.

- Thank you. I'll think about it. I've got a few things to do . . .

He sounded more abrupt than he meant to.

- You're welcome.

A little laugh, then a crimping of lips that were touched with pink gloss. He was flustered now, trapped by his untruth. As the woman locked up the cabinet, Keith pretended to inspect an ornately carved Burmese rocking chair. A family of five - parents and three kids - in wellingtons and fluorescent jackets came in and began fussing around a large oak chest. *But can you date it*, the blonde woman kept saying, *accurately, I mean?* He made his escape, tilting his head in farewell he found the door and exited under the *chang, chang, chang* of the bell. The dog looked up and then went back to sleep.

It was cold. Late afternoon. A bitter little breeze was stirring litter in the town square. His face was flushed and his ears felt hot. As he glanced back through the window, the younger daughter, hand on hip, was asking the older one a question. The older one shrugged, fingering the key and glancing towards the door. He was sure they were talking about him. He'd dreamed about them once. That there was another room deep in the shop with a four-poster bed in which all the women slept in long cotton nightshirts. There were candles and velvet drapes. Weird. He'd forgotten about that until now. It was strange how things came back like that. Random thoughts. Fragments that made no sense. Unless you believed that dreams meant something. He moved on quickly from their line of sight.

Three-thirty. Too early to go home to an empty house and microwave something. Too late to catch the rugby on TV. He was wearing a decent pair of brogues and wondered about the river walk. He could use some exercise after that lunch. It squatted in his stomach, pressing against the coat that was slightly too tight.

Keith went through the village square, past the new out-fitters, which catered for all sexes. *Quinne & Starkey*. A made-up name meant to sound traditional, dependable. In fact, it was run by some middle-aged dandy in tight trousers who dyed his hair and wore paisley-pattern waistcoats. The lane led down to the river walk. There was just time to make the circuit before it went dark. Keith felt a pressure on his bladder from the pint and slipped into the public conveniences. They were few and far between these days. The smell of ammonia and disinfectant stung his nose. He stepped carefully over the wet tiled floor. He'd bought a shirt at that new shop last summer and the man in the waistcoat had offered him a complimentary fragrance. *Fragrance?* Keith had looked blank. He wasn't about to start wearing perfume at his time of life. He drew the line at sandalwood shaving cream. There was none of that sort of rubbish about Darvesh. You knew where you stood there.

Keith passed water in one of the cubicles, holding back the wings of his coat with his elbows. He zipped up and flushed the toilet. The plumbing groaned as if there was a demon trapped in the piping. A *djinn*. Was that what they called them? He washed his hands. No soap, of course. The hand dryer was broken and he dabbed them on the damp roller towel, trying not to think of the germs. He buttoned his coat, his fingers slipping on its tight buttons.

When he left the toilet the dandy in the outfitter's was reaching into the window for something. His hair was thinning like everyone else's. You couldn't hold that back. Vijay knew what a man wanted and he wasn't about to start stocking handbags and cosmetics – or *fragrances*, for that matter. Meg would have laughed, of course, flicking back the grey hair she'd started to wear very short, cut into her neck. *Why not, you silly thing?* She'd got him pulling his nasal hair and trimming his eyebrows. That was enough. Funny, how all that hair sprouted as you got older.

It was a degree colder if anything. Keith tucked in his scarf and pulled up his collar, leaving the town centre on a path that led past a new housing development. Just boxes, really, each one had a black solar panel on the roof, but not a chimney amongst them. The path dipped down sharply then curved towards the old stone bridge. In summer, kids jumped from the parapet into the river. The pool below was flanked by rocks where couples sunbathed or urged their Labradors into the water. You could see the youngsters daring each other, then there'd be a cheer as one of them found the courage to fall. It had become quite a spectacle, like the dozens of motorcyclists who gathered for tea and bacon sandwiches at the mock Tudor café further along. In summer they made a killing.

Just before the bridge on the left-hand side, there was a kissing gate. Keith went through it to the river path. He held the gate open out of habit, then let it close with a clang. They must have done this walk a hundred times. The river was high. Brown with peat, it surged between boulders and outcrops of limestone. A woman came past with two muddy beagles on a lead, dragging the dogs away from him with an apology. Keith smiled at her, catching their wet tang. He moved on, turning sideways to allow a couple and their kids to get by. The path had been recently gravelled and made for easy walking. His shoes crunched. Satisfying. At one time it would have been a quagmire. The council had got some things in hand, at least. There was the cricket ground on the left with the little timber pavilion. It'd been a good few years since he turned his arm over. He'd played until he was fifty-six, bowling leg-spin and batting low down the order. Coming home late for dinner, falling asleep in the bath with a whisky. Meg hadn't minded. She understood why he still had to do it. Because there had to be more to life than work. A torn back muscle had put paid to all that. He still felt it when he got in and out of the car.

The path was badly eroded in places, where the river curved and undermined its banks. In different phases of conservation, the council had laid concrete blocks, driven timber piles and dropped wire cages of boulders to protect it. Unchecked, it would wash everything away, eroding the banking, bringing down the town above it. Further on it parted around a little island overgrown with willows, then joined itself again.

Sometimes there was a heron waiting in the shallows. In the deep pool at the far end of the walk, salmon and sea trout rose or leapt clear of the water. Fisherman waded out from a gravel bank to stand thigh-deep with their rods and landing nets. But not today.

Light was fading now, the river supple, gleaming like eel skin. Keith went through another gate, stepping down awkwardly over the rocks on the far side. Here there was a house set back from the water – a converted mill of some sort – then the path ended in a row of iron railings where the banking became too dangerous, dropping away to the current. Next to the house was a churned mud paddock. A white horse tapped its hooves against the metal gate, a restless ghost in the dusk. The gate tolled like a bell. Then a long climb of steps led up to the viewing point and the churchyard. Keith set off up them steadily, feeling his heart rate rise. *What doesn't kill you* . . . well, maybe. He paused gallantly to let a stout woman in a purple fleece get past on her way down. Then he made it to the top, chest pounding. The woman had smiled at him, ruefully. As if they were in it together. Old age. But it was in them, really.

The viewing point overhung the banking and showed a perfect view. Picturesque. The river had planed a wide flatland, leaving a curved terrace in the middle distance in front of which nestled a farm. Beyond that, a line of dun-coloured hills with those streaks of snow. The side of the sheet-metal barn was painted in outrageous candy-stripe colours. That was about planning permission being refused, the farmer's way of hitting back. He'd seen something about it in the local paper, laughing with Meg one Saturday after they'd lain in bed a little longer, then breakfasted on coffee and toast and soft-boiled eggs. One of their rituals now that getting up didn't matter much. They still fitted together nicely in bed, her face against the pillowslip like the face of a girl in the dim light. Making love gently and without haste. Strange, how he still saw the girl in the woman, as if time hadn't flowed on at all. Somehow the rainbow-coloured barn had become a local feature, a quirk of humour that people had appreciated and become fond of. After all, it did no harm in the end, upsetting the way things were. The colours glowed now in the setting sun.

Keith turned into the graveyard where a granite church was surrounded by yews. There was a low perimeter wall and beyond it rows of stone-built houses, yellow lights burning. The vicarage was set in a space of its own to the north side, accessed by a cobbled lane. A set of iron gates led back into the main street. The gates had an ingenious self-closing mechanism. Pushing the gates allowed them to rise on rollers that went up a greased iron slope. Gravity made them roll back down and close again. No special effort needed. It all worked beautifully, elegant and simple. He'd pointed them out to Meg whenever they passed this way. He'd probably bored her with it all.

It was gone four-thirty now and the lights were on in the bookshop and cheese factory, the ironmonger's and the Age Concern shop where he'd taken Meg's things. Then, without quite realising it, he was crying, sobbing out little spasms of air. He turned back into the graveyard before anyone could see him and made for a bench in the church porch, loosening the buttons on his coat to sit. It could happen anytime. Things working away inside you. Things you weren't really aware of. Thoughts of the future didn't go anywhere now.

They couldn't. There was only really one end to it all, to grief, to memories.

Keith sat for a few minutes, catching his breath, feeling the cold strike into his buttocks. There was the stone coffin with its chipped edges. It had been cut for some bishop in the Middle Ages. Meg used to joke that it was about his size. But people were smaller in those days, malnourished, their bones crooked with disease. He was a respectable five foot ten. There was an inscription around the church porch in Latin, but it was eroded and impossible to read. Even if he could have remembered what he'd been taught at school. Centuries of rain had eaten it away. The mower had left clumps of dead grass between the headstones. A thrush was hopping and stabbing for worms, cocking its head, listening to the earth seething. There were tiny pearls of moisture on its back.

Now there was a commotion at the iron gates. A long, high cry without words. A shriek that went right to Keith's chest, visceral, like the distress of a baby. The thrush took off and perched in a yew tree where it sent out an alarm call, repeating the same phrase. A boy of about fourteen in a red puffer jacket was being led through the gate in a group of five kids and two adults, probably from the special school up the hill. The boy dragged back from the group and called out again. There were mangled words, but Keith couldn't make them out. The boy had glasses and walked with a jerky gait. One of the adults led him to a bench and he let out another howl of anguish, inconsolable, his hands clenched up in front of his face as he was pulling down on a blind.

Keith hunched back against the stone of the church porch. The other kids stood in a half circle: another lad and three girls. They gazed at the adults as they tried to soothe the boy. Keith was trapped by the boy's shrieking. It was dredged from the bottom of his lungs. It was another kind of grief. One of the adults tried to take the boy's arm, but he pulled away, letting out a scream that carried all the way back into the town. People were pausing in the street now, looking anxiously towards the churchyard where the little group was hidden.

Keith rose, buttoning his coat, getting ready to slip away. The paving stones were treacherous with moss. He looped back through the churchyard to the viewing point where he could find another path back into town. That way he wouldn't have to pass the boy rocking there. Wouldn't have to feel this helpless shame. He stood for a moment. Frost seemed to crackle in the grass. Dusk was thickening. There was the moon pulling clear of the horizon, huge and white above the line of hills. There was the glimmer of the river, the outline of farm buildings, the candy stripes blurring. And there were the boy's cries, raising goosebumps on Keith's neck as he veered down a back lane that took him onto the main street between the wine merchant and Vijay's.

Back in the shop, he could have sworn they were waiting for him. The mother lingering in the lit window, watching the street. The dog curled on the cane chair, the dark-eyed daughters hovering at the counter. Keith didn't even speak, he simply nodded at the back room and then followed the eldest daughter there and watched her unlock the cabinet. His glasses misted with the heat in the shop. He could smell her perfume again, stronger this time. Lavender.

She smiled and handed him the silver fern with a faint curtsy. Her eyes seemed to shine. Feverish. When he paid for the brooch, they all gathered around to congratulate him. The older woman in attendance, the daughter who wrapped blue ribbon around Meg's neat little parcel, the daughter who rang up the till and took his debit card. It was the way they all stood so close together exuding … *something* … he couldn't describe what it was, that feeling. The way they were so perfectly *demure* – not the right word either – and yet seemed to give off a glow of their inner selves, a hint of pleasurable appetite. Perhaps that was pride in what they did, what they knew, a kind of worldliness about *things*. There was no harm in that, after all. The older woman touched his arm.

– Give my regards to your wife. I hope she enjoys the brooch.

– Thank you. I will.

– Bye! Bye!

A chorus. He half turned in the doorway. That ironic gentility overcoming him again.

– Until next time.

Keith gestured with the package, tipping it up then slipping it into a side pocket of the coat. He smiled at the young women who stood side by side, regarding him inquisitively. Then he was in the street, seeing them drawing down the blinds and locking the shop door, realising he'd kept them past closing time. He wondered if they knew about Meg. If they'd known all the time.

The bell faded as it jangled to a standstill. He tidied his scarf and tucked his hands into his pockets. Then he made for home, flattening his fingers inside the tight fabric, against the little package that fitted snugly there. Cars pulled away from their parking spaces in the town square, swinging the white scythes of their headlights. There was the moon, voyaging above chimneys and roof slates. There was a single star, pulsing with light. A star that might no longer exist. That old illusion of life after death. He'd learned that on one of those TV documentaries. When we look at the night sky we're really looking back in time. It was unimaginable. Even the mathematics seemed fabulous.

Everything was connected in the end. Salmon and sea trout nosing upstream in the river, leaping the weirs, scenting their birth waters in minute traces of peat. Returning to breed and to die. Their gleaming bodies pinned to the river's surge. The rainbow colours of the barn fading. Cattle herded into ship-pens, mired with dung, blowing out gouts of steam, pulling hay from iron mangers. Sheep straying on the hills, white-faced where darkness was falling. Little owls calling from that island where the river forked. It was all going on around him, beyond him. Life was just messiness, really, but we saw patterns in it. Had to.

It'd be Christmas soon. He'd be invited to stay with Katherine or Simon, when what he really wanted . . . when what he really wanted was somewhere else now. Somewhere in that current of time that they'd trailed their hands in so carelessly.

Keith paused, irresolute, drawing blades of air into his lungs.

Home.

He moved on, his shoes rapping against the paving stones.

Home.

The night pressed a cold mask against his face. He thought he heard the clank of a horse's hooves tolling against a metal gate.

Homeward.

There was that cry again. A little lower, like the yelp of a fox carrying towards him from the churchyard where the boy was.

KARÎN

T HE RIVER FLOWED through level fields. It went
under an iron bridge to her left, a quarter of a mile away.
Then it flowed on, a ribbon of crinkled foil. Zoe had left her
car in the street at the B&B, then walked. She'd almost collided
with a milkman leaving pints of milk and orange juice on the
step. She hadn't seen that in years. The place was chintzy, the
landlady fussing over her. She didn't fancy the breakfast. It
was always like that after a trip, that lingering sense of self-
sufficiency, self-hate.

Clay was sticking to her boots. She could see the town
on the skyline, light catching the windows of tower blocks,
the minaret of the new mosque with its crescent moon. The
women in the mountains had invoked Allah as they gave her
their stories. *Praise be upon him. We will meet again, Insh'allah.*
But they hadn't met again. She'd walked back to the SUV,
following Shamal, her translator. Two days later, there'd been
a Turkish airstrike and the village had been bombed into a
smear of scree – breeze blocks and plaster, dried blood and
thorn-trapped headscarves blowing out over the valley. And
shit. Human shit you could tread in if you weren't careful.
She'd been warned to get out of there. It was *unpredictable*.
Which was ironic when you thought about it. It was all too
predictable.

Zoe clapped her hands together in fingerless gloves, feeling
her palms thud. She sniffed, tasting salt, feeling in her pocket
for a tissue. The footpath slipped downhill and she emerged

from a stand of sycamores into a stubbled field where heaps of manure had been dumped. It steamed in the air, the earth smouldering. There were crows picking through the dung. One took to the air and gave a call to the others, like a grating manhole cover. One by one, they sighted her and took off, following the river towards the sea. She stood to watch a hare loping between furrows, the dark fur on its face parted by wind. It hunkered down, lowering the tips of its ears, as if it knew to a millimetre the dimensions of its own body.

The woman called Karîn had green eyes, the skin of her face pocked with tiny marks from some childhood illness. One eyelid drooped. She had the strong wrists and swollen knuckles of a woman who'd worked the land. The Ba'athists had taken her husband away and looted their possessions. She told how she sat in the emptied house at night with a knife in her lap to protect the children. How her milk had dried up. How she'd walked into Iran with her sisters. *A refugee, imagine! A wanderer.* Stepping along the mountain trails with her baby tied to her back, holding the hands of her other two children – a boy and a girl who hadn't eaten for days. Stumbling from exhaustion, she'd laid her dead baby in the snow and walked on. *I felt nothing. I could not feel.* At the next village the women met a group of neighbours from Rawanduz and shared the little food they had. Some stragglers joined them, one woman carrying a baby she'd found by the path. It had moved its hand and there it was, alive. A miracle. *Praise be. God did not want him to die.* He was grown up now, a Peshmerga soldier, an officer. He'd lived and thrived, somehow.

Zoe crossed the field towards a stile, catching the sharp scent of dung. The path was rutted and there was water in the footprints other walkers had left. This was supposed to be a short-cut, but she felt suddenly uncertain. She took out her phone to get a GPS location, but there was no signal. Lost in the English countryside. That was ironic, too. They'd found a group of women and children huddled in a stone enclosure near the Turkish border. A sheepfold. The old men who had struggled up the mountain with them were trying to weigh down a canopy of plastic sheets with rocks, but the wind was defeating them, tearing the sheeting, shredding speech. One of them had spoken with Shamal. But what they said she never knew. The man's face was etched like stone under his headscarf and she noticed that there were no buttons on his jacket. It was fastened with brass safety pins. They'd left them there, promising to tell the Peshmerga that they needed help. They thought she was a journalist, but that wasn't why she wanted to hear them speak. She'd come for stories of the past. *Al Anfal*. Genocide. Now the present was repeating the past, as if time itself had curdled. *The Kurds have no friends, only the mountains*. That was the saying.

Two days later, she was driving down through limestone gorges, over miles of abandoned farmland to Erbil, racing the weather to catch a flight home. She had their stories on her hand-held recorder. Three weeks of interviews. Snow had fallen into the gloom of the gorge and they had to wait as a shepherd drove his flock of goats past them with two shambling mountain dogs. He'd glanced in at them and the driver had raised his hand to greet him. There was a café opposite a waterfall, a man standing in there alone under a naked strip light. They approached the city through checkpoints, the soldiers hefting Kalashnikovs, peering down at her, a foreigner. Then the suburbs with packs of stray dogs gathered under lampposts where snowflakes whirled. Then security queues, the flight to Istanbul, just in time. Winging through darkness over Turkey, Italy, France. Then England in the rain, patched fields tilting below the plane, drifts of cloud, the runway glistening. Thinking about home and where that might be. Thinking about Emma.

Zoe stepped from the stile to the road. Now there was something familiar in the way the ash trees almost touched together across it. Their branches were tipped with black buds. Emma's house was down a side lane. It was close by. There was rubbish in the hedgerows, thrown from passing cars: cigarette packets, beer cans, polystyrene takeaway trays. She's seen that below Korek, where picnickers thought nothing of throwing their empty bottles at the valley, broken glass glinting in scree, under new almond blossom. Grey streams swollen with melted snow. Now there was a tilted signpost and she was sure, stepping past it to find the driveway on her left. Emma's old Fiesta was there, parked at an angle to the cottage. It was like the houses she'd drawn as a child: four windows and a door, a chimney with a scribble of smoke. The house was still. No smoke. Zoe stamped mud from her boots onto the road. A jackdaw settled on a chimney pot and watched her watching the house.

It was too early to wake Emma and the baby. Although Siobhan wasn't really a baby any more. She was clinging to the furniture, trying to walk, Emma had said in her last email. She'd sent a picture of her chortling in a yellow Babygro or whatever those all-in-one suits were called. Zoe pushed through the garden gate and sat on a bench under the cherry tree. She found a cigarette and lit it with the lighter she'd bought at the airport in Istanbul. She blew a stream of smoke and the jackdaw jerked its head and looked at her, then took off. The curtains of the house were drawn. Sun was just beginning to glint on its windows. Her B&B was about a mile away, on the edge of town. It was where she'd stayed last time, when Emma was pregnant with Siobhan. When everything else was out of kilter, it was good to repeat things, to retrace her steps, to have some familiarity. The landlady had remembered her, or pretended to, and greeted her like an old friend. Now here she was. She'd found the house again. All she had to do was wait, which was doing nothing really, for once in her life.

Damp began to seep through from the timbers of the seat. Zoe stood up and pulled her jeans away from her thighs. She'd fractured her ankle as a kid and in weather like this it ached. She was grinding the cigarette stub under her heel when the curtains of an upstairs room parted and there was Emma in her pyjamas, startled, then waving down at her. Then someone was unbarring the door and she was there, smiling, her blonde hair unruly with sleep, her arms wide. The pyjamas slipped against her skin as Zoe hugged her. Her body felt fuller, more complicated.

– *Brrr!* Bloody hell, you're early!

– Didn't sleep much. Hang on . . .

Zoe unlaced her boots and left them in the porch. Now they were the same height. Emma was pushing the door shut, pulling on a cardigan that was slung over the back of a chair as they entered the kitchen.

– You could have stayed with us, I did say . . .

– I know, I know.

Zoe was pulling off the gloves and stuffing them into her jacket pocket, the same jacket she'd worn at Rawanduz and Sulaymaniyah. She wondered if there were particles of Kurdish soil in the seams or at the bottom of the pockets. There was a Kurdish flag folded in her luggage still, like the one painted on the mountain near Soran. She dropped the jacket over a chair. The house was warm, the radiators heating up. There was an Aga in the kitchen, and she stood with her back to it, watching Emma put the kettle on then find cups.

– Siobhan?

– She's at my mum's. We do a sleep-over every Friday night. She'll bring her round later. Didn't I say in my email?

Emma turned to smile at her, pulling her hair into a bunch over her shoulder.

– Anyway, it's nice to see you in one piece! Good trip?

– Yes, pretty good. Amazing, actually . . .

In one piece. Was she? She felt as if she was in many pieces most of the time. She wanted to kiss Zoe on the neck, just above the collar of her pyjama jacket, against the line of her clavicle where the skin was creamy and smooth and flushed from the kitchen's heat. She could see the outline of her body through the thin fabric when she turned against the light.

– Jordan?

Emma stiffened but didn't turn.

– Oh, he comes around when he feels like it. Same old, same old . . .

– That's tough.

– That's Jordan, remember? A river to be crossed.

Emma turned with the spoon in her hand.

– It's Earl Grey. No sugar?

– No sugar, just a dash of milk.

Emma put the mug of tea on the table.

– I guess I'm getting used to it. Him being fucking useless.

And she laughed, a little laugh of abandonment. A blue vein showed for a moment at the side of her throat. Zoe remembered their nickname for him when they'd been students.

– His Excellency?

– His Excellency!

It'd been Emma's way of dealing with him, even before she got pregnant. *His Excellency's late.* Or, *His Excellency requests that we meet him at seven.* Or, ruefully, when he'd let her down again, simply, *His Excellency, eh?* Spoken with a mixture of affection and scorn and resignation. He'd been charming with his floppy dark hair and quizzical eyebrows, tight-fitting clothes and Doc Martens. With the public-school erudition that he wore so easily. But he'd been a fuckup from day one. They'd been studying for their PhDs. Before Zoe's job at the Peace Institute.

Emma sat at the table. The cuffs of the cardigan came over her hands and she rolled them back. Zoe realized it must be Jordan's.

– Did you get much stuff?

– Lots. It's all to be translated. We've done some of it. But, yeah, lots. Pretty harrowing.

– I'll bet.

She been interviewing older Kurdish women about their experiences of *Al Anfal.* Not the women who'd fought, who were on the TV news every day. But the women who'd fled with their children, the woman who'd survived Saddam's onslaught through the Eighties and early Nineties. But she'd got caught up in a new situation. The Peshmerga fighting ISIS in Syria, the Turks taking their chance to bomb YPG and PPK strongholds. It was only two years since ISIS had murdered thousands of Yazidi men and boys at Sinjar. There were still Yazidi refugees in Soran, where she was based. She told Emma how she'd found them sheltering in the Christian church in Dayana. The way the children had looked at them with their huge, dark eyes. Then she was sobbing ridiculously, and Emma's hand was on her arm.

– Hey, hey, don't cry.

Her voice was convulsing in her chest and she couldn't catch her breath.

– I'm sorry. I don't usually. Fuck!

She dug in her pocket for a hanky, then remembered she didn't have one. Emma passed a box of tissues and she blew her nose. *After they dropped gas, I came back from the fields and gave them milk, my father and my children. They brought it up like cheese.* That was Karîn's story, which wound in and out of all the others somehow. Flowing through past and present. A river swollen with grief. Emma was waiting, plucking at the sleeves of the cardigan and watching her.

– Sorry.

Emma shook her head.

– It's OK, don't . . .

– It was pretty full-on at times. Amazing women. I'll tell you some time . . . when it's easier.

Zoe smiled, dabbing with the handkerchief.

– Sure. I'd like that.

Emma's fingers were warm against hers.

– Come here.

Then they were hugging, and Zoe could feel Emma's body again through the pyjamas, stroking the fabric. Emma giggled.

– Silk! My parents . . .

Her parents were probably paying the rent as well. Emma's body had changed. She'd had a baby, after all, had carried it for months, given birth, then fed it from her own breasts. Zoe saw Karîn laying her baby in the snow, a line of refugees trudging on.

– Come on!

Emma was tugging her hand, leading her upstairs to the rumpled bed that was still warm from her sleep. They undressed and slipped between the sheets, their arms and legs entangled. Then the slow kiss that seemed to stop everything and start everything again. Everything Zoe wanted and couldn't bear. Finding each other again. The lightness of their touch. Skin to skin. Their bodies slipping together like the lost parts of a puzzle. Like they always had. Uncomplicatedly. Making love despite everything. Silencing the things that clamoured. Before Jordan, during Jordan. Now maybe it was after Jordan. Though that was something Emma would never say. She lay against Zoe, smelling of warm skin and sleepiness, her fingers tangled in Zoe's short hair.

– It's probably filthy.

– What is?

Emma sounded sleepy.

– My hair.

– I'm sure it isn't.

Emma pretended to smell it, running her tongue gently around Zoe's throat, until it was unbearable, and she was laughing and begging for mercy and pinning Emma against the pillows all at the same time. Sunlight was still faint at the windows, as if the morning was leaving them to themselves. The house was still, peaceful, apart from the tick of the Aga downstairs as it heated and cooled.

They rose just before lunchtime. Emma showered and Zoe made coffee and toast and boiled eggs, searching for egg cups and plates. They ate together as a band of light slanted between them, talking freely now. The women's stories would be translated into English at the Institute where there was a Kurdish-language expert who also knew Sorani. They'd get versions back to Shamal for checking and then they'd form a research archive. Testimony. A record of a particular time and place, bearing witness. The women's responses to violence and the memory of violence. There'd be a paper to write, but that felt secondary. What mattered most was the women's stories. Their indelible images, their contradictions and silences. What mattered was not anything *she* could say about them, but their own words. Zoe remembered jolting down to Erbil in the back of the pickup on the journey home, the radio blaring, the heater full on, snowflakes driven against the windscreen. The driver shouting incomprehensibly in English, adding, *Insh'allah! Insh'allah!* Everything was in the mind and hands of God. Then the plane rising above city lights and her long flight home through darkness to what little she'd left behind.

Zoe had wanted to see Emma, but she'd deliberately stayed in a B&B, hadn't wanted the temptation of her. And there was Jordan, of course. Jordan who came and went. Jordan whose patina of charm had worn through to a kind of emotional poverty. She'd thought of Emma on the long flight. She'd longed for her. Now here they were, back in the old complications that touch had made simple once upon a time. Though that wasn't true, either. And once upon a time was a fairy tale. She remembered Karîn seated on a low settee, a tray of mint tea between them, a bowl of apples and pomegranates, sugar dissolving in swirling veils. *God spared us*, she'd said, *God wanted us to live.* She remembered that old lady in Erbil, almost deaf, who spoke of an honour killing when she was a girl. How a cousin had been killed by her own brothers, her bloody ear thrown into her mother's lap. She'd framed the story as a traditional tale, seen through a window. *I looked through a small dalaqua. I saw the man striding in the orchard. It was dawn and the birds were singing brightly.* She'd worn a pair of silver earrings, leaning forward to hear Shamal's replies and confirmations. She could neither read nor write, but her memory had shaped the story.

Emma was glancing at the kitchen clock. Hours had passed as they sat at the table. They rose to go for a walk before the cold closed in again. Zoe's boots were still damp. They walked arm in arm along a wooded trail. There was a dead pigeon beside the path, rooks calling from tree tops. Then the crackle of pheasants as they came in to roost. A breeze stirred fallen leaves. Lights came on in the town behind them. Emma snuggled her face against Zoe's shoulder. They met an older couple walking their Labradors, one black and one pale gold. Emma greeted them, but they returned an odd look.

– Spooky pair!

Zoe shrugged.

– What the fuck!

– Question mark or exclamation mark?

– Exclamation mark!

It was an old game. They stopped to kiss, their mouths full of breathlessness and body heat. Then they turned for home through the gaunt trees. Emma skipped on ahead to pick up something she'd seen glinting beside the path. It was a child's plastic bracelet. *Finders keepers!* She used to say that when things turned up. Even if it was the last drop of milk in the fridge when they shared digs. Even if it was Jordan, waiting for them at the bus shelter or in some café. They'd made love in Zoe's attic room with its sloping ceiling, scattered books and papers, the laptop open like a clam, the electric heater filling the air with that dry, dusty smell of winter afternoons. But Zoe had been put down whenever Emma had picked something else up.

The Kurdish women had been fascinated by her short hair. Even the Peshmerga women who fought with Kalashnikovs and rocket launchers wore braided plaits slung over their shoulders. *Where is your husband?* they asked. *You have how many children?* Zoe would shake her head, setting up the little recorder, placing it between them, checking the battery. No husband, no children. *One day*, the women had said, *one day he will come to marry you with wedding gifts, Insh'allah!* Emma put the bangle in her pocket. Emma who'd kissed her so hard that her lips felt bruised. Now she was looking at her as if she'd never seen her before, a look Zoe remembered too well.

They'd argued about it once. Their *situation*, as Emma liked to call it. An act of God or nature. Something they found themselves amongst, as if they'd got lost somehow.

– It has to stop, Zoe.

That was Emma, suddenly pulling away from her when they were riding home on the Metro.

– What? What has to stop?

– It. Us. We have to stop.

– Why now. Why all this now?

They were heading back after a seminar. The train had paused at a platform to let a group of commuters off. Office workers with rucksacks, reading their novels and newspapers standing up. Now a group of girls in short frocks and high heels got on, crowding the doors as they hissed shut. Then into the tunnel, their faces stark in the white lights.

- It's not fair on Jordan, you know it isn't.

- Jordan? Not fair on Jordan? *His Excellency?* Are you fucking kidding me?

Silence, Emma stooping to lift her bag.

- Jordan?

They'd got off the train and walked home in silence, through Newcastle where the Tyne threaded under its seven bridges. That time they'd avoided each other, hadn't spoken more than was necessary for three weeks. Sharing the same house, scrupulously polite. Leaving the bathroom cleaner than usual. Until one day Emma turned up at her door with a bag of apples. *James Grieve*, she'd said, almost shyly. Apples of all things. In Kurdistan, at Christian weddings, the bride threw an apple to the bridesmaids. Zoe had her let her in, pulling the door wide.

- The truth is . . .

And Emma had undone the top button of Zoe's shirt.

- . . . we want each other, don't we?

Zoe had pulled away, trying to disentangle herself.

- Is that it? It's OK now, but it wasn't then?

- Shush!

Emma's smile was mocking her, her hand unbuttoning her again. Then it was stroking her nipple, her brown eyes quizzical and amused. Afterwards, that had seemed so unforgivably off-hand. Picking up where she left off. They'd gone to bed, of course, because she was a pushover, wasn't she? She'd got lonely. She said that, like a fool. *I missed you, I really missed you.* Murmuring into Emma's hair. The smell of it. Feeling a moment of peace settle on her. Then Emma was rushing to

meet Jordan for a film-club screening. *Il Postino.* That film
about Pablo Neruda in Italy. She was going to be late. Leaving
the paper bag of apples on the table, their scent filling the
room so that Zoe woke to it, alone in the single bed. It all
seemed so merciless. And years later she'd seen the same film,
which was all about seduction, and poetry, of course. That
was typical of Jordan, talking the talk.

Now there was Emma pocketing another trophy. A child's
plastic bangle. It might have been the diadem of a queen. Why
was that so annoying? She wondered if she'd ever said it to
Jordan. *Here's Zoe. Finders keepers!* She doubted it. Jordan
seemed entirely oblivious to them. To their situation. He didn't
know about it because he probably didn't understand love – he
really didn't, Emma assured her – or maybe he knew something
and didn't care. After all, Zoe was taking on some of the work.
The work of loving somebody. The work of *making* love, which
wasn't work at all, though it sounded like it. Emma would
never really be with her as long as Jordan was around. Now
there was Siobhan. Now there was Emma's mother.

A thin skin of ice was forming on the dirty puddles. A
cock pheasant sprawled from the trees, squawking in alarm,
its plumage flustering green and bronze.

Back at the house, they took off their boots and coats,
sitting quietly in the warmth. Then Emma's mobile was
ringing and there she was, Emma's Mum, ready to deliver
the child in half an hour. Then the kettle was drumming on
the stove and there was condensation on the kitchen window.
Emma was upstairs, making up Siobhan's cot with new sheets.

The Kurdish women had carried their babies strapped
to their backs for warmth. One woman had shown her a
woven bag made by her own mother. *We carried goat's cheese,*

firewood, milk in it. We carried our babies. She was there in the photograph, stout with age, the bag slung over her shoulder, its colours glowing. He son had lost his legs to a landmine. She hadn't needed a translation for that. The woman had wept, chopping her hands against her thighs to show where the surgeons had amputated. He was in America now, studying. An engineer. *Come,* she said, wiping tears on her shawl, *you are welcome in my house, now we must eat.* Then they sat down to dumplings and meatballs. The woman urging her to enjoy, her sons gathering round to thank her. Another woman, a teacher, had given her a piece of honeycomb from the hive in her garden. She'd passed it to Shamal for his family and he'd thanked her, quoting some lines from a Kurdish poem about blood and honey, salt and sweetness.

Emma's stockinged feet were pattering on the floorboards upstairs. The kettle gave a series of little shrieks and Zoe poured hot water over the teabags. There had been stories and there had been silences. *Lacunae,* her supervisor would have called them. You couldn't ask. She didn't need to ask what it was like to be a refugee, to rely on the favours of foreign men. Those silences were thick. Like curtains hanging between them. The women had left with their children and returned with the ones that lived. That was their story. The Yazidi women and girls who came home had been forgiven for what was done to them. They'd been caught in the glare of the Western media. But for the older women, those stories were pressed into silence. Sometimes a husband would be present at the interview – a man who'd fought or been imprisoned by the Ba'athists – and he would reach out and take the hand of his wife. To honour her suffering. To honour her silence.

Zoe was startled by feet on the stairs, Emma's sudden entry

into the room. She was struggling into her coat, pulling her hair clear of the collar, working her feet into a pair of slip-ons warming under the stove.

- Mum's on her way.

- Are you going out?

Exclamation mark or question mark?

- Just to pick up Siobhan. It's easier if I take her straight from the car when she's asleep in the baby seat. She usually is . . .

Zoe had never been a good liar. Or any good at hiding things. She'd seen that hooded look in Karîn's face as she praised God when they left her. She'd seen it in another woman's eyes. Their last interviewee. She'd been waiting for them in black robes and hijab outside her house. The woman whose husband and son had been ambushed in their car. She'd watched them burn to death across the valley. The woman whose twelve-year-old daughter had been killed by a stray bullet as she played outside. The woman whose life had been one sorrow after another. She was a mourner now, comforting others. After they'd interviewed her and taken her photograph against the failing light, she'd hugged them. *You are my son my daughter. Peace be upon you!* Then the courtyard had filled up with her daughters and daughters' daughters, the youngest child a baby that Zoe had cradled in her arms, bubbles of saliva forming at her lips. They'd left as darkness drifted into the mountains.

Zoe watched through the windows where Emma wrapped her arms around herself, stamping her feet, waiting for her mother to pull up. She was expected to stay away from the windows. She was somebody and something that had never happened and never would. *Never say never.* Shamal used to say that, an English phrase he'd picked up from somewhere. Zoe reached for her boots and shrugged into her coat. She left quietly by the back door, pulled the Yale catch closed, tying her laces, hearing the crunch of tyres on gravel. Then she was finding her way back through the fields. She had a lot to do. Collating, organising transcripts, checking the translations as they emerged to make sure they worked in English. Sometimes the flaws were obvious, and you had to go back to the source and start again.

The sun was very low on the horizon, a scarlet blaze shading to orange and lemon, then hazing into pale blue. She felt the cold insinuate, walking briskly, watching the river redden. She remembered how Karîn had told her that a man had stood in a mountain torrent where blocks of ice were coming down in the current. How he'd thrown her own children to her, one by one. *God be praised, they all survived!* Karîn who'd laid her dead baby in the snow, only to have it returned to her alive. Karîn whose silences would always be unredeemed.

Emma would be stepping into the house with Siobhan asleep in her arms, her mother driving away to join the traffic on the main road. The town lay ahead, nested in electric light. A three-quarter moon rose above the horizon, huge and yellow. Like the moon above Korek, burning bright as a lynx's eye as they came down from the cold of the mountains, loose stones treacherous underfoot. Karîn told her how they'd used it as their guide, travelling by night, following the mountain trails. *So we are not seen.* Zoe walked towards it now, feeling it irradiate her with light, frost forming on the fenceposts where she climbed the stile. She found the gloves in her pocket and pulled them on. She thought of Siobhan still sleeping, of Emma calling out to her in the empty house.

LIKE FADO

LISBON, THE OLD quarter. We were a steep climb above the city, staying in a family-run hotel in a cobbled square with jacaranda trees and yellow wagtails. Jill was at a conference at the university and I'd tagged along for a few days. I wasn't planning to do much, just mooch about with my camera, catching up with myself.

Largo do Carmo was the square where the revolution ended in seventy-four. The coup started in the army, then took to the streets. They put flowers in the guns of soldiers. *Revolução dos Cravos*. The carnation revolution. Almost bloodless. It spread to Africa, stopping the wars in Angola and Mozambique. Just a few carnations and the will to change things. I was still at school, but I remembered it all on the news. Unlike Jill, who seemed to have no recollection of it at all. But then I was two years older than her.

The hotel rooms were spacious and modern. Ours had a glass-faced bathroom with a shower you could see into from the room, unless you pulled down a blind. That was weird. It took us a few minutes to work out how the taps operated. A sign of age, maybe. But the towels were soft and the hot water plentiful and there was a mini-bar and a kettle, tea and coffee. The restaurant looked half-decent and the breakfast was excellent: croissants, fresh yoghurt, crispy bacon, scrambled eggs and little pork sausages. The coffee was good and you could even make toast on one of those heated conveyor belt things, though it took forever, waiting for the transformation.

Opposite the hotel was a shop that sold guitars, mandolins, sheet music and high-gloss pianos. Further along was a boutique selling hand-made shoes, though the fittings were too narrow for me. Then a barracks with a sentry in metal helmet and curiasse. One day a man, the next a woman. Very fetching in either case. The cafés spilled into the street and at weekends musicians set up little PA systems and serenaded the tourists. We kept remembering that Portuguese wasn't Spanish. If we slipped into Castilian people looked at us in puzzlement. It reminded me of Jacqui, our daughter. She was learning Mandarin, but when she came home, she got her grammar mixed up. *Chinglish*, she called it. In Lisbon, most people spoke a bit of English anyway, so it hardly mattered.

We had an evening to recover from the flight and the hassle of airport security and baggage carousels. We were knackered, and Jill had work things to check. Oddly enough, we ended up in a Spanish restaurant a short walk from the hotel. We ate braised rabbit with shallots and drank one of those dark Dao wines, all brambles and jam. Jill's teeth went purple like that first time she got drunk with me in a wine bar in Liverpool and told me to fuck off. Right out of the blue, as if she'd just recognized me and we had an old grudge. We weren't sleeping together then. The bar was called The Corkscrew and we drank two bottles of Côte du Rhône, which was going it a bit in those days. We were students living on our grants, making do. When you think of the debt kids get into these days with tuition fees, we were lucky. We didn't realize we were a blip in history, that working-class kids would never see such days again. When I graduated, I owed the bank thirty-six quid and paid it off in three weeks, working in a factory that made pork pies. I've never eaten one since.

The second day of the visit, Jill had a full day at the conference. It was some European network to do with child abuse. Or sex trafficking. I should have known more, but I hadn't asked too many questions. I'd been pre-occupied with my own meltdown. We'd called by at the university on the way from the airport, just to meet her Portuguese colleagues. Three elegant women, professors in trouser suits and high heels who spent a lot of money on their hair. It was a bit embarrassing with Jill explaining that I wasn't an academic. It's hard for some academics to imagine that, like they were born to it. As if there's nothing else.

The fact I'd just been made redundant was another matter. I was secretly glad, actually. I was getting uneasy, working in advertising. Too much bullshit. Maybe everyone gets there in the end, cynical and jealous of the new generation. I'd specialized in working for what we used to call Third World charities. We ran campaigns on a shoestring, but the company still creamed off a profit. Then those youngsters muscling in, fresh from their college courses, wanting to change everything, talking about the same things in a new language.

The receptionist at the university looked at us sideways when Jill introduced herself, stumbling over the Portuguese names of her colleagues. She picked up the phone to call for help. Of course, the professors all spoke perfect English when they stepped out of the lift, tilting their heads towards us, struggling with our quaint pronunciation.

After breakfast on that first morning, Jill came out from the bathroom shaking her hands to dry her nail varnish, trying to fasten her necklace. For a moment she could have been twenty again, her cheeks flushed from the shower. The necklace was one that Jacqui had brought back for her. Yellow jade set in silver. The clasp was awkward. Jill wasn't wearing the earrings that matched the necklace. They'd come without fixings and I'd spent ages on the internet finding hangers and bails, but they'd never been quite right.

Jill flicked back her hair and tilted her glasses. She hadn't worn those when we were courting, though she'd had a pair of sunglasses that we thought were very cool the first time we'd caught the ferry to Caen with our rucksacks and that tiny tent. That was before her PhD and my first job writing adverts for skin products. Which Jill thought was hilarious, but we got by, even when she was pregnant with Jacqui. Looking back, we might even have been happy. At the time, just surviving was enough.

– How do I look?

– Great!

She sighed a little theatrically.

– What I mean is, do these go together?

She was wearing a dark maroon scooped top and a navy-blue suit with flat-heeled shoes. The shoes were silver. So, she was a bit nervous. I kissed her and stroked her shoulders.

– You look great, honestly.

I remembered the three professors on high heels like flamingos. I remembered Max.

– OK, I'll try to believe you.

– Believe me. You look lovely. Very . . . professional.

– Arsehole!

I'd run out of ideas when it came to how she looked. I liked it. The way she looked. Jill grimaced, picked up her briefcase and checked inside.

– OK, got my phone, my laptop, got my purse and the taxi should be on its way. Come down with me?

- OK, just a sec.

I slipped on some shoes and a windcheater.

When we got to the lift, I saw Jill staring at me in the mirror as if she'd never seen me before. I could see my bald patch. When we stepped out a woman in a pink twin-set was pushing in a folded wheelchair. I stopped to give her a hand and got to the door just in time to see Jill getting into a black Mercedes. She wound the window down.

- Be good?

It sounded like a question.

- You, too.

She rolled her eyes and put on her glasses, as if not being good was unthinkable. It was an academic conference, after all. I wondered if Max would be there and that's why she didn't fancy the conference dinner this time.

It's funny how you just know things. I didn't need to check her mobile phone messages or anything like that. I just knew. We'd met at another conference dinner. He was a neat looking guy with grey hair, hooded eyes, one of those linen jackets that academics love. He'd been Jill's PhD supervisor. A professor of Sociology, an expert on something or other I'd forgotten. When he shook my hand, he just glanced towards Jill who was leaning against the wall with a glass of prosecco. That night we'd driven home in silence, our headlights slicing through the dark of country lanes. Jill had reached out to touch my arm, but I couldn't speak. I never asked how it started or when or how it ended. There was a little owl in the road and when it flew up in the headlights it seemed to stare in at us. We never talked about Max. Not once. Whatever I felt about it I'd buried somehow, somewhere. The owl had seemed mesmerized, staring at us through the windscreen.

I waved the taxi off and went back to my room to check some emails. I'd put a few irons in the fire with some of the bigger companies. I didn't hold out much hope, but not working wasn't an option. The wi-fi was superfast. Nothing doing. I sent Jacqui a quick one to say where we were. She was back in Guangzhou working in telecoms. I should have known more about that, too. I was a bit dismayed she'd ended up in that line of work, but I couldn't have said why exactly. I was proud of Jill and what she did, even the dark side. Or especially that. It was that thing about making a difference that haunted our generation. We'd both tried in different ways. I didn't have a PhD, of course. I wouldn't have known where to start.

I took my phone off the charger, packed my camera and slipped my wallet into my camera bag. I'd got until about four o'clock when Jill would be heading back and we'd go out for dinner. She was supposed to be researching that. We were determined to listen to some Fado. We'd been to Lisbon a couple of years before and I'd fallen in love with the music, its darkness, its extravagance. Like the wine, there was nothing frivolous about it. I don't think Jill was as keen as me, she found it all a bit sentimental. She was probably just humouring me because I'd come along when I didn't have to. There was a good music shop down in the city and the CDs the owner had recommended last time had been spot-on. Amalia Rodriguez, Ana Moura, Carminho and Gisela Joao, along with a couple of compilations. One of them was an arrangement of Fernando Pessoa's poetry, the guy with over seventy heteronyms. I liked to listen to them when I was cooking, drinking wine and waiting for Jill to get home, always hours later then me. Thinking of Pessoa slipping from one persona to another. Sometimes I was half-pissed by the time the dinner went on the table.

It was April and there was still a slight chill in the air, so I kept the windcheater. The woman on the desk had clocked me as I left. Being middle-aged had started to make me look and feel like everyone else. I was pretty much indistinguishable from any other guy over fifty. And I had to be careful in the sun. Still, I'd kept fit and was only a few pounds overweight according to that BMI thing we were all supposed to be taking notice of. If you exaggerated your height just a tad, it all worked out fine. I hadn't actually measured myself in years, so why not?

I walked down the street from the hotel, passing the shoe shop. There was a young woman in a grey scarf seated at the counter, reading a book. It all looked very peaceful. Very expensive. The shoes were tiny, like many of the Portuguese. I wasn't tempted. I veered right and took a set of steps that led down to the main road. On the left was a fantastic Gothic building that looked as if it had been the original town hall. The railway station was close by, and dotted through the city were those trams that took you to the higher streets, hauled along on steel hawsers. *Elevadors*. The suspension springs were all seized as if they hadn't been serviced in years. My dad had worked in engineering and believed in maintenance, taking our Hillman Minx to bits every weekend. I could hear him muttering how bloody useless they were. Charming in their way, but probably deadly. I preferred to walk.

I'd been down to the waterfront on that previous visit: same thing, Jill at a conference, me exploring, kicking my heels, trying to keep out of the bars, trying not to log into my work emails. I'd picked up a map from the hotel and, this time, I decided to head across to the opposite side of the city. Lisbon had been pretty much destroyed by an earthquake in 1775 and the central section – Chiado and Bairro Alta – had been rebuilt in geometric patterns. But they'd kept out the big international chains and there were lots of little shops and cafés. Curio and millinery shops, stationers and wine merchants. The sorts of places where you could buy sealing wax or antique books. I checked the map, turning to face north, keeping the sun on my right. I was at Marqués de Pombal, and the area beyond that around Estefania looked promising.

I went up a street that slanted back from the main road, climbing steeply. There was a little square with concrete seats and a row of African guys talking and smoking. They were watching a woman in a purple kaftan carrying a baby strapped to her back, trying to stop another little boy from running ahead into the road. They were laughing at her. I remembered Mozambique, Angola. One way or another, they must have lived through those old colonial wars. I wondered what it was like for them here in Lisbon, at the dark heart of the old empire.

The thing with Max had probably ended after that evening. Jill knew that I'd picked up something between them. Maybe something that never even got started. Maybe something that was all in my mind. Or perhaps I *wanted* her to have an affair because that gave things a bit of excitement, a bit of the passion that ebbs away as you get older. Although passion is about the self, really. Love is about someone else. That's what I wanted to say to Jill, that I'd kept on loving her because I couldn't help it. But, mostly, we didn't say anything.

There was suddenly a lot of graffiti on the buildings and

the classy shops selling clothes and handbags were replaced by tiny cafés and grocery shops with produce set out across the pavements, so you had to walk in the road. Trays of dates and oranges, courgettes, tomatoes, avocados. A trickle of soapy water went down the gutter where someone was washing their windows. Some of the houses were beautifully tiled and I took a few shots. I was using a little Fuji camera with a fixed lens. I'd got a Canon with a big zoom, but it stuck out a mile. You could slip the Fuji into your pocket. It was discreet and the images were excellent.

There were some black kids with dreadlocks in a doorway, laughing at me. I'd forgotten my hat and was probably looking a bit pink after that climb. I'd have loved to take a shot of them, but you couldn't. Sometimes I carried the camera openly and that way you might get asked. I'd got some great shots at a hair-braiding salon when I was in Nairobi. *Muzungu, photo me, please!* But you had to be careful. Especially these days when images could end up on the internet.

The kids were gorgeous and full of fun. But, sure enough, their dad appeared to bring them inside. He wore a white singlet and was lean and tough looking. He gave me a curious look. Not hostile exactly, but *What the fuck?* all the same. We used to talk about that in the advertising game. That little gap between the pitch the ad made before the audience quite got it. Then puzzlement turned to gratification and they were hooked. With the new-wave ads you hardly know what they were advertising other than the consumer experience itself. The products were pretty much the same, so it was about the art-form, not the product. Or the *idea* of the product. Or its consumption. It was a different advertising skill, alright. Like that glass-walled shower that meant nothing in the end.

Voyeurism at best. It was bullshit when most people had so little. Except desire.

My job had been to make people feel good about giving. Close-up images of smiling African women and kids, personal stories of salvation, of healing. And if I'm honest, of gratitude. Sometimes I wasn't sure if that was much better than selling the latest Audi. Whether the moral ground was any higher. If there was any moral ground. But at least there was a human connection, and that seemed worth something at the time.

I moved on, zig-zagging through the streets as they rose higher. The *elevador* went past, painted red like a British fire engine. A row of faces looked back at me. I wiped away a trickle of sweat and took another right turn. Occasionally you'd get a glimpse of the city laid out below. Rectilinear. Beyond that, the wispy clouds beyond the sea. I remembered those equestrian statues, glaring white in the city squares. Portugal might be a small country, but it had a huge imperial ego. It had taken a few bunches of flowers to damp that down. Well, not really. But it was a good story and there were some great photographs from that time. A revolution has to be promoted like everything else and all revolutions have a certain style.

I came to a street where a line of houses had been demolished. There was something new going up, covered in green plastic netting. Next to that, a house with ornate blue and white tiling and a fabulously weathered front door. I crouched down to take a couple of shots. The door opened. There was a woman standing there, slightly built, squinting a little in the sun as if surprised to see me. She had cropped hair and earrings made of peacock feathers that dangled on either side of her face. She was dressed in a white sleeveless blouse and striped skirt. I raised my hand feebly, as if to apologize for intruding. Her slow smile seemed to make time for me.

– *Olá.*

– *Olá.*

She said something else. Her voice rose up at the end of the sentence, so I guess it was a question, but I'd used up all my Portuguese. I gestured to the camera.

– *Mi scusi.*

It wasn't Portuguese. It probably wasn't anything. Italian? She looked a bit puzzled and repeated whatever it was she'd said earlier. I shrugged and put a hand to my chest, fingers open in what I hoped was a gesture of repentance. She turned sideways and signalled at me to enter the house. I showed her the flat of my hand, to say, No, *that's* OK. But she signed more urgently, wagging her fingers. I followed her in, but my heart was thudding.

The street was bright, the inside of the house startlingly dark. There was a spicy smell. Maybe fenugreek. Maybe cumin, cloves, cardamoms. The windows were grimy on the outside and not quite closed. Their net curtains billowed into the room. There was a settee with a bold tartan pattern and a clothes-horse hung with children's things: little vests that buttoned at the shoulder and miniature socks and trousers.

– *Venha!*

The woman was leading me into a back room, a kitchen, which had a steel sink with crockery neatly stacked. She was silhouetted against the light that came through tall windows at the back of the house. Her face was almost invisible, apart from a flash of eye gleam. Her dark skin seemed part of the shadows that suffused the room.

The woman went up the stairs ahead of me, stepping lightly

in canvas shoes. The stairs were made of wood that had once been varnished, but the gloss had worn away. A ring on her finger clicked against the bannister, her shoulders bunching and relaxing. And I followed her for no reason. What was I even doing here? There was a faint patch of sweat in the small of her back. Again, that faint scent of something. Her bare shoulders gleaming in the shaft of sun that fell from a skylight. I felt suddenly hot, cold sweat dribbling down my sides, my hand moist against the camera.

The woman stepped from the stairs to the landing and pushed open a door, clucking softly, as if there was a small animal underfoot. She paused in the doorway and smiled back at me, curling her fingers to get me to follow her. I could feel my heart bumping against my ribs. Inside the room she was pulling on a rod to tilt the Venetian blind, allowing light to slant into the room. There was a double bed with a carved headboard. My mouth had dried out. I half turned to say something, but there, propped up in the bed was a figure lying back against a stack of pillows. A glass of water stood on a little table and what looked like a bible, the edges of the pages gilded. The sleeper's eyes opened slowly. It was an old woman. She wore pearl studs in her ears and the skin hung loosely from her forearms. On her wrist was one of those plastic diver's watches with all sorts of gadgets sticking out. She had no teeth and her lips were crimped inwards, crumpling her face. The younger woman leaned over her to adjust the pillows and turned to me.

- *Mãe*.

I could see the resemblance in the shape of the women's heads, the finely formed temples, the shape of their eyes. She smiled at me again.

– *Bonita* . . . be-ootiful . . .

The English took me aback and I was stammering.

– Yes . . . beautiful!

The old woman *was* beautiful in the way that only the very old and the very young can be, her skin exquisitely creased, her irises and pupils dark, merging to the point of invisibility. Her hair still black, apart from a crinkling of white at the temples.

I stepped towards the window and saw a group of school-children in the street below being chivvied by their teacher. He wore a lanyard and a straw hat. Inside the room it was hot and still and the sun made wedges of dust where it penetrated the shutters. The younger woman was pointing to my camera, turning to tug at the blinds to let in more light. She cupped her hands towards the figure in the bed. The old lady was emitting short, hoarse breaths.

– *Por favor, senhor?*

She pointed to the camera again. The old lady turned her face to me, without expression. It was then I realized that she was dying, that the scent in the house was the sweet scent of someone passing from this life to the next.

I took some shots, nudging the window shutters open a little, taking a couple with the aperture closed down, then some wide open, so that only the old lady's face was in focus. Then a shot of her hands where they were folded on the white sheet, tangled in a rosary. The colours in the room were muted. It felt almost pornographic to look at her through a lens. The younger woman was pressed into a corner. Although the old lady was looking at me, she seemed to be watching a far distance. A desert traveller or a sailor nearing home, cross-ing the seam between this life and whatever lay beyond. As

I worked, her eyes drooped and her head turned to one side, breath softening as if she was no longer able to make the effort of wakefulness. Her daughter put her hands together at one side of her face to show me she was sleeping now.

Downstairs, I showed her the images on the camera's live view. The light in the room made the old lady look as if she was floating in space, the texture of her skin like softest leather, her eyes huge and luminous. The woman clapped her hands silently and gave me that brilliant, dimpled smile. She wrote something on a slip of paper and gave it to me, pointing to a folded laptop on the table. She wanted me to email her the files.

– *Obrigada, obrigada.*

– You're welcome.

The woman looked at me, puzzled.

– She really is beautiful.

I pointed at the image of her hands folded against the white sheets.

– *Bonita . . .*

Beautiful and so close to death it was tangible. The Portuguese word had come back and she smiled at me delightedly. There was that smell of fenugreek again as she leaned close, pointing to the email address, then pointing to herself. I wondered about my own smell. Last night's wine and aftershave, probably. We shook hands and her skin was smooth and cool. I went to the door and she let me into the street, waving goodbye. Smiling as if we were friends parting, the peacock-feather earrings vivid against the dark interior of the house.

I walked down from the neighbourhood through patches of shadow and searing sunlight. Near Pombal I found a café and ordered some lunch. It was a local fish served with slices of potato, onion and red pepper. Simple, but delicately cooked, with lemon wedges and sprigs of samphire. I stuck to fizzy water with ice instead of wine. The waiters all spoke English, so no problem. I took my camera and scrolled through the images of the old lady, remembering the sweet, cloying stillness in the room. The heat. The tumbling motes of dust in shafts of light. The way her eyes seemed to be looking beyond everything. The way we all have to die but don't know when.

Back at the hotel I plugged the camera into my MacBook and downloaded the images. I adjusted a couple of the exposures before sending them off in batches to the address I'd been given. Funny, but it felt like a secret, intimate and somehow clandestine. It was four o'clock by the time I'd finished. I checked my mail to find I'd been offered an interview with a firm in Manchester who were interested in my CV. That might do it. I got in the shower and let the hot water stream over me, remembering that I hadn't worn a hat. I was packing away my camera when Jill came through the door with one of those canvas shoulder-bags they give you at conferences with a notepad and a biro and a bottle of water and a map of the campus. Bullshit, really. Stocking fillers. We must have had dozens of them at home.

– Hiya, how did it go?

– It went . . . how about you?

– Good, just mooched about really. Nice lunch.

– That's good.

– Fish in a little café.

– Nice. I need to get under the shower.

She looked awkward. I wondered who else had been there,

at the conference. The three professors, obviously. I thought about the images in my camera, on my hard-drive.

Jill showered and changed into slacks and halter top. We sat next to each other on the bed and checked the map. I wanted to make love. To reclaim something. Right at that moment. I nuzzled the back of my hand against her breast.

– Hey! We're going out!

She was smiling, pushing my hand back. Patting it as if I was a child.

– Maybe later . . .

I kissed the damp hair she'd tucked behind her ear.

– Later

– OK, later . . .

Jill had made some enquiries with her Portuguese colleagues. So, they were good for something. There was a fado café in Chiado, along from Bairro Alto. It was walkable. I thought of those elegant women stepping in their high heels. Flamingos. Smiling at our northern English, our lack of sophistication. I thought of the old woman lying in shadow and light, wreathed in a kind of chiaroscuro. I didn't know how to tell Jill any more than I could tell her the other stuff. The stuff about Max. That I'd known about it. About *something*. That I didn't even care anymore. Max was an annoyance. A cliché. I guessed she'd been hurt by it all in the end and hadn't shown it.

We linked arms and set off into the evening. The sun still hot. The square was coming out in purple blossom. There was a bird I didn't recognize singing close by. A girl in a white apron was setting tables at a restaurant for the evening customers, polishing wine glasses, laying out knives and forks. It was tempting to stay just where we were. To let everything else flow past us, to hold onto the moment. Maybe to talk, at last. We walked on, following the streets downward, Jill holding onto my arm.

We found the café up a cobbled street opposite a little baker's shop and an old-fashioned milliner's that sold lace and cards of pins. The idea was that you booked in for the evening meal and the fado was served up between courses. It all kicked off at eight o'clock, so we had an hour. We booked a table, the waiter struggling with our surname. *Monaghan.* I had to spell it out for him. We paused in the street.

– Drink?

Jill took my arm.

– Try to stop me!

We walked to a bar and ordered a couple of drinks and some peanuts. I had a beer and Jill went for white wine. *Vinho Verde*, faintly green. There was another British family there, the father burned brick red, two kids sitting with bottles of Fanta, a smelly baby in a buggy that kept pushing away its bottle of milk away as the mother bent over it. *Just like Jacqui*, Jill said, smiling at me, remembering something I'd forgotten. I thought of her out there in China and that suddenly felt very far away. Then Jill was telling me about the conference and the research network they were trying to set up, but I was only half listening. She knew that. She probably expected it by now. I never mentioned the interview or the old lady. I don't know why. Maybe tomorrow.

When we got back to the restaurant the band was setting up. A woman singer in a long tight frock, cut low in the back. Two guitarists, tuning up. We got a plate of starters – little pastries and olives and more white wine. We clinked glasses and I remembered just how much of our lives we'd spent together. We'd been together longer than before we knew each other. We'd survived together and grown together. And after all, love changes. It changes for the better in some ways.

Jill's eyes looked very dark in the candlelight. When the band lilted into the first song there was this amazing texture as the guitars wove into each other and the singer's voice rose and fell. Like the sea. Husky, plangent. I remembered the old lady dying in that dim room, flooded by darkness and then by light. I still hadn't said anything to Jill. Maybe I never would. It was too intimate, too difficult somehow. But it wasn't really a secret either, just something for later. Like that interview. Maybe I'd show her the pictures some time. Maybe. For a moment we were lost in the music, the way you get lost in a book, in a story. Out of time. Even though music keeps time, it moves us beyond it. We didn't know what the woman was singing about. Except that we did. She sang for the sea and for lost love and for the life that was leaving us and that we were leaving. *Saudade*. That was the word. And the word was almost untranslatable, meaning fate, nostalgia, sorrow, the passion of remembrance. When the red wine arrived it was dark crimson, a Barraida.

After the last applause when the band stood up and bowed low to the audience, I paid the bill. I used a credit card but left a tip in Euros. I hated tipping. That false sense of privilege, like acting a part. Being called 'Sir' when really you were no one. The singer was outside smoking a cigarette. She stared at us for a moment as we left.

We walked back to the hotel, pausing to look in the shop windows. I remembered that Jill had spent the whole day indoors and hadn't really seen the city. The statues were huge and frost-white under their spotlights. Families with tired kids were still eating at restaurants along the waterfront. There were the faintest stars struggling beyond the city lights. *We should have stayed longer,* Jill was saying, *it's so beautiful.* Her hands were stroking the hairs on my arms and I felt that old frisson, despite everything. Despite age. Despite whatever had happened. She spoke as if our visit was already over. As if we were already back to our lives. I squeezed her arms and kissed her there in the street. There was still something inexpressible about the feeling of another body against mine. Jill's body that I knew so well. Or thought I did. I slipped my finger under her blouse at the shoulder and there was her warm skin, a pale band showing her suntan. I put my lips to it tasting the heat of her.

Jill pulled away, laughing, her lips glossy. She put a hand to her ear, checking her earrings. She'd put on the jade ones that I'd tried to fix and that always hung at a slight angle. She took my hand. My phone buzzed in my pocket and I thought it was probably Jacqui getting back to me. Tomorrow morning we'd be in the air, heading for England. Heading for Manchester, landing under low clouds.

The air was suddenly much colder as a chill came in from the sea. Jill shivered.

– Come on, Paul. Let's go.

– Do you want to go straight back?

– Yes, to the hotel. Home.

Later, she'd said. She was getting cold, impatient, rubbing at goosebumps on her arms. She'd been carrying her cardigan but put it on now, shrugging herself into it, straightening it. The hotel wasn't home. It was just a temporary space. Back in England our other home was waiting. The fridge murmuring in its sleep, the answerphone bleeping, the freezer growing ledges of ice. Dust on the windows, rain quenching the garden.

Jill's hand was in mine as we walked. She gave me a sideways smile that told me we'd make love later. That we'd wake together in our room with that slight surprise at where we were before packing our things and heading to the airport. What I felt wasn't regret, exactly. It was that sense of fate, of melancholy. Of *saudade*. Jill was saying something, but I didn't catch it. I was thinking about that old woman nearing journey's end, staring into her future, like a flower's petals closing for the night. They'd be deep crimson, roses or carnations, the colour of wine or blood. That faint sweet smell, seeping through rooms where light slanted through the shutters. The tumult of her fading mind. Like all of life replaying itself in moments and memories. Like fado.

PEPÉ'S

THE GLASS WAS streaked with water and foam. When the black rubber squeegee went across it, there was Victor's face behind the suds. He had straight dark hair and wire-rimmed glasses, just like when they were in CM1. They'd shared a desk until secondary school. Yvette pulled her skirt down and turned back to lining up the glasses on the bar. She could sense his eyes on her. She stooped to bring more glasses from the washer and straightened to find Madame Gauthier watching her with those hooded eyes that were the colour of pitted olives.

– *Il attend.*

– *OK, OK, je vais . . .*

Yvette, said it nervously, taking the ten euro note from Madame and wrenching the door open to pay Victor who stammered his thanks.

– *Mm . . . Merci, Yvette.*

– You're welcome. Have a nice day.

She smiled ironically and twirled away. He was trying not to look at her. And he was blushing. When she re-entered the bar, there were Madame's eyes. She looked as if nothing could ever surprise her again. Everything that could happen had already happened. There was nothing new under the sun. A new day was just another day. Yvette took a tea towel and began polishing the beer glasses, catching reflections of her face and wiping them away.

Pepé's was just over a kilometre out of town. A bar/

restaurant with a pull-in for cars and lorries. The road barged through on its way to Alençon, Rennes, Chartres, the south. It ran away to whatever lay beyond the middle of nowhere, the back of beyond.

Yvette had no idea who Pepé was or had been. There was the neon figure of a Pierrot on the wall of the restaurant. He had a white ruff, red lips and tunic buttons and a tragic, downturned mouth. The name flashed on and off above him, as if it had flown from his mouth. But that was all. Madame Gauthier had a husband, for sure. Bernard, a big bluff guy who worked as a mechanic in the local dairy. But Pepé was a mystery. Yvette wondered if this lack of a namesake for the café bothered anyone else. She guessed it went back to the Seventies when Madam and Bernard were young. Maybe it was Bernard's nickname. Maybe they'd come up with the name after making love, lying on their backs, cigarette smoke curling, planning the future together. Now there was a thought.

Madame's hips brushed past her as she shook an ashtray into the bin.

Yvette had got the job after leaving school where she hadn't been very good at anything, except mocking the teachers and bunking off to swim in that crook of the river with Anna and Martine. The water flowed over flat grey stones, clear and deep, chilling your bones on sunny days of stolen freedom. They were attending the Lycée now, Anna and Martine. Anna had a boyfriend who drove a green Fiat.

Yvette's mother had sent her down for the job after spotting an ad in the local tobacconist's. She'd had a cursory interview with Madame Gauthier, who flicked ash from her Gitane and made it abundantly clear that she was to be addressed as

'Madame' and nothing else. That bit hadn't been cursory. It had been as clear as the glasses stacked above the bar, fresh from the dishwasher. *Remember, she can be a real bitch!* her mother had called to her before the interview as she was putting on lipstick and brushing out her eyelashes. Never a truer word.

Dust spiralled in a band of sunlight that struck through the glass doors. Eleven-thirty. Another thirty minutes before they could expect customers for lunch. There was a pizza menu and a plat du jour. Entrées were taken from the chilled salad bar that stood at one end of the dining room. Then it was meat and veg, a slice of cheese if the customer had room, followed by ice cream or coffee. Madame wasn't a bad cook and it was good value for thirteen euros. The customers were mainly local office workers who drove out to escape the town, a few passing routiers, English or German tourists who'd got lost, juggling their maps and cameras and children who needed the loo.

Yvette got her own lunch at about two o'clock when the place calmed down, then it was a long afternoon with Madame taking a nap. Then another quiet evening with Bernard and Yvette serving behind the bar. It was all over by nine o'clock, except the odd barfly. They usually let her go at ten p.m. Then it was a twenty-minute walk into town along a poorly-lit road to the crooked house on Rue Montgomery where she lived with her parents and younger brother, Dominic. Sometimes she borrowed Dom's bike. If it was raining, she got a lift with her dad – if he was in the right mood.

Yvette hated walking home at night, seeing her shadow cast on the road by approaching headlights. Sometimes a car would slow down, then speed past. That sense of being looked over you got from older guys in the bar who were bored with their wives or didn't have one. There were wild peacocks in the woods at the ruined chateau. Their shrieks raised the hair on the back of your neck. In the mornings, buzzards and kites tumbling over the pine thickets, fighting off the crows. All this summer the sky had been a polished blue sphere, beaming down the sun's heat as she trudged to work.

But it was a job.

And that was something in a town that was already half empty and getting emptier. She carried a mobile phone in her shoulder bag and she was careful never to leave that behind.

Madame was arranging olives and paté in the salad bar and checking the temperature. Yvette heard a lorry pull onto the gravel car park: scrunching tyres, the hiss of airbrakes. Then the bell jangled on its spring as the door to the restaurant opened. A dog ran in, scurrying around the legs of the oak tables. Madame's face was a picture.

– Morning Giselle!

It was a short guy dressed in overalls with a fluster of curly black hair that he pushed back from his face. The dog – Lulu's dog – was dashing around the restaurant, its claws scraping on the tiled floor. Yvette bent down to tickle its tummy and it went belly-up in delight.

– Morning Yvette, *ça va?*

Madame nodded curtly, laying the last place in the restaurant and straightening the paper tablecloth.

– Good morning, *Monsieur*.

Lulu raised his eyebrows quizzically and grinned. He knew very well that it was more than Yvette's life was worth to address him informally. The dog was an English Jack Russell bitch.

– Mitzi! Mitzi!

He put a hard edge on his voice, like stropping a knife, and the dog slunk back to him. Yvette filled a tin bowl with water and the dog lapped at it, then curled up on a newspaper next to the door.

Lulu had been to school with her father, back in the day. Which reminded her of Victor for some reason. Whenever she told her father that Lulu had been in the bar her father would shake his head and laugh. He came in a couple of days a week, depending on his route. He delivered materials for a local building supplies company and Mitzi went everywhere with him, sleeping in the cab, leaping down as soon as the door was open to pee on the grass.

Lulu played bass guitar in a band and every last Friday of the month they appeared at Pepé's to play British and American rock covers. Lulu wore his shirt open to the waist and crocodile skin winkle pickers. Bopping up and down to the music with his eyes closed, then opening them to beam at an audience drunk enough to dance in the space Bernard cleared between the tables. That was a late night for everyone. A couple of times the band had given Yvette a lift home. Smoking, arguing about the gig, drinking cans of pilsner they'd cadged from Bernard, along with the roll of euros he took from the till. Yvette made a space to huddle among the equipment. The amplifiers still hot, reeking of sweat and cigarettes. Smelling of men.

Mitzi looked up now as Yvette passed, then lay down, her flank twitching. Her eyelashes were long, her eyes like buttons. Lulu was at the buffet, piling his plate with chorizo and boiled eggs and cornichons. Yvette put a carafe of water and a basket of bread on his table. She noticed that Madame was watching Lulu with pursed lips, hitching her waistband. Her eyes had that drilled-out look again. The radio behind the bar was playing a song by Johnny Halliday. There was Lulu, munching cornichons and tapping his fingers to the beat like an aficionado. She'd seen the video. Johnny strutting in a leather jerkin. *Requiem pour un fou . . .*

It was another quiet shift. By nine-thirty Yvette was walking back into town. It was July. A hot day had softened tarmac on the road and raised the scent of larches. An owl flew from the trees, its ghostly wings startling her. She quickened her step, clutching her phone, that familiar prickling at her neck. It was a dark night, no moon, the sky crisscrossed with aeroplane lights or satellites. It was hard to tell them from the stars at first. But there they were. A life beyond this life. People up there, looking down at her. That was weird. She'd be invisible, of course. A nobody walking to nowhere.

The next day, the same. Apart from no Lulu.

Wednesday brought a minibus full of American tourists on the wine trail. Yvette could hear them speaking in slurred English before they came through the door with their guide, a middle-aged woman dressed in high heels, a flared red skirt and a tight black top. Madame greeted them with a wide smile, narrowing her eyes at Yvette to hurry her to the kitchen and back. The Americans were made up of half a dozen retired couples, their skin leathery from Florida sun, their clothes brand new. The men wore moccasins, check shirts, cargo pants and heavy gold watches. The women wore a female version of the same outfit. They were polite in an insincere, American way. Not like the Brits who fell over themselves to say please and thank you in terrible French. Not like the Germans who were remote and buttoned-up. The Americans left a mess of breadcrumbs and spilled food and stained tablecloths. But they tipped generously and called her *madmoswelle*. A heavily built man with a bush of white hair and bleached blue eyes squeezed her elbow as he left, fumbling in his waistcoat to scatter change on the table. His chinos were spattered from the urinals, but he hadn't noticed. The bell chimed as the door shut behind them and there they were, milling good-naturedly at their minibus in the car park. The guide emptied gravel from her stilettoes before climbing aboard.

Thursday was quiet again. Routiers. A few reps. An Italian couple who spent the entire lunchtime arguing over a road map while their children fought over a comic in the background. The woman looked thin and stressed-out, speaking in rapid, jabbing phrases. The man was laconic and vague, sipping mineral water, clinking the ice and looking at his wife pityingly over his glasses. He had pinched nostrils that turned white in exasperation. Yvette could see how annoying he was.

Madame went for her nap at two-thirty and Bernard appeared at six. He took a shower and came down unshaven, his hair slicked back, smelling of pomade. He ate some leftover casserole in the kitchen, then joined Yvette behind the bar, pouring himself a glass of Kronenbourg. He looked out of sorts. A long way from his usual amiable self. Yvette knew to keep her head down. Madame was one thing, but Bernard was quite another after a long day at work.

At five past seven a vehicle arrived in the car park. The lights glared directly through the windows and Yvette flinched. When the driver turned them off, she saw a blurry green after-image. The door opened and Lulu came in, letting the door slam behind him, nodding to the other customers. Bernard looked up from his newspaper and offered his hand but didn't move. Lulu wore a white polo shirt and jeans. For a man of his age he still had a neat figure. Yvette put a bowl of crisps in front of him and poured him a beer. He chatted to Bernard about the football, but it was like pulling teeth. Lulu looked at Yvette, letting his eyelids droop. He shrugged. The television flickered. The newspaper rustled as Bernard licked his finger and turned the pages.

Now there was the sound of a moped buzzing into the car park. The rider cut the engine. When the door jangled open, it was Victor in a new leather jacket, carrying a crash helmet. His glasses misted in the heat of the bar. He took them off to wipe them, looking like a kid again. The phantom of a smile passed across Lulu's face. He patted the stool next to him, speaking in exaggerated American English.

– Hey, bad boy, how's it hanging?

– OK.

It was probably the only English Victor knew. He wrinkled his nose and mumbled something else, sliding onto the bar stool, laying down his helmet. Bernard looked up without interest, nodding a greeting, his jowls sagging. Yvette pushed up the bangles on her arm and gave him her brightest smile. He still reminded her of the Victor she knew from junior school. He'd given her a lucky-bag ring once, in the playground. Stammering. Making the other girls laugh. She'd given it back, watching him blush deep crimson as the other kids mocked him. Afterwards she'd regretted it. He was nice, after all. On the other hand, they were just kids. And kids were cruel. But it was funny she still thought about it, still felt a pang of regret.

The football match on the TV made a patch of green in the corner of the bar. A few more customers drifted in and

Bernard roused himself to greet them and pull their beers.
Yvette was tidying the tables, noticing how Lulu had his hand
on Victor's shoulder and was talking earnestly. She wondered
what they could possibly have to say to each other. Victor's
foot slipped off the foot rail as if he was only half-listening.
Lulu bought them both another beer. Yvette went outside for
a breather. The air was cool and there was Lulu's Jack Russell,
its nippled belly pressed up against the window of his car.
Mitzi. A couple of customers left the bar, lighting cigarettes
and blowing smoke into the night air as they went.

Then Lulu was beside her, rubbing his bare arms, shaking
his head and smiling at the dog.

– Look at her, that's love for you!

Yvette laughed.

– She's cute!

Lulu turned as he pointed his keys at the car.

– Need a lift?

Yvette glanced at her watch. There were still things to do
before Bernard would let her go home.

– No thanks. I've got to work.

– The bar's empty!

– It always is, but it's more than my job's worth to ask.

– OK. Say hello to your dad, eh?

She watched Lulu get into the car. The dog was jumping
up to lick his face and he was laughing. Then the headlights
bloomed. Yvette turned back into the bar. What *was* her job
worth in the end? It was a dead end. Just like the town. She
wondered what it would be like to sit up in the cab of the
truck with Lulu, driving from town to town, doing something
different every day instead of working for Madame.

There was a sudden flurry of colder air. It scattered litter across the car park and raised goose pimples on her arms. She went back in the bar and collected the last glasses. Victor was engrossed in the closing moments of the football or pretended to be. Bernard was drooping his eyes. He drew his finger across his throat. Victor rose to leave. Yvette collected her jacket from the back room and waved goodnight as she left. Bernard was locking the door behind her, his skin greenish in the strip light. He waved and went cross-eyed, like you do to amuse a kid. She smiled to oblige. Then the neon figure of the Pierrot was extinguished.

When Yvette got to the main road, the town was faintly lit against the sky. Victor was waiting astride his moped. He held out his helmet to her, Yvette considered the road. She was tired. It had been another long day. She'd got her period that morning and needed a shower. A car went past, slowing briefly, as if in two minds, its rear lights blinking like rubies.

– Thanks. She took the helmet and put it on.

It was a size too big and smelled brand new. She got astride the bike as Victor held it steady. The headlight came on, a white beam slicing the darkness. She remembered him in a circle of girls in the playground. Holding out the silver ring that was made of plastic. The way everyone had laughed at him. He started the engine and the moped lurched. Yvette had to put her arms around him to keep steady. Her knees were on either side of him and her skirt rode up. It was OK, because he couldn't see. His shoulders hunched over the handlebars. Her breath misted the plastic visor and when the bike slowed or braked, she was pressed against Victor's back.

Darkness dwindled behind them as the town came closer under its aura of light. First streetlamps, then outlying houses closing up for the night. Then the school, the fire station, then bumping over the bridge where the river flowed like ink with the lights of houses sunk into it. Then the long main street where the church spire was lit up and the bars were open and there were still customers lingering over cognac in the restaurants. She thought of Madame and Bernard in bed together. Sleeping, breathing each other's air, their dreams mingling. She remembered Lulu's little dog, its pale pink-nippled belly pressed against the car window.

Now Victor was steering the bike into a layby close to her house and she was climbing off, pulling her skirt down, struggling with the helmet. He leaned the moped on its side-stand.

– Here.

And his fingers were under her chin gently teasing the strap through the buckle.

Yvette shook her hair free.

– Thanks.

Without thinking, as if he was her brother, she was leaning forward to kiss him. His face was cold from the ride and his eyes went dark with surprise. But he kept his hands by his side. Yvette pulled back.

– That was sweet of you. Sleep well!

And she was gone, walking towards her house in the slightly exaggerated manner of someone who knows they're being observed.

Back home her parents were watching television. Dom was in his bedroom with the door open, playing on his Xbox or whatever that thing was. His room had that fusty smell of boys. He was wearing headphones and didn't even look up as she went into the bathroom to shower and clean her teeth. She looked lost in the mirror, her eyes hollow. She'd never liked her nose, which was too thin and made her look like a bird. Her hair needed washing. It was always greasy this time of the month. There never seemed time for that. Maybe tomorrow, if she got home early. The helmet had flattened it against her head. She flicked it back with a comb, trying to put more body in it, which it didn't have. She remembered the feel of Victor's body hunched on the moped. The way he hadn't said anything to her. The way her breasts had tingled. Then that brief kiss he'd flinched from.

The days went by and Victor stayed away. His boss came to clean the windows instead. Then it was July the twenty-eighth, the last Friday in the month. By six p.m. Bernard was re-arranging the tables. With Yvette's help, he pulled everything back a few yards, table legs screeching against floor tiles. A transit van appeared in the car park and the band were stretching, flicking away cigarettes, lifting out their gear. When they were playing, they had to stand in front of the toilets and members of the audience edged between them all night. It wasn't very cool. They'd be playing a smoochy number and some guy would appear in the doorway checking his flies, patting down his hair.

No wonder Lulu played with his eyes closed, swaying to the beat, wincing occasionally. Yvette could never tell what that was. If he made a mistake himself, he'd look at someone else in the band, incredulous. They'd told her about that trick last time in the van, what an arsehole he was. Lulu had laughed, almost choking on the beer, flicking ash. She'd realized that you didn't have to grow up after all. And she wondered if he took something else, apart from beer. His pupils were always wide and dark on band nights.

The singer was setting up a microphone stand. He was tall

and gangly. Good looking in a goofy way. The drummer was a squat guy with a shaved head who was almost hidden behind his kit. The guitar player had receding hair and bounced on the balls of his feet as he played, a row of effects pedals in front of him. Then there was Lulu with his shock of curls, his open shirt and medallion, his fingers rippling on the neck of the bass. You had to admit, he still had something.

There were a few families finishing their meals. Yvette brought them their desserts and coffee. The band was doing a sound check in English, the PA echoing. *One, two. One, two.* They thought it sounded cool, but it was just something annoying she'd learned at school. She could count to twenty and ask the way to the museum or the supermarket. Crazy. She remembered Anna and Martine speaking in English to piss her off, their tanned bodies knifing the river. The singer was fixing a set of floor lights that came on and off to the beat of the bass drum, casting the band's shadows against the wall. By the time they got halfway through their set, the windows would be running with sweat.

At eleven-thirty, there was a tight group on the dance floor, everyone dancing alone, but the whole group moving like some kind of ectoplasm. Most of the oldies had gone home. Bernard had got through a few drinks and was in a good mood. He pushed Yvette towards the dancers.

– Go on, go on. Enjoy!

Maybe he liked to watch her dancing in her short skirt. Older guys were like that, pretending not to look. Madame had long gone to bed with her earplugs. The lights were flashing red, purple, blue and green as the drummer pounded his kit and the guitarist flashed out a long solo. The singer had stepped back to give him space and there was Lulu, blissfully in the moment. The song finished with a descending run on the guitar, then vibrato on the final note. Now Lulu was looking at the guitar player. He seemed annoyed.

Then the singer announced the last song over the opening bars of 'Gloria', a song by that Irish guy whose name she couldn't remember. The audience joined in on the chorus, stamping their feet, raising their arms, saluting another Friday night. Yvette danced at the edge of the crowd, letting her body loosen. Then there was Victor, who seemed to appear from the flux of bodies, dancing beside her, the lights glancing off his glasses. He looked pleased to see her, but she couldn't remember him coming to the bar for drinks. To her surprise, he was a good dancer, hardly moving, turning from the hips, flexing to the beat without effort. She remembered their bodies spooning on his moped. He faced her and for the last few choruses they danced in unison, smiling at each other. There they were, in the playground again. She touched his arm as the song ended, liking the feel of her skin on his. Then Lulu was pulling off his guitar, holding up his hand, milking the applause.

Yvette was clearing the bar. The band were loading the van, the drummer taking down his kit at the far end of the room. There was Mitzi up at the window, her head cocked expectantly. Lulu went by with a PA speaker in each hand, bumping them against the doorway. Then there was some commotion and the singer had his arm around Lulu, who was stooping forward, sitting down on one of the speakers. Bernard was watching with narrowed eyes.

- *Putain!*

He dropped his tea towel and went outside to investigate. The dog was yapping now, short, sharp cries as the door opened and closed. Then Bernard was back, shaking his head, picking up the phone.

– It's Lulu. Not good.

He spoke rapidly into the mouthpiece. Yvette finished stacking the dishwasher and switched it on. It lurched as it came to life. She went to the doors and cleared a patch of condensation from the glass. The drummer was out there now. The singer still had his arm round Lulu. The dog was watching them, pawing the gravel. Then there was a blue light flashing up the road and the paramedics were there. They laid Lulu flat on a stretcher, pumping his chest and fitting an oxygen mask. All the time the blue light turned on and off, round and round, clashing with the neon Pierrot. Until they were loading the stretcher and the ambulance was heading into town with the siren shrieking.

After that, everything seemed very still.

The band finished loading, carried Mitzi to the van, and drove away. A few young people were still milling around, waiting for taxis or phoning home to say what had happened. Bernard was out there, shooing them home. Madame had come downstairs in her nightgown and hairnet and was asking Yvette what had happened.

– *Qu'est-ce qu'il s'est passé? Qu'est-ce qu'il s'est passé?*

When Yvette told her, a strange look went across her face and she pulled her nightgown tighter as if she was suddenly cold.

– Good Christ!

Just for a moment her eyes softened as if a memory was dissolving them. Yvette could have sworn she was about to cry. But then, they went back a long way. Madame, Lulu, Bernard. Everybody did in a small town.

Then Bernard was counting out her tips and changing them into notes. She pushed the little fold into her bra and went outside, slipping on her jacket. There was Victor's moped, leaning on its side-stand in the empty car park. The last taxi had pulled away. The lights in the bar where Bernard's shadow moved were going out, one by one. But the Pierrot was still pulsing in his baggy trousers and floppy hat, his mouth twisted down in a grimace of unutterable sadness. *Pepé's*. Yvette looked at Victor and her chest went tight. He seemed just like a child again.

– *Ça va?*

Victor stood up from the bike and his voice faltered as he replied.

– *Qui, ça va, Yvette.*

Victor was almost whispering. Yvette's heart fluttered as if it could break free and fly. She put her hand on his arm and at that moment the Pierrot extinguished and a flush of darkness entered the car park.

– I didn't know you could dance like that!

Victor shrugged, embarrassed. He was nine years old again, showing her the ring.

– You were great!

Yvette stepped closer, put her arms around him, pulling him into a long kiss, feeling his mouth warm and moist and soft, his hands fumbling against her waist. She remembered the Jack Russell bitch, watchful, loyally pressed against the van window. She saw Lulu, white-faced on the stretcher as the neon Pierrot blinked in perpetual astonishment. Then she was whispering into his neck.

– Victor.

– *Oui.*

That was all he said. *Yes.* As if he was answering a question, as if he was recognized. As if he'd been waiting to be all this time. Yvette felt the little wad of euros scratch against her breast. Her lips found Victor's mouth again and she was amazed at the way it yielded to hers, the way he was another person now. Something washed into her, suffusing her with sudden heat. She thought of Lulu, staring at the white tiles of a hospital ceiling. Or maybe worse. Maybe staring at the dark end of eternity. She remembered the stricken look on Madame's face, that unreadable look. She wondered where Mitzi was now, whimpering as Lulu was loaded into the ambulance with its flashing blue light.

Then Victor touched her arm and they were on the bike together, enveloped in the engine's vibration, the sharp scent of fuel. On Sunday she had the day off. On Monday he'd be cleaning the café windows again. So little time between now and then. Between one moment and the next. Between this moment and the future. Her arms tightened around him. He twisted the throttle and the bike buzzed like a bumble bee trapped in a foxglove. Her helmet bumped against his head and she laughed deep in her throat. They headed back to town, its halo of lights smouldering in mist that came off the river.

DAZZER

DAZZER PICKED UP his pint and tilted it.

— It made me sick, that . . . sick as a dog. But it had to be done, mate.

Dazzer. Darrell Grady. How many years was that? He looked into the bottom of his glass then drained it. He'd put on a lot of weight, standing there in a khaki gaberdine and corduroy trousers. Slip-on shoes. Plenty of silver-blond hair. I remembered his small flat teeth, his dimples, the way his thumbs had always bent away from the things he gripped. There they were again as he grimaced and put the glass down.

I raised my eyebrows and pointed at the empty pint. He shook his head and rubbed his stomach. He was wearing silver cufflinks.

— Got to go, Ian. I'll see you, eh? Give me a bell.

He patted my arm and went to the drizzle outside, pulling up his collar as he slipped through the rotating door. I finished my pint and ordered another, watching as it foamed and settled, the golden liquid streaming upwards. Dazzer. Bloody hell! It'd been years. It'd been half a lifetime. He'd been standing at the bar stubbing out a cigarette as I walked in, looking just like his father, Pat, an accountant who'd worked for the council. The Gradys were a big family. Catholics. *But not religious*, my mum always said in a particular tone of voice. As if they'd seen the light. They rented an old farmhouse a few fields away from our house. We were at the far edge of town where building had petered out at the end of the last century. My dad had done some work for them, putting in new kitchen units. I remember him cursing the old hand-made bricks that were so hard they'd blunted his drill. The place burnt down after they left. Then it was demolished to build a sports centre.

Dazzer was left-handed. Well-built, even as a lad. He had an old cricket bat bound with black electrical tape that had belonged to his older brother. *Sean.* My brother had shown me how to bind a bat with string, tightly wound at the edges, then tied off to stop the wood splintering. We played on the field below our house. Dazzer made my leg-spin into off-spin. No technique. Cross-batting and slogging as hard as he could. He didn't like being out and he couldn't bowl for toffee. He'd always been handy with his fists when he needed to be. Though I never had him down as a bully.

Imagine a shallow river valley running roughly north-south. A group of mills clustered in the south, the town on three sides, but open fields to the west. We were the last terrace of the town. Ladysmith Terrace. All the houses were built in the early nineteen hundreds and named after battles in the Boer War. Opposite was a scatter of farms scraping a living from the last patches of agricultural land. The foul little river ran between, a fugitive.

Running on an east-west axis was the railway embankment, slicing the valley in half, allowing the river through twin culverts like the muzzle of a double-barrelled gun. At one point the canal ran under the railway and then over the river on a high aqueduct. Another piece of Victorian engineering, like the quad of cotton mills where my grandfather had worked. Their chimneys had gone cold in the Fifties, before I was born. Kestrels nested there and hunted over the waste tips and fields. The river banks were overgrown with Himalayan balsam and rosebay willow herb. Cattle bawled behind gap-toothed hawthorn hedges, mended with barbed wire and old gates. When the blossom was out it looked as it had looked for centuries, before the mills and canals and railways. But it was winter now and everything was laid bare.

There was one farm left, beyond where Dazzer's house used to be, squeezed up against the railway embankment above a heart-shaped field where a few cows still grazed. You could see the moors in the far distance, nestled in a blue haze or whitened by snow. Even the pub I was drinking in had once been a farmhouse.

Dazzer had older brothers, a sister and a good-natured mother who always made a fuss when I went round. The boys had thick unruly hair and the sister a chestnut ponytail that she sometimes wore in a braid. I can't remember their names now or even how many there were. Their father was a bluff, friendly guy, originally from Ulster. Even my dad liked Pat, and that was something coming from a bloke who didn't like many people. Or any people. Every morning Pat followed the milk wagon down the lane in his Morris Traveller, pipe smoke drifting from the quarter light. They seemed happier than us, more prosperous, more themselves.

The barman was trying to catch my attention with the pint. I turned back to him.

– There you go. I'll need to top that up.

He had a buzz cut and wide brown eyes.

– Cheers.

I was home. I was in a pub. There was the pint glass at my elbow. I should have been content. Like a pig in straw. If only.

I dropped some coins on the bar and the barman took the

pint back to raise its crown of foam. A perfectionist. Old school. Few and far between now.

– Nice pint!

– Cheers. Enjoy.

Credit where it's due. But he wasn't interested. He had enough to do. *Sufficient unto the day.* Whatever that's supposed to mean. It was something my mum used to say. I put my nose to the pint and caught the scent of malt and hops. The beer slipped into my throat the way a river finds its estuary.

I put the pint down, watching rings of foam cling to the sides of the glass. I remembered it was Dazzer who'd given me my first taste of beer on a school trip. He was allowed to drink at home, which was unheard of in my family. *They've nowt better to do. More money than sense*, my dad said, because he only ever took a bottle of Guinness on a Friday night and felt guilty about that. Which was bullshit, because he didn't feel guilty about much else. But he was always quick onto the moral high ground. *Like a ferret up a downspout*, my older brother Teddy would say, rolling a ciggy in the Rizzla he kept hidden in a bedroom drawer.

Dazzer got some older lads to buy the beer. They weren't eighteen either, but they looked it. It was brown ale and when I tasted it, I didn't know what the fuss was about. It was dry and bitter. But I was fourteen and it was a new thing. It was *cool*, which was all that mattered. We were on a field trip at one of those outward-bound centres in the Lake District. There were a group of girls from Dewsbury on the same outing. We were at a single sex school and girls, apart from my sister and her friends, were a mystery. I had my first kiss with a girl called Emily, as well as my first taste of beer. We met in the woods behind the hostel after her friend passed on a message. I remembered the feel of her body, the scent of her. *Emily.* An old-fashioned name. Her hair clung to my face when we kissed. Her mouth was wet and warm and tasted of spearmint.

We wrote to each other afterwards and I phoned her a few times from the local phone box that stank of piss and cigarettes. It didn't last more than a few weeks, but then how could it? We were practising for something, I guess. For life, for the real thing. Turned out Dazzer had married Pamela Johnson from our primary school. She'd always seemed the brightest kid in the class, but she never made it to the grammar. She's still there, peeking between us on the school photograph, with Miss Cooper watching over us under the chestnut trees in the playground. We picked the conkers and threaded them and fought with them in autumn. Something else Dazzer always had the knack for.

I took another pull of the beer, watching rain fall through the haloes of streetlamps outside. That afternoon, my dad had discharged himself from hospital. I'd got a call from the district nurse to warn me, so I was home before him. Letting myself into that smell of stale food and stained carpets. When the taxi arrived, he lurched out with bandaged feet, carrying a plastic bag attached to a catheter. He was still in pyjamas and a nightgown. Now he staggered towards the front gate like one of Napoleon's guys on the retreat from Moscow. He leaned on the garden wall where my mum had tended the privet hedge and grown a few sickly bluebells. It was only three days since he'd thrown his walking stick at my brother, shouting, *I'll see the fucking lot of you off!* He was nice like that. Mad as a box of frogs when it suited him. Cool and collected when that served him better. They'd run some psychiatric tests on him and he'd run rings round them. It would have been funny in a parallel universe. Which is what it felt like sometimes.

I paid the taxi driver, lifted Dad's suitcase and got him into the house. I didn't mind the catheter and the bag of piss, deep amber and murky. But I did mind that the only help he'd accept was from family. He'd been a difficult man and – in his own estimation – had led a difficult life. But then so had most working people who'd been brought up before the war and missed out on an education. Some of our neighbours had served in Burma, fighting the Japanese. They'd seen terrible things, and probably done them. But my dad didn't think so. All that was cushy compared to National Service in the air force on a Hebridean island. All his life he'd blamed things on somebody else. In fact, everyone but himself. Pat Grady had missed military service, somehow. *Soft Irish bastard.* And you have to remember my dad liked him. Enough said.

I'd been at primary school with Dazzer, along with Pamela and a red-haired girl called Judie Brown, who I'd really liked. I never saw her again after we made it to the grammar school. That was full of working-class kids and pretty rough by any standards. The boys were that fateful mixture: intelligent and functionally ruthless, hunting down any weakness. Chanting at the deputy head in assembly every morning. Trapping a kid called Jeremy in the playground after school every day and kicking footballs at him until he sobbed for mercy. No teachers ever seemed to notice, especially the headmaster, a five-foot martinet. Len Cahill. Old school, again. But not in a good way. He ruled by fear and probably had to. We survived until the sixth form, when the most violent kids left and we could grow our hair and learn the guitar and share LPs in the common room. I remembered Dave Hillier crying at the bus stop the day Jimi Hendrix died. September 1970. We'd started a new term. It was the beginning of the Seventies, and the Sixties were just catching up with us in the north.

The territory of your childhood never leaves you. I read that somewhere. Maybe not those exact words. But it's true, like all clichés. One feature of our territory was a disused canal, a ribbon of black water that used to carry coal and cotton. It circled the mills and bisected the mosses in-between. It was overgrown in places, reed beds sprawling from the towpath. We used to fish it for perch and roach after school or at weekends. There were pike and tench, too. Legendary giants.

I used to walk miles back then, just to be out of the house. At weekends, I'd run into Dazzer, or he'd call by with his rod and creel and keep net. Stuff we couldn't afford. He'd adopted me, I suppose. Our favourite spot was by a ruined lockkeeper's house. The old timber gates were rotting, letting the water spray through. It was a near a riding stables that had used to be a pub, The Top Drum, where my grandad must have drunk in-between shifts at the mill. All that was out of reach now. Time and space. Space and time. You couldn't force a blade between them.

Dazzer was knowledgeable about birds, spotting wagtails and goldfinches and reed buntings, knowing a meadow pipit from a skylark. It was part of his family lore. My dad wouldn't have known a swan from a farmyard duck. But Dazzer's clan had the knowledge and passed it down. I remember that curious curve of his thumb as he forced a treble hook through the spine of a roach, using it as live bait to lure a pike from the reeds. If he caught one it was thrashed to death with the rod rest, its devil's face gaping rows of teeth.

One night, we were packing up the gear to go home. I can't remember if we'd caught anything. Lapwings were calling through the dusk, dipping low over the fields, their cries piercing and eerie. Turning to leave, we spotted a couple lying full length in the grass behind the old lock house. I remember Dazzer smiling and making a gesture with his hand, as if he knew something I didn't. It was a cynical smile, like the grin on a jack pike. So what was happening was something secret, something forbidden. He was worldly like that, always seeming to know things beyond my reach.

We'd grown up in a house with no bathroom for most of my childhood and we had to carry piss-pots down the yard to the privy. Some mornings, there was a condom floating in the one my dad set down outside his and mum's bedroom. They appeared in the river when it flooded, hanging from the hawthorn branches. Was that love? I'd lie awake in that stifling house, listening for trains on the embankment, hearing wind shrieking in the telephone wires. Summer nights were long and hot and there were cats fighting outside or having sex, our own grey tom among them. He'd come limping home with a torn ear or scabby leg. In winter there'd be a glimmer of frost along the outhouse roofs when the moon rose beyond the town, its promise of elsewhere. My father's voice from the next room bitter and low as a saw.

Now there was this couple full-length in the grass, oblivious of us. We stood in the shadows. They moved together, their bodies twined. It took me a while to realize that it was two girls. I could hear their low cries, see their pale thighs where their skirts were pushed up. I turned away, ashamed.

It was Dazzer who took a backward glance, who made that gesture, shaking his head, smirking.

We set off along the canal, balancing on its coping stones. The moon rose above the mill chimneys and the railway embankment. We went under the railway tunnel, parting company at the track that led to his house. I walked on over the river and up the lane. The hawthorns were in bloom, lining the field boundaries like underslips hung to dry. It must have been a Friday because my sister was washing her hair over the sink with Linco beer shampoo when I got home. I felt that little tug of shame that came all too often now.

I was one of the first kids to leave that neighbourhood and go to university. My brother, Teddy, was working in electronics by then, building circuits for fighter jets. Christine had got on the ladder at a solicitor's firm, training on the job. I went to Leeds to study geography and became a school teacher. Dazzer had gone straight into work. He'd been good at chemistry and was taken on by the local brewery. It was family-owned and had resisted takeovers from the bigger firms. Twenty-odd years later he was still there. Sales manager. Prosperous, self-satisfied, genial, just like his parents had been. He'd got a couple of kids. One still at college. One working for the brewery as well. She'd got an MBA, I think he said. Dazzer wore a heavy gold wedding ring. I noticed it as he gripped his beer glass, asking me if I'd ever married. He gave me an old-fashioned look as he asked, as if he'd never expected it anyway.

I told him about my nephews and nieces. But I didn't tell him about Angela. How we'd met at the staff party at my first school where she taught physics. She was from Rutland, a county that had appeared and disappeared with each boundary change. I didn't say how I'd got her pregnant through being a bloody fool and knowing nothing. Then the Registry Office, then the miscarriage after two months, which she somehow blamed on me. All our colleagues thought it was a whirlwind romance when it was really sex, recrimination and waste.

It hadn't been about anything in the end. No infidelity. No betrayal, except the failure to love each other. Our marriage was loaded with long disappointments and longer silences. Something like hatred had begun to weep from it like fluid from a wound. So, I had no kids to boast about. I felt like a child myself, my father back there in that terraced house, dozing in front of the TV, his catheter draining into the plastic bag that rested on an offcut of Axminster he'd picked up from the local market and spread in front of the fireplace.

I was trying to share the weekends with my brother and sister. This time I'd got the short straw. Teddy was on holiday and Christine was busy with her children. That was fair enough. I drove home straight from school. It was about thirty-five miles, so I hadn't fallen far from the tree. I went at a snail's pace, dreading the state of the house, the fingerprints smeared on the toilet walls, the pans of burnt food coagulating on the stove, the shopping I'd have to do in the supermarket they'd built when I was growing up.

Home was a nowhere place now, a ghost of the busy little mill town where my dad had been raised. It'd been gutted by town planners. The old municipal gardens replaced by twin traffic roundabouts and an underpass. No one in their right mind would have visited that on a community. *Back-handers*, my dad said, the way he said *left-footers*. *They're all as bent as each other*. There were those with influence and those without.

Those on the make and those with sod-all but a thin wage packet at the end of the week. If they were lucky.

Driving down to see my dad was one thing. Driving home when I'd done my duty was another. I'd floor the accelerator and then stop off for a couple of pints when I got close to home. I was seeing someone about the time I ran into Dazzer. Sheila, who taught English, and who eventually got sick of me being away at weekends. Or maybe she'd just got sick of me. It hadn't meant much. And maybe you just get past being able to love someone. I went back to microwaved meals and screw-top wine and football on the telly. Waking up on the settee, streetlights shining through the orange curtains that Angela had put up and that I could never seem to get rid of.

Most Sundays involved a steady hangover and a stack of marking. After the separation, Angela had married the solicitor who'd divorced us. You couldn't make it up. But her mother would have been delighted to see the back of me. The way I struggled with the cutlery when I visited their detached house, a Volvo estate parked on the driveway. The way I dropped strawberries onto the table linen or cut the nose off the Stilton and helped myself to wine without asking. I watched her dad's face as I filled my glass. He was some kind of company director. They had a Filipino home-help, Theresa, who did the washing and ironing and helped out at dinner parties when they entertained. *Of course, we pay her nearly twice the going rate.* I felt like blowing bubbles in the fucking Bordeaux. We are who we are. You couldn't blame Angela for hating my attitudes. Or for the solicitor. In fact, I quite liked Alec, though I always wondered if he'd told Angela to dig her heels in over our settlement. She'd taken me to the cleaners in the end.

I finished my pint and looked around the bar. Mock Tudor beams and faux plasterwork finished with a brush to look rustic. My dad had done some work on that too, if I wasn't mistaken. They'd given him a bottle of Mateus Rosé. A flat bottle in woven straw. We kept it for years afterwards. I wondered if the pub was full of blokes I'd been to school with and just didn't recognize. Passers-by, now. They'd built a massive housing estate on what had used to be open fields when I was a kid. It'd been settled by people from slum clearances in Manchester. *Folk from town,* my mother called them. Even the local accent had changed, losing its Lancashire brogue, taking on sharper tones. I'd delivered post up on the estate for a time when I was a student. Alsatians dogs prowling behind leylandii hedges and lattice fences. Jack Russells yapping behind frosted glass, shredding letters as they went through. I'd never got that thing about dogs, front lawns littered with shit and kids playing there.

I picked my coat up and nodded to the barman who ignored me or didn't notice. Out into the rain. I crossed the road where streetlamps blurred into wet tarmac, finding my dad asleep in front of the electric fire. Slumped in an armchair, the television blaring. I turned it down, watching to see if he'd wake. He was well away. The bag would need changing soon. He'd come home with a promise that the district nurse would call. I unplugged it all as he dozed. The new bag went on easily, but emptying the full one was a nightmare. My parents had had a little extension built onto the house with a kitchen, bathroom and toilet, but it had no heating or double glazing and it was freezing in winter. I managed to discharge the bag into the toilet and flush it, then went out to the dustbin. The rain had picked up, lashing the brickwork.

I had no idea what was supposed to happen next. Waiting as my dad snored in a chair, the new bag gradually filling. *What was I going to do?* Dazzer said, *a lezzer sniffing round my daughter?* I saw his thumb against the pint glass. *Right under my fucking nose.* I thought about Angela. I hadn't really been a bloody fool out of ignorance. I'd thought children might be a part of love. That was the stupidity. Thinking that other people could feel the same as you did. She was the dumb one, forgetting her cap. But that wasn't fair either, I knew that. The whole thing felt like shame again from this distance. *She was making me look a real cunt, mate. Right there in the office. I wasn't having it.*

My dad shifted in the chair, dreaming of something. Maybe my mum. She'd been a cook at the local infirmary. I thought about getting him to bed. I thought about smothering him with a pillow. Would anybody even know? I got a long way down the road with that idea as he dozed. Even imagining defending myself in court. I was pretty sure I'd get off. He'd been a selfish get, expecting my sister to look after him, just because she was a woman. He couldn't do a thing around the house apart from poke about with the Hoover. Nothing I ever did was good enough. No wonder I drove home like a maniac after every visit. No wonder I drank.

One time I'd been called to the hospital urgently. I arrived to find his bed made up and empty. For a moment I thought he must have passed on. Then, at the far end of the ward this little figure appeared, coming back from the washroom, swinging his towel, joshing with the other guys as if they were all out on some jolly or back in the army. I'd dropped everything to get there. He'd got lost after Bury market and thumbed a lift from an ambulance, so it wasn't an easy visit, digesting that. Then I was heading home through Burnley and there was this big flash of light as the speed camera went off. Sixty quid and three points on my license. Double fuck.

It was only nine o'clock. I watched him snoring in the armchair. He needed a haircut. Maybe a lot more than that. He didn't have to worry, because I was worried. I was dreading that freezing little bedroom where my sister had slept. The mahogany bed-head, creaking springs, the floral wallpaper. The past waiting for me at every turn. Like Dazzer. *I wasn't fucking having it. No way. Making a twat out of me after I'd brought her up.* That twist of a smile as he raised his pint.

My mum had died in that bed. We'd got it downstairs somehow, because he didn't want her in care. The mattress jammed in the stairwell before we pulled it loose. He kept her for three days afterwards, without telling anyone. The doctor looked at us as if we were all insane when he came to sign the certificate.

After a struggle, I got him to bed. He kept calling me Teddy, which was good in a way, because he wouldn't know which son I was when things had gone missing or hadn't been done properly.

I managed some sleep before the morning when the nurse had promised to call. When I opened the curtains, there it all was. The last farm cringing against the railway embankment. The new sports pavilion and playing field built where Dazzer's house had been, where they'd lived and seemed to prosper. Before Pat had lost his job in the Eighties and taken a bus to the reservoir. My mum sent me the newspaper cutting. You had to hand it to him.

Dazzer's mother had moved into a council house on one of the new estates. But that wasn't what he wanted to talk about. *You know how it is, a young lass and an old lezzer. I wasn't having that.* He told me the story with a faint smile. I remembered that look he'd given me as we turned from those girls in the field, making love all those years ago. *I found out where she lived and paid her a call.* He rapped the back of his hand into his palm. Left-handed, his thumb curling back.

My dad was shouting something. The cows looked up from the heart-shaped field, as if they'd heard him call out. There was a loop of rope still hanging from the sycamore tree. But it didn't look as if the local kids played there anymore. We'd spent hours in that tree, taking it in turns to swing out over the emptiness below, watching the sun go down behind the mills. The cows bent their heads again. A freight train taking on the embankment arrived level with them. When I was a kid it'd been steam trains, moving through the night, streaming sparks and smoke into darkness.

My dad was shouting again. Croaking over the early morning traffic. *Ian! Ian! Help me with this bloody thing!* And I was helping an old man out of bed, taking the urine bag away and fitting a new one. Making tea in the little kitchen where my mother had cooked and cleaned and used the washing machine. There was even a fridge, which we'd never had as kids. I watched steam obscure the view of the last fields that the town was waiting to engulf. *Give us a call sometime, next time you're home to see your old man,* Dazzer said, watching me pretend to enter his number into my phone. *We'll go for a pint and catch up properly.*

I cleared a patch in the moisture on the glass. There was a row of empty plant pots on the windowsill. Dead geraniums and dried soil. A man was walking his dog up the lane. I thought about that couple in the dusk all those years ago, their low voices mingling with the cries of lapwings. I envied them, then. I still do. The way one of them leaned over to place her finger across the lips of her friend to quieten her. The way their bodies had fitted together. Now there were the cows grazing, heads down in the field. There was my father calling me again. Then the district nurse was ringing the doorbell, neat in her green uniform. I remembered the dark waters of the canal as night fell over those girls making love behind the ruined cottage, Dazzer's face twisting into a smile, as if he'd always known everything.

THE APRIL SUN

THE OLD MAN came up behind us on the rocky path. He was big and square-set and walked with a stick. Swaying slightly, labouring, stumbling. His feet knocking on the loose stones underfoot. He wore a dark suit and a tie splashed with scarlet poppies. Silver-rimmed spectacles low on his nose. He was bald and had the scar of a deep head wound that must have healed a long time ago. He met us on a humped bridge that went over a dry stream. Just below a wayside shrine where primroses grew. The shrine held an icon of the sacred heart, plastic flowers and electric candles behind a Perspex window.

– *Buongiorno.*

– Good morning, ladies!

He came back at us in English, even after Monica had tried out her Italian. He must have heard us talking as he followed us up the path.

We'd walked out of the village along the road, past the spa hotel that rose up like a fascist monument. Then we'd taken a mule track that climbed steeply, passing a ruined church. The hills were wooded with all sorts of broad-leaved trees – hazel, birch, oak, alder and others I didn't recognize. Wild flowers grew thick on the verges and there were goats grazing in the meadows, their bells clanking.

When we sat on the apartment balcony in the evenings, the woods simmered under a blue haze and swifts screamed by in gangs, so close we could have reached out to touch them.

Last night a pillar of cloud had appeared, turning pink in the falling sun. There were other villages on other hilltops, their clock towers painted white, their gilded hands striking the hour just moments out of time, so that the whole valley echoed.

The old man leaned his stick against the parapet of the bridge and sat down. He took out a folded handkerchief and wiped his forehead where it glistened with sweat.

– You are on holiday? English?

– Yes, English. We . . .

– I'm Australian, actually. Originally, I mean . . .

But the old man wasn't interested in what she meant or in the New World or Sydney. Maybe the bright timbre of Monica's accent bothered him. The way her sentences rose up at the end like questions. She was tall with freckles and a bunch of tawny hair screwed up onto her head. She had one of those neat little noses and shallow blue eyes that were too ready to meet your own. I'd had a job keeping up with her long-legged pace on the way up.

The old man rose and sat down again, settling himself on the limestone parapet. I noticed that his shoes were scuffed at the toes. Black shoes, like a priest's or lawyer's.

– Ah, I was in London once, in Trafalgar Square. It was so interesting.

– Did you stay long?

He didn't answer me straight away but put the handkerchief back in his pocket and patted it, as if to make sure it was still there. It was hard to guess his age. Over eighty, anyway.

– Not long. Just to visit some Italian friends, then I come home.

- Your English is excellent.

- Ha! You're kind. I never speak that.

There was a pause. The old guy took out the handkerchief again and wiped his face. He put it back in his pocket.

- It's very heat!

I laughed just to be polite. Then Monica chose her moment.

- But it's very beautiful.

Now the old man laughed, rocking a little against the stone bridge and reaching behind him for his stick again.

- It is Italy. Everywhere is beautiful!

We smiled in appreciation and he gestured to the village above, the green cupola of the church, the ochre and pink houses.

- You went up to those village?

Monica slung her little rucksack.

- Not yet. Tomorrow.

- Tomorrow? *Molto bene!* Is good to visit there.

We stood up and the old man smiled and shook his head gently as if we'd invited him to join us.

- I will rest. I am not young!

We shook hands and said goodbye.

We'd come to look at the church and to wonder why it had fallen into ruins. It was plain by Italian standards – white walls and a broken pantile roof showing the rafters. All or-namentation had been removed and the walls were scrawled with graffiti in several languages. German, English, Italian. Even some Arabic script. Some campers had lit a fire where the altar must have been, and the smoke had blackened the walls as if the place had been sacked.

There was a stumpy tower with a set of stone stairs. The steps were covered in fallen plaster and rubble. Monica was keen to explore.

- It looks dangerous.

- Ah, c'mon Keri. Don't be so soft!

And up she went. I followed her. If she fell, I fell. She kicked plaster dust into my face and down my shirt-front and into my bra. We clung to the rough walls, sweat in our eyes, until we were standing on a little landing. It was open to the sky where the tiles had fallen away and gave a view of the valley though a ruined window. Spirals of smoke drifted against the deep green of the trees. Scattered farms nested in clearings and there was a faint smell of burning olive wood. In one field we saw a black horse flicking its mane and tail, as if an insect was plaguing it. Its hooves tore up clods of earth. Monica was soon bored. She touched my arm.

- C'mon Keri, Sandra's gonna be wondering . . .

We descended warily, our boots skidding in the dust. We took the bridleway back to the spa, then up the long drag of tarmac to the apartment.

Sandra had stayed back with a headache, making lunch from the things you could buy at the village shop. Cheese and ham and fatty sausages. Sometimes fresh onions, aubergines and green beans that were displayed in trays outside. Bunches of parsley or basil. Fresh bread if you got there early in the morning. It was run by a woman with dark rings under her eyes and grey streaks in her hair who spoke a little English. We pointed to things and she'd repeat their names in Italian slowly, as if we were children. When we asked for wine she pointed to a row of bottles high on a shelf then told us that her husband ran the local bar. When we asked for eggs she spread her hands slowly and frowned until I did the chicken dance and she pulled them triumphantly from behind the counter.

Monica and I had caught up with the old man as he laboured back down the path. There was something heartbroken about him. Something defeated in the stoop of his shoulders, the way the stick felt its way ahead of him like a blind man's. But he wasn't blind. His eyes were clear behind the glasses. The wound in his head seemed to pulse in the sun. Every now and again he'd stop to wipe his face. We passed, greeting him once more, and when we were about twenty paces ahead of him, he called out to us.

– Ah, ladies. Ladies.

He waved the stick.

– Remember me some time!

Monica looked back, shading her eyes. We murmured something back to him. Then we were walking on at her rapid pace. She moved like a cat that had the perfect body weight, skimming over the ground. She wore shorts and ankle socks as if she'd been born in them. Whereas Sandra looked as if she'd been dressed by her mum, legs white from lack of sun. She always said I was lucky to have a permanent tan. Very funny. But at least we could laugh at each other.

I lingered with my camera, trying some close-ups of thistles and wild flowers and hazel nuts, catching my breath, then catching up. *Remember me some time*. Only someone who knew that they were going to die could say that. He was going to die here, where everything was beautiful. I felt tears prickle under my eyelids, but Monica was already ahead of me, moving with that impatient twitch of the hips, her leg muscles flexing like a horse.

We'd started out from Leeds, flying to Nice with one of those cut-price airlines. Everything stripped to the bone. The seats didn't recline and the cabin crew all wore blingy wristwatches. *Please do store your luggage in the overhead locker. Please do take care leaving the aircraft. Please do have the correct change for refreshments.* We watched the bursar with close-cropped hair tease the younger cabin boy who had dimples and perfect teeth. He used the gangway of the plane as a catwalk. Despite the rubbish conditions, they were nice to us. And you wouldn't want that job. Clearing up everyone's crap, putting up with rudeness, even eating those bloody awful aircraft meals. No wonder they camped it up.

We got a taxi at the airport at Nice. We'd agreed to just bring cabin luggage, except Sandra had risked an extra carrier bag that seemed to be stuffed with hair products. She had a short bob cut into her neck. Low maintenance. My dad was half Nigerian and I had a head of curls that were a nightmare to wash and dry. His dad was from Port Harcourt, way back. Hair's a big deal at any age. The taxi driver had a shaven head sprinkled with dark moles. I wondered if that was the sun. He looked bored and bad-tempered

When we were close to the hotel, we passed a group of squatters camping under polythene sheets in a little park next to a dazzlingly white church. Purple blossom tumbled from the walls. *Bougainvillea*, Monica said. They must have that in Australia. The squatters looked like Syrians or Libyans fleeing the war. The driver muttered, *Les coleurs!* I knew that meant 'all sorts' in French, but there was a racist slur, a sneer to his voice. I looked at the skin of my arm in the sun and wanted to tell him no one gets on a boat and risks their life for nothing. That you have to be desperate and afraid to test the sea. There was a guy in a wheelchair who had no legs, pulling on a tee shirt, muscled from pushing himself along. How he'd got here was unimaginable. But then other lives are.

We stayed overnight in a grubby little hotel near the Promenade des Anglais, where there was that awful terrorist attack a year later. We had a vile breakfast of instant coffee and stale croissants that put me in a temper for the rest of the day. We could have gone around the corner to a decent café, but Sandra kept saying she was exhausted and just needed to get herself together and could we please just eat in the hotel? She looked like she'd been awake all night, though we'd shared a bed and pretty much fallen asleep at once. I dreamed that I was sitting my A-levels again but had done no revision. My books were in a steel locker, just like the ones we'd really had at school. Miss Kennedy, my old geography teacher, was watching me, wearing a long black academic gown. Weird.

I woke with Sandra's arm across me, though she was fast asleep. We showered in tepid water, fumbling with those stupid shower-gel containers, then dressed, bleary-eyed, pulling on crumpled clothes, traipsing downstairs for a distinctly un-Continental experience. Then there was a panic because Sandra thought she'd lost her passport, which was in her hand luggage all the time. But not before she'd been down to reception to ask if they'd found it, getting me to translate. In fact, we had the sort of shitty experience that almost always comes with travel. Unless you're loaded, I suppose. But we'd done it on the cheap. We were social work students, not millionaires, like those guys who were crossing the bay in their white yachts.

Monica didn't say much over breakfast. Just dunked her croissant in the awful coffee and traced our route to the railway station on the map she'd brought.

– It's about half a kilometre.

Sandra looked blank. She didn't look as if she had any idea

what a kilometre was. She hadn't put in her contact lenses and her eyes had an unfocussed, faraway look. Monica snapped up her wrist to show her watch.

– We'll need to get going in about twenty.

– Twenty?

Sandra was looking bewildered. She'd smeared lipstick all over her mouth and looked half-witted with tangled, damp hair.

– *Minutes*. Twenty minutes?

There was Monica's voice rising up again with impatience. For some reason I turned my coffee cup upside down on the saucer, as if I was trapping an insect.

– Good. Can't wait.

Monica grinned and folded the map. She didn't give a monkey's, really. Hard-core Australian. Or maybe that was the impression she was aiming for. I hadn't known her long. Didn't really know her, in fact. It had been Sandra's idea to bring her along. *Straight as a die*, she'd whispered. *But she's OK. You'll like her.*

I didn't know what Monica was used to. Maybe she was just good at making the best of things. But you don't go to France for terrible coffee when it's so plentiful back in the UK.

The leery guy behind the desk watched us as we brought our bags downstairs. We handed in the keys with what I hoped was ironical politeness. The homeless men were gathered in the street around that guy in the wheelchair. They had a teenage girl with them, her hair covered with a headscarf. They slept in the grounds of the Church of Our Lady and the priest ran a soup kitchen on the promenade. They were mainly Arabs from what we could tell.

All in all, there was something oppressive about Nice. Those gaggles of beautiful tanned girls heading for the beach, walking as if they owned the future. But you could feel the sun burning you up, generations of its worshippers growing old and wrinkled. Its glare on plate glass and the stone bulk of the church. It wasn't anywhere I wanted to be for long.

We set off for the train station, following Monica, trailing our luggage. A few stops beyond Ventimiglia we'd catch a bus up into the mountains. The train was a weird two-storey affair. We bought sandwiches at the station and piled aboard, hoisting our bags up the stairs. The countryside flitted past. Industrial sidings, graffiti, then low fields with rows of vines. Sandra went to find the loo and got lost and hadn't taken her phone. *For fuck's sake, Keri, she's the giddy limit!* When she didn't return, Monica decided to go and find her. Eventually they appeared just as we were approaching the Italian border, entering Liguria, where the train slowed and stopped. We shrugged and ate our lunch and opened the windows to get an airflow into the carriage. It was stifling. When the train started again it crawled into Ventimiglia station. An announcement in Italian, French and then English told us that there'd been a power line failure and that buses would take us to our destination. Hundreds of passengers spilled into the blinding sun.

We waited for hours in the heat. Buses arrived and passengers besieged them, trying to get aboard even before they'd parked up, the drivers gesturing angrily. It reminded me of that footage from Saigon after the Vietnam war, those people clinging to helicopters as they took off. There were *carabinieri* on duty, slouching about in shades. They had white pistol holsters and smoked cigarettes, eyeing up women's breasts and doing absolutely sod-all to help the old people or children who were being shouldered aside. By now Sandra was overheated and wailing and Monica's jaw had set into a firm line. I went to the loo and had to queue, and when I got a cubicle it was foul and scattered with toilet paper. The fiasco went on until the crowds gradually thinned, with the Brits trying to form a queue and the Americans and Australia hanging back in the shadows. The *Continentals*, as Sandra called them, surged forward, then were gone. There was a French boy behind us with a double bass who stood no chance. Twice Monica strode off to try to find out what was happening and twice she came back looking as if she could kill. Shaking her head. Checking her phone.

Eventually, well after noon, the bus came and took us up through the mountains, stopping at villages to pick up locals and a few tourists on the way. We got to the town at four o'clock in the afternoon and there, waiting for us, smoking and grinding her cigarette butts into the dust, was Aniela. She was a Greek woman living in Italy, a painter who made a living selling her work and looking after holiday flats for her clients. She was about fifty, burnt dark by the sun, tousled hair, tight leggings, a tee shirt with a picture of Kurt Cobain on it, a gap in her side-teeth. She grinned and dropped her cigarette, stepping on it as we approached.

– You are welcome, welcome!

– I'm so sorry we're late.

She held up her phone to show us she'd been keeping track of the situation.

– Don't be sorry. It is Italy!

She shrugged, her breasts loose under Kurt's face.

– Come!

She hauled our luggage into the boot of the battered Datsun she was leaning against and we piled in. No aircon, of course, and by now we'd all started to sweat. Aniela gunned the engine and we set off on a white-knuckle ride through villages, round hairpin bends, up gradients, over little bridges, past market gardens shrouded in black netting, through dense forests that bristled on the hillsides.

I'll swear Aniela never once stopped talking, throwing her hands off the wheel, laughing, jerking her head back to make sure we were listening. By the time we pulled into the village square, even Monica looked nauseous. Sandra was chalk-white, dragging her bag from the boot of the Datsun, glaring spitefully at the village. Then there was the apartment. It was up a short flight of steps that fanned from a green door above the cobbled street. There was a long corridor with ground floor apartments, then two crooked flights of stairs that led to ours.

The first room was a lounge and kitchen with a little balcony that smelled of sewage. The walls and canvas chairs were covered in green algae. Then a small bedroom with bunk beds leading to a toilet and shower en suite with no shower curtain. Then a double bedroom reached only through the single. It was awkward. Sandra and I dumped our luggage in the double bedroom whilst Monica slung hers onto the lower bunk. *I've seen better fucking stables!* I felt a bit hurt at that. After all, I'd made the booking. Well, me and Sandra. Everything had looked great on the website. When we looked from the window, which overlooked a kind of plaza, there was washing hanging on the balconies and a group of boys playing soccer, the sound of the ball echoing off the walls.

That first night we found the shop and bought biscuits, some ham, a hard cheese, tomatoes, avocados and a bottle of red wine. We ate at the little Formica table in the kitchen and laughed at our predicament. *We'll survive*, Monica said, *even if it is a fucking holiday!* That night Sandra and I huddled on the hard mattress in the double bedroom listening to Monica snoring on the bunk bed next door. We'd booked the flat for a week. Of course, it wasn't terrible. It wasn't the end of the world. Maybe it was even *authentic* in some way, but we couldn't help feeling taken advantage of. When I put my arm around Sandra in the night, she clung to it, muttering something in her sleep. In the morning, we woke to Monica chasing a cockroach around the kitchen. *Little fucker! Uggh!* Then the slap of it crunched under her sandal. Sun was blaring through the thin curtain and already in the plaza there were old ladies sitting out in their doorways. I thought how cruel it was to grow old on a mountain, those pensioners labouring through the steep streets, hobbling to the shop from a house half a mile away or more.

You can get used to almost anything, and we did. We switched on the gas cylinder, got the cooker working, found the immersion heater and discovered hot water, then walked out to the little bakery in the lower part of the village. There was a café that served nice coffee. Lower down, an old-fashioned *gelateria* that offered almost any variety of ice cream you could think of. The road there ran straight to the coast and the café was full of old men in Lycra cycling gear, their new carbon frames gleaming in the cycle stands on the little plaza. It was odd to see the grizzled old guys with their stringy legs dressed in the latest gear. They looked oddly camp. They drank espressos, spoke in the local dialect, a cross between French and Italian, and stuffed bars of chocolate into the back pockets of their singlets.

We walked a bit further to the spa hotel with its 1930's architecture, all curving clean lines and polished glass, watching the rich guests lying out beside the pool. Monica whispering in admiration, *That is so fucking pampered!* We could have used a bit of that. I saw Sandra taking note. We hadn't brought the map, so didn't go any further. But the walk looked promising, the verges thick with yellow and purple flowers, huge butterflies settling and rising again in the sun. We bought fresh bread and pastries on the way home and some slices of pizza. People were friendly and hand-gestures and pidgin French got us through. Things were looking up. None of us had slept that well, but we were in Italy, a long way from the university and work placements and long days where we hardly saw the sun. Sandra and Monica walked ahead of me. Monica striding along, Sandra with her miniature Marilyn Monroe walk, hips swinging. She could look very sweet. They were laughing, and just for a second Monica arm went around Sandra's shoulders as she leaned down to say something.

It was Thursday when we decided to walk up to the village above the church that the old man had pointed to. It was another hot day. We climbed above the spa, the blue rectangle of the swimming pool shrinking. A light breeze came to stir the leaves. The black horse was there, its coat gleaming, grazing peacefully. It was possible to reach the village by road, but that way was much longer, since the band of sticky tarmac curled around the hillside, rising as it went. We decided on a direct assault, past the ruined church, up a steep path through open meadows. As we neared the village we saw someone had thrown pieces of pasta onto the path and a flock of pigeons were pecking at it. They weren't afraid of us. They rose and settled again just a few paces ahead. The draught of their wings was surprisingly powerful. Sandra was clutching the small of her back, climbing with grim determination, whilst Monica sauntered a few paces ahead, her long legs making easy work of it.

The track curved into the village and then through the houses that had been above us. There was a little bar on our right where a wild-looking red-headed girl was serving at table. She was unruly and beautiful, wearing a tie-dye top and blue harem trousers. She served us iced mineral waters, laughing at us where we sat sweating and catching our breath. I saw Monica watching her and wondered how she felt being alone in a threesome. I guessed it wasn't ideal, especially in that cramped little flat with its awkward layout. The girl knew she was being admired and was enjoying it. She carried on laying the tables in the restaurant, straightening tablecloths, setting cutlery, her shoulders tanned and freckled, her hair burning in flashes of sun.

The mineral water was ice-cold and slightly salty. Perfect. We drained the glasses and crunched the ice until our heads ached. Sandra held a cube to her temple, wincing at the pain as we laughed. We picked up our hats and the rucksack Monica was carrying and set off into the village. Just below the houses was a little square with flower beds and two granite monuments. On one was a bronze plate with a list of names. The other was dated September 1944 with some lines of a poem. All in Italian, of course. It was all hard to decipher. An old woman passed us carrying cardboard to the recycling bins. She paused on her way back. She only came up to my shoulder and her eyes were black and bright. She spoke to us, turning her hands towards her chest. Her words blurred into each other and even I could tell she had a strong regional accent. She tried English.

– Where . . . where from?

I pointed to Sandra and myself.

– English.

Monica stepped forward into the little circle we'd made.

– *Sono Australiana.*

– *Bene, bene.*

The old woman pointed to the monument where there were over thirty names. Names of the dead. When she turned back to us her face was already wet.

– *I Tedeschi . . . la guerra . . . Mia sorella, mia madre, mio fratello . . .*

I realized afterwards that she'd thought we might be Germans. We'd seen them down at the gelateria in their VWs and Mercedes, feeding their kids ice cream, touring the valleys. The old woman went on haltingly, with Monica trying to help.

– *Per calpa di Stella Rossa.*

She said that over and over. *Stella Rossa.* The Red Star. Later we found out that at the end of the war, the German had retreated through Italy, destroying everything before them. The Stella Rossa were a partisan guerrilla group. The massacre here had been a reprisal for one of their attacks. Over thirty civilians, men, women and children. They'd been dragged from their hiding places, white-faced into the sun to face extinction. I saw them, calling out to their children in fear, huddling. I saw the stones of the square running with blood.

– *Ero una bambina, una bambina!*

She'd been a small child. She gestured, lowering her hands towards the ground. She'd been too young to be killed but had watched it all. Someone had spared her, but her whole family had died in moments. As she said goodbye, the woman took my hands in hers. Our skin was almost a perfect match.

We watched the old lady walk slowly back to her house, wiping her face on her apron. We were watched in turn by three old men who sat in the shade wearing straw trilbies and smoking, their faces impassive.

We lifted our bags and walked into the village, not speaking. It was a warren of houses and streets. It was peaceful now with hardly any traffic. Cats sleeping in doorways, the church clock tolling the hour. They'd dragged them out from their hiding places to shoot them. Families, neighbours, friends. The cobbler, the butcher, the tailor, the baker. Friends and people who'd fallen out with each other over nothing. Lovers, siblings, spouses, and those who'd not spoken together for years, lined up to die. Their last moments of life spent in terror and bewilderment, overlooking the valley with its wild flowers and pigeons and lazy smoke scribbled on the sky. *Everywhere is beautiful*, the old man had said. I realized now why he was so full of melancholy.

We ate lunch in one of the local cafés, close to the church, then walked back through the meadows. The path was strewn with barley straw and there were sweet peas overhanging a wall, their scent filling the air. We passed the little shrine and reached the ruin of the church and paused for a moment on the bridge, looking back to the village that was partly hidden by the hill. Then we walked down to the spa and the *gelateria* before slogging up to the apartment on the hot road.

Sandra was struggling. I'd taken the rucksack from Monica and could feel a half-empty bottle of water sloshing against me as I walked. I couldn't get the image of red stars out of my mind, the cobblestones splashed with blood, a little girl watching her mother, brother and sister die. We stopped at the bar for a beer and the locals welcomed us incomprehensibly. We were given peanuts with our drinks. There was a montage of photographs on the wall, mainly showing red-eyed men drinking in the bar. Then one with the owner with his hands around his wife's throat – the hollow-eyed woman who ran the little shop. I suppose he thought that was funny.

There was water everywhere in the village, running under the pavements and between the houses. A waterfall fell almost vertically about half way down the long hill, its water splashing over moss into a basin of rock. Just below our house was a little square with a deep well in it. When you looked down, it seemed as if the moon had fallen there to reflect your face. Those damp places were haunted by bullfrogs and they set up a racket every evening, enveloping us in pulsing waves of sound. Like rubber bands being pinched together. A kind of machismo that was also abandoned and sad.

That evening, we sat on the mouldy little balcony drinking wine, ignoring the smell, watching a Dutch theatre company set up a stage on the plaza below. They were tall people, taller even than Monica, and they cast long shadows in the setting sun as they worked. In two days we'd be going home, but we'd catch their performance before we went. It was all to do with a lost child and friendship between two villages, even though the people couldn't speak each other's language. The tall actors got up on stilts in frock coats and top hats and striped waistcoats and everyone loved it, especially the village children who were given sweets and balloons.

Monica had taken a photograph of the words on the

monument and was trying to piece them together into English with the help of an app on her phone.

– *The April sun will . . . continue to rise and shine its . . . brilliance . . . from the blue sky and the light, pure air over woods and green pastures . . .*

She looked up.

– I think that's right. Jesus, that's beautiful!

Sandra covered her hand with hers. We held the last of the wine up to the light where it glowed. It tasted of burnt cherries, of yesterdays, of a kind of regret that's hard to find in words.

That night I couldn't sleep for the sound of the bullfrogs. Then, when they went silent, it was the thought of those villagers dragged into the sun to die. When I eventually woke up the bed was empty. I must have been fidgeting again. When I went to the loo, Sandra was sleeping in the bunk below Monica, her hair catching in the sun that came through the shutters. Flushing the toilet must have woken her, because when I came back her eyes were open. She turned them upwards towards Monica, warning me not to wake her.

Sandra's eyes were hazel in that early-morning light. She watched me calmly, not speaking, just pulling the sheet over her shoulder as if she was cold. A gesture of indifference or of intimacy. It was hard to tell. We were leaving tomorrow. Leaving to catch the bus, then the train, then a plane back to Leeds where our essays and supervisors and clients with their messy lives were waiting for us. I remembered the chaos at Ventimiglia, the French boy with his double bass, the *carabinieri* strutting their stuff like pigeons on that path to the village. It was our last day in Italy. Italy, where everything was beautiful. I leaned in to kiss Sandra, wondering what love was. What it meant. And I knew it was something you forget, then find again in a moment through a memory, a look, touch. *Remember me some time*, that old man had said. And I would. I will.

SHOO

I WAS EIGHTEEN. Old enough to vote. Though I
never had. Old enough to marry. Though I'd never been
on a real date. Old enough to die for my country (people still
talked like that back then). But why the fuck would you? Pete
liked to say. And I'd only been abroad once, to Paris on a
school trip. We'd marvelled at the French girls, their flawless
skin and flawless French. Eighteen, just. A virgin, of course.
About to become a student when being a student meant you
were a bit special. I'd bought a donkey jacket from Millet's
with my first wage packet. We were a new wave. We were on
the edge of the rest of our lives.

I'd got a summer job in the supermarket that had just
opened up on the site of the demolished shoe factory. It'd
come out like a blackened tooth. If you couldn't work, at least
you could shop. It was the future. They only had one music
tape when the shop opened – Stevie Wonder's *Greatest Hits*
– and it drove us crazy all summer. It was 1976 and there was
a gang of us, getting ready to leave home for the first time like
swallows on the wire, febrile with the sense of change. Mainly,
there was me and Pete.

We spent our days stocking shelves or wheeling trol-
leys in the warehouse. Maybe a stint on the bacon counter
with its smell of cold grease, the women mocking our long
hair. *Bloody hell, lad, you favour a mop head!* Then a couple
of pints before going home as the evening light streamed
through the windows of the Sun Mill Inn. The beer flowed

through half-measure pumps at the bar like liquefied gold. The lads from the engineering works jumped up on the tables in stained overalls, swung their hips and pumped their fists to the beat of Gary Glitter. *Come on! Come on!*

Long days started at seven a.m., clocking on in the smell of detergent that still reminds me of those days. That moment slotting the card into the machine, a whole day of work ahead. Time mortgaged. Stacking shelves for two hours before the shop opened, the aisles empty of shoppers. Filling the gaps until everything was in place again. It was timeless. A cornucopia of never-ending plenty in a town that had been dying for as long as I'd lived there. And that sound track: *Shoo-be-doo-be-doo-da-day*.

About a week into the job, I was dragging another pack of tinned beans from the forklift, slicing it open with a Stanley knife.

– You'll have to move a bit quicker than that to keep Jackson off your back!

Then that quiet chuckle.

– Move them up two at a time.

Linda crouched down beside me, our shoulders touching. She wore the blue suit of a supervisor. I caught the scent of perfume, felt her hair brush my face. It was blonde and she wore it in a bob.

– Like this, see?

She swung two cans with one hand. Out from the pack and onto the shelf, then did it again, then again. I gave it a try and dropped a can, denting the rim. She tutted theatrically and pushed it to the back of the shelf.

– You won't be studying retail sales, then?

– History and politics.

Linda pretended to be impressed but she was laughing at me.

She came just a little higher than my shoulder. Dimpled. A little cleft in her chin. She had even teeth, as if she'd worn a brace when she was a kid. She didn't use makeup. Her eyes were full-on, and I was blushing. Pete was stacking breakfast cereals further down the aisle and smirking across at us. Then Linda was turning away to spare me, her calves brisk above flat-heeled shoes that might have seemed staid on anyone else. But not on Linda. On Linda they looked just right. They looked tasteful.

She must have been twenty-eight, though she seemed younger. She had a way of getting the best out of everyone without hassling you. Unlike Jackson, who was a twat of the first order, as Pete often said, declaiming from one of the stacks in the warehouse, fingering his new beard, his hair falling over his shoulder as Irish Lil, the tattooed cleaner, cursed him.

– You useless feckin' gobshite!

Pete put his fingers in his mouth and wolf-whistled back at her, until she delivered the ultimate indictment.

– Cunt!

Catharsis achieved, Pete was delighted. No one messed with Lillian, but Pete seemed to get away with it. We'd been friends since primary school when we'd sat next to each other. He was a Twomey and I was a Tattersall. Then surviving grammar school, where we both kept our heads down, where we were processed rather than educated. The headmaster bullied the teachers, the teachers bullied us, we bullied each other. And we bullied the teachers when we could. The nice ones didn't stand a chance. Now the supermarket, where days passed in the boredom of work. Clocking on at seven a.m., clocking off at five, getting a taste of the world of work, just to remind us what we were escaping.

The town had been on its arse ever since I'd known it, the rotting cradle of industry. The old mills were empty, their chimneys coming down, collapsing into dust and debris, making headlines in the local paper. There was a future in demolition, at least. The shoe factory was gone. The pottery where Pete's mum worked went bankrupt and the stock was sold off. The linen mill was home to a new gym and a couple of mail-order companies. Corner shops closed as the factories closed. Lines of workers who'd queued in overalls for bacon butties or corned beef sandwiches had vanished. It was a town of ghosts. *The Undead*, Pete called them.

Then the supermarkets and shopping centres came to strip off the last meat from the bone. Retail outlets. The town, once famous for manufacturing, became famous for unemployment and racial violence. A minor riot had started in a pub called The Goodfellows when some Asian guy got glassed by a crypto-fascist. That said it all. *Crypto what?* Linda said, laughing at us in the canteen. *They're just arseholes, aren't they?* So, when I say *us*, I really mean me and Pete, who'd grown a Ché Guevara beard and was heading for Reading University to study philosophy. Another reason Lillian thought he was a cunt.

I lived with my mum and dad and a cat called Marmalade in a semi-detached house on a council estate built in the Fifties. It had replaced an infamous slum, pulled down after the war when the town got a Labour council. I'd never lived anywhere else. My parents were both locals. They'd met at a dinner dance in the days before rock and roll. It was hard to imagine. My parents dancing to a swing band or a string quartet.

We had a beige Austin Maxi and an asbestos garage that, in point of fact, was perfectly safe. A garden with a square lawn and privet hedge and rockery and a lattice fence to separate us from the neighbours. They cooked some kind of foreign food in the evenings when we left the windows open to cool the house, and blackbirds sang from garden to garden. *Curry!* Said with a sniff and a toss of the head as my mum set about liver and bacon, slamming the HP sauce on the table for my dad to slather over everything. She always seemed cross with him. A state of perpetuity. Just like the way we'd always lived there.

My mum worked as a school secretary and my dad was a clerical officer at the magistrate's court, though he'd been a police cadet for a time before I came along. You couldn't imagine that, either. My dad in a uniform and helmet. Radio protocols. *Roger, over and out.* The long arm of the law. He had serious hair loss and used to rub Bay Rum into his scalp. It smelled of cloves and desperation. They must have loved each other once, but their lips squeezed together like traps whenever anything like that came up on TV.

Mostly, I didn't want to imagine any of that stuff, listening to Hendrix and Led Zeppelin and T Rex on Radio Caroline in bed, thinking about girls. Thinking about Linda, actually, who was much more than a girl. I wanted it to pass: childhood, adolescence. The teenage years of yawning boredom and repetition and tellings-off from parents and teachers and rubber-necking neighbours if you so much as farted in the garden when they were lying in their deckchairs, shutting out the smell of chicken tikka masala from *you know where*. They were hoping they'd be proved right about things. The miners. The anti-apartheid mob. Anyone who was bolshie. Anyone with bell bottoms or hair touching their collar. We wanted to prove them wrong. Me and Pete, who had a pair of velvet loons and a paisley waistcoat.

That summer my parents went on holiday to a B&B on the Pembrokeshire coast and left me alone for two weeks. It had never happened before, and you could tell my dad didn't like it one little bit. But then I had a job and was earning money for the first time in my life and that meant something. To them and to me. It stood for something. I could cook simple dishes – omelettes, and casseroles with a tin of steak – so I wouldn't starve. The nice neighbours, Geoff and Edith, had a key. In case I left the gas on or wanked myself to death, I suppose. My mum looked upset when they were leaving, leaning from the window of the car to remind me about locking the back door at night. As if the Sikh family who lived opposite would swarm through the garden under cover of darkness with the knives they kept hidden in their turbans. I could be murdered by bus conductors before my life had really started.

The other thing about Linda was crosswords. Pete and I laboured through the *Daily Mirror* in our tea-breaks. Whenever she was around, she was a dab-hand at supplying us with the most perplexing words. She got *mainmast, perturbation* and *watercress* in one session, leaving us with one clue to go. *Sixth-form English*, she said, smoothing down her skirt and straightening her name tag, winking at Pete as she left. *Sort that last one out yourselves.* Six across, five letters: *Mediterranean jellyfish.*

Pete wasn't the slightest bit interested in girls. But you

didn't talk about being gay back then. Not in our town. Not if you had any sense. Not if you had a head to kick in. That was a cross he had to carry for a bit longer. One that he'd eventually lay down when we were hitching in Spain after graduation. Before they had gap years, which we'd never heard of. I told him about Linda on that trip, too. Sitting up in the tent with our gas light, drinking red wine from a NATO water bottle I'd bought at the Army and Navy shop, eating squashed baguette, our shadows cast against the nylon as if we were giants.

In both cases it was probably the wine that loosened up the past. We had our degrees. I'd got a 2:1. Pete had got a first and was about do an MA. My mum wanted to know why I wasn't doing an MA, when you could get a maintenance grant. Remember those? I didn't know what I wanted to do, to be honest. Pete and I hadn't seen each other that much in three years and were finding out just what had changed about us. If anything ever really changes. *Comes to the surface*, might be a better expression. Things rise up that are sometimes better forgotten. But not always. It wasn't all about the future. We were reminiscing about that summer before we finally left home, the way young people do. Squatting on our sleeping bags, slugging back the wine. Even then, just into my twenties, I was full of longing for the past.

I'd been back to the supermarket, getting ready to seem surprised, wandering the aisles, dangling a basket, pretending to shop. But Linda was long gone. She was far too smart to stand still in one place. There was a West Indian family in her little house, the kids laughing at me curiously when I knocked on the door to ask for her. The mother bustling through to say she was gone. *Sorry*, she said, smiling sadly, *we're sorry fer real.* As if someone had died.

Back in '76, it was a hot summer. A blistering summer in a stifling little town where the slate roofs seemed to soak up the heat and you lay awake at night sticking to the sheets and pillows. Sometimes, in the late afternoons after work, I went swimming at the local baths. They'd been built before most houses had bathrooms. Slipper baths. Turkish baths. It was all a bit mysterious, but it was the pool I was interested in with its chilly waters and tang of chlorine and yelling kids, their mothers cruising. I'd take my towel and swimming shorts into work. Pete would rather have jumped off a high building than go swimming. But there I was, not wanting to go home, counting the hours to when I could clock off.

I was a pretty hopeless swimmer, but it passed the time, and it was cool. And there were girls. It was always pretty crowded there and you had to make way carefully, crawling down the length of the baths, the blue tiles wavering and glimmering, the hubbub closing over you. It didn't take much to put me off my stroke so I'd be spitting chlorine. One day, something or someone shot into the water beside me and overtook me with rapid, efficient strokes. When I got to the other end, Linda was grinning at me, her hair plastered to her head. She ducked down below the surface, emerged again like something reborn, then set off with the breaststroke. Lazily powerful. Her shoulders creamy in the filtered light. Later I noticed her on the diving board in her black one-piece costume, her body neat and compact, knifing into the water.

I wondered if she'd come here as a kid, like I did with my mum. Shivering at the cold, drinking hot Bovril in the café. I decided to get out of the way before she saw how useless I was. But she didn't hang about either.

– Well, well!

She was strolling towards me as I waited for my bus, her swimming kit dangling in an orange carrier bag. Jeans. A man's collarless shirt.

– Do you?

– What?

– Come here often?

Her eyes wide with mock surprise.

– Not really, I'm a crap swimmer.

– You are, I couldn't help noticing.

She was teasing me again. I must have blushed because she touched my arm.

– I could teach you.

There was my bus approaching.

– I don't think *anyone* could teach me . . .

– No, maybe not . . .

A group of school kids pushed past us with their satchels. I pulled myself up onto the platform, wondering if she'd follow. But she stayed put, pushing the bracelet of her watch up her arm. She looked nervous, for the first time.

– I'll see you, then.

– See you later . . .

I wish I'd thought of something smart to say. *Alligator?* My mum used to say that. It was what you said to kids. I noticed Linda didn't wear a wedding ring. She didn't seem afraid of anything, but she grew smaller as the bus pulled away.

My parents left on Saturday, my day off. Mum was fussing about everything as my dad packed the car. He was fanatical about anything rattling in the back. He was trying to pretend that leaving me on my own for two weeks was nothing special. I had money to pay the milkman, I had to pick up the papers, which my dad usually did on his way to work. I'd need to remember to get some shopping and not live on takeaways or the chip shop. I waved them off. That first night alone was eerie. Pete came across and we turned up the radiogram. He was getting into King Crimson and Free and Curved Air. It was strange, being in charge. It felt like the end of something and the start of something. But I had absolutely no idea what. I can't remember what we talked about, either. It was just another moment in our long conversation about leaving.

I do remember that on Sunday I was working again. Leaving our empty house, which was a weird feeling at first. In those days, supermarkets closed on Sundays and it was a day of shelf stocking, stocktaking, getting ready for the Monday rush. Linda was on duty and she came to work dressed in casual clothes. A pair of old jeans and sneakers and a tennis shirt that looked as if it'd seen action on the court.

She told me once she'd been to the girls' grammar school, just after slotting some crossword clue into place with mock triumph. Pete and I had been to the boys' grammar, before they merged with the girls as a co-ed comprehensive. If you were good at metal work, they marched you down to engineering drawing. I scraped through with French O-level and a clutch of subjects that sent me down the other route to study English, geography and history.

The shop was always quiet on Sundays, like trespassing in an empty church. And, thank God, Stevie Wonder was turned off. It was the day most stuff went missing, Jackson had once said, significantly, eyeing us up as we stretched out our tea break.

- Like we'd nick anything from this shithole.

Pete slung his tea bag into the sink and let water run into his cup.

– Instant coffee, toilet paper, nappy sterilizer, tampons, pre-cooked pastry cases, Weetabix, family pack . . .

Pete flicked his cup upside down.

– . . . oh yes, the list is endless, Jackson.

But Jackson had already gone and Linda was there with her quizzical smile, hands on hips, as if she didn't quite get us.

As it happened, Pete was off work that Sunday, so the day dragged more than usual. Linda and I did the crossword together in an empty canteen, our heads almost touching over the table. The scent of her hair wafted close, her eyelashes flickering in concentration. Her closeness, the warmth of her skin, a faint perfume I could never quite place. Her neat hands on the biro, filling out the clues or scribbling a word in the margins. Those frank eyes that seemed to be narrowed at me the whole time, as if she was holding back laughter.

In the afternoon I did a stint in the warehouse arranging pallets. Heavy work. I was resting on the handle of the truck when I felt someone come up behind me and push something into the back pocket of my jeans. By the time I turned around, they'd slipped away down one of the aisles. I didn't have time to think about it because Jackson was on the prowl, putting us under pressure just for the sake of it.

– Come on, Michael, we don't pay you to pat your arse.

I did the wide-eyed look.

– Get on with it!

He had a stupid moustache, a whippet's stomach and Terylene flares. I pressed the lever to lower the forks and the pallet sank to the floor as he watched me. By the time I'd shifted the rest of the delivery I'd forgotten about whatever it was in my pocket. I remembered Linda blanking me as we clocked off at four p.m., but I thought nothing of it. She just looked a bit preoccupied.

I was waiting for my bus, standing in the sunshine we'd missed, when I felt in my pocket for change. I found a slip of paper. It had *Linda* written on one side and her address and something else written on the other. *27 Boar Hill St. 7 o'clock*. My chest went tight. Linda's hand-writing slanted to the right. We'd been taught it should slant the other way. When I looked up, the bus was there, panting diesel into the heat, the conductor looking at me from the platform as if I was an idiot.

I could see a faint reflection of myself in the window as we bumped towards home. I kept telling myself that I was eighteen. Eighteen. I remember telling my younger cousin when he was nine that I'd been nine once. He'd looked at me as if I was nuts. *Everyone used to be nine*, he said, as if it was blindingly obvious. Now everyone used to be seventeen.

Boar Hill Street was down by the stinking grey river in the old town. Cobbled streets radiated down from the parish church that stood on a low hill, its stone darkened by soot and rain. I knew where it was because my mum's mother had lived nearby. She ran a sweet shop from her front room, and we'd visited when I was a kid, my mum leaving me with her sometimes to go shopping or visit the doctor with some ailment they spoke about in whispers. Seven o'clock. That left just over two hours. My gran had found me stealing sweets once and slapped my legs.

I got home and ran the bath. My mum had ironed a few shirts for me and I chose an old blue one, made out of crisp cotton poplin. My favourite jeans were clean and I remember standing at the sink scrubbing my teeth, watching the cat stalking something in the garden. Mum had bought me a deodorant stick after one of our little talks and I lashed it on. Old Spice, with a picture of a sailing ship on the label. I sat in a deckchair after that, watching the sun dip behind our neighbour's greenhouse, killing time.

Linda. She was half my age again. Beyond that fact, nothing was obvious. She'd chosen her moment. I must have let drop that my parents were away. Accidentally-on-purpose. It was a ten-minute walk to Boar Hill Street when I finally left the house, putting down some milk for the cat, which was rubbing against my legs. There were jet trails across the sky, converging somewhere beyond the town. Somewhere that wasn't England. I'd waited until the sun fell behind the laburnum tree. It trailed remnants of yellow blossom like streamers left over from a party. Every part of it was poisonous, my dad had told me. Locking the house felt like a betrayal. I didn't know why.

Linda's house had net curtains in the sashes and a dark maroon door. There was an old watering can planted with flowers outside. The house was one of the two-up, two-down terraces, with a kitchen and bathroom added on where the back yard and the old long-drop toilet had been. There was a brass knocker, no bell. I could hear footsteps thudding softly as she came down the stairs that spilled into the little hallway. She smiled at me and pulled the door wider. She'd changed into a summer frock, deep crimson with yellow flowers and blue parakeets. She was barefoot.

- Hi! Come in.

She sounded surprised, as if none of this had been arranged. I followed her, noticing the freckles on her shoulders, a trace of talcum powder. The front room had a plain three-piece suite and a coffee table laid out with two glasses and a bottle of wine that I recognized from the supermarket.

– This is nice.

– We do our best!

She smiled again, flicking a wing of hair back from her face. Her arms were bare and sun tanned and I could see a paler stripe where her wristwatch had been. Showers were rare in those days, so I guessed she'd just got out of the bath.

There was a bowl of olives on the table, something I'd never tasted, but recognized from stocking the fridges. The open fire had been replaced with a gas fire and in one alcove was a Philips Dansette record player. There was a line of swimming trophies on the mantelpiece and a cup with crossed tennis racquets. The other alcove was lined with books and records. The last rays of the sun made a faint haze as they fell though the net curtains that shielded us from the street. I watched Linda go to the record player and drop the needle onto an LP. The room thrummed to the chords of flamenco guitar. Then she was pouring the wine and I was perching on the edge of the settee. I couldn't really describe how I was feeling. We never had wine at home. I'd only ever tasted it at family weddings or christenings. As she stooped, I could see a blue vein between her breasts.

You can guess the rest. How there was an awkward silence as we sat with dry mouths, not saying much. How the wine mixed with the slight bitterness of the olives. How we shifted closer on the settee until our bodies were touching and how our breath quickened as the music stopped and the stylus clicked and I was kissing her, tasting her, fumbling with the buttons on her frock. How the bed was neatly made with clean cotton sheets and how she guided me that first time when I came too soon, then waited patiently, then guided me again until we were moving together and her body was the only thing I'd ever wanted, kissing her breasts and lips, her eyes closing, my hand under her waist as we made love with the last light of the sun rosy against the bleak parish church that filled the top quarter of the window.

Then how we dozed, waking hot and sticky, until she kicked off the sheets and we cooled together, my face nuzzling her clean-smelling hair, our fingers and legs intertwined. Then it was chilly, and she pulled the sheets back and we lay together as darkness sifted into the room and the streetlights burned yellow like cats' eyes the length of the street. There should have been a faint sickle of moon with that old cynical smile of approval as the world turned under it. But I never saw it.

In the morning the room was shaded, the light lemon-coloured on the sycamores under the church. There were sparrows squabbling in the gutters and when I woke up, she was still sleeping, her lips pressing together and relaxing as if she wanted to say something. Then she awoke and pulled on some knickers and went to the loo. Then I did, slipping into my jeans, then slipping them off again to get back into bed. We held each other, her breasts soft against my chest. I kissed them and put my hand on her belly, but she pushed it away.

– Not now, we'll be sore!

I put my lips to her throat and felt the blood beating there. She laughed, pushing at my head.

– You're sweet . . .

She kissed the tip of my nose.

– But trust me.

And I did. I was about to speak, but she put her finger against my lips and said.

– Not now. Tonight. There's always tonight, sweetheart.

Sweetheart. She said it plainly and simply with a Lancashire burr that made her sound so sensible. *Sweetheart.* Like a fact. Like something incontrovertible, obvious, something in plain sight.

But she was right. There was Monday night and every night for the next two weeks, as long as my parents were away. I left the table lamps on at home for the neighbours' sake. Staying over at Linda's, walking home light-headed in the early hours, through empty streets as the milk floats went to work filling up empty doorsteps across the town, the bottles clinking. Most days the cat was already waiting for me and I'd feed him in the kitchen, rinsing the tin clean as my mum had shown me so the dustbin wouldn't stink, making a cup of tea before work, lying in the bath, steaming up the windows, thinking about what had changed. After three days I got a postcard asking if I was OK.

At work Linda and I hardly looked at each other now. After work, I made my excuses to Pete – I can't even remember how I put him off. He'd guessed something anyway. He'd shrug and smile and put his finger to the side of his nose. Linda had lent me a key, so I could let myself in without half the street knowing. I must have looked surprised, but she'd shrugged as if it wasn't a big deal.

So, it was no surprise to find that Pete had known pretty much everything when we sat up in that hopeless little tent, sipping sour wine from the plastic bottle. We were in Spain, close to the Portuguese border, looking down on the Minho river that we'd have to cross tomorrow. The young guy who served us in the village bar had asked us, *Where you go?* We pointed to the river and beyond. We knew he'd be here forever, working for the family, growing old. I'd watched him and Pete exchange glances. Now Pete slugged the wine, grimacing in a little shudder. *Everyone knew,* he said, *you silly bugger, what did you expect?* What did I expect? I expected everything, but I could never have said what that was. The days were taken by work, but the nights were ours, hot and sleepless, and still somehow unbelievable.

I know I'm supposed to say that one morning I woke and noticed the lines on Linda's face and was overcome by a wave of existential sadness, realising it couldn't last. Or that her ex-husband came to the door one evening and punched my lights out. Or that we failed to connect again after that first time and avoided each other in embarrassment. Or that my parents came home suddenly and found her address on that slip of paper on the kitchen table, putting two and two together. Or how she took me out for one last meal to end it, overcome by bitterness and regret, sipping the last of the wine, envying my freedom when she was tied to work, growing older alone.

But she wasn't tied and none of that happened. It didn't happen because we weren't in a story that had to end with a whimper or a bang or a clever twist of the plot. There wasn't even an ex-husband to turn up. Linda knew when the time was right to end things. Or maybe it was blindingly obvious that we'd only ever have those two weeks. And friendship is so much less destructive than love. The only other person I've ever known who realized that was Pete, who was wise in his own way.

The day before my parents came home, we made love for

the last time and she stroked my hair as I lay against her and whispered, very simply.

   – It's time now, Michael, sweetheart. Thank you.

I lifted my head. I don't know what I'd imagined. I suppose I'd been waiting for this. Dreading it. But maybe it was all there was to say. I felt dazed all the same, kissing her cheek, wanting to cry.

   – Thank you. You've been . . .

   – I *am*. Just say I am.

She pushed me gently away, her hands lingering on my waist, and I got dressed and went downstairs for the last time, leaving her key on the kitchen table, closing the door, passing the watering can full of peonies that she'd forgotten to water. Suddenly, I felt very small, like a child again.

Then walking home through the dawn chorus, the moon looking like its own ghost. The house smelled empty and the cat had caught something and was waiting for me, a tail hanging from its mouth, making that low grizzling noise. The cat set it down, but the mouse was too bewildered to run away. It moved feebly, staring with its shocked eyes until the cat caught it again. I left Marmalade to it and went into the house. Making my bed look slept in. Throwing away the food my mum had left in the fridge. Rumpling the newspapers as if I'd actually read them. Cutting the lawn, watering the window boxes, trying to remember the other dozen things I'd been asked to do.

I never saw Linda again. She was on holiday during my last week at work, then we were packing the car for my first term at Nottingham. Pete knew that something had happened to me, something momentous. But he never asked what it was. Of course, he didn't have to because he already knew. We took up where we'd left off for that last week and he put up with my silences.

I'd lived a lie, for sure, and I felt guilty for reasons that were hard to put in a neat row. I was all over the place. But on one level, things had been simple. Unaccounted. Now they were over, nobody owed anybody anything. What had happened was part of the past, where the present moment had slipped without me ever really noticing until Linda had pushed me gently from the bed.

Then me and Pete again, meeting for a pint after work, watching the cocky young guys from Pearson's firing back the beer, dancing on the tables at the Sun Mill Inn, cigarettes dangling from their lips. Watching the summer drain away into our futures, the tables strewn with empty glasses in the sinking light. Linda was gone. I knew that was her way of never growing old. *Come on! Come on!* That was Pete, laughing at me from behind his beard, raising a glass of bitter like an ingot. I replied almost without thinking, feeling the pint cool in my hand.

Shoo-be-doo-be-doo-da-day!

TEMPESTADE DE FOGO

SOME MORNINGS SHE just wanted the day to end. Some days she just wanted life to end. Though it would be like a dominant seventh chord, jangling on into emptiness. Unresolved. And maybe it had already ended. Her life.

Maybe this was the afterlife, lying in the sun like a lizard, absorbing heat and light until she felt irradiated. Eternity. Endlessness. Illusions, because the only thing that went on forever was forever. Which you didn't actually experience. She dabbed sun cream onto her arms and smoothed it into her skin. They carried the white marks of old mosquito bites. Of course, they'd never bothered Hywel. Something to do with blood groups, he said. That way he had of knowing everything. Or seeming to. A world-class bullshitter. The cream was cool. Soothing. Sunbathing was foolish, of course. Christina's sister, Delia, had warned her about it, babbling down the phone from England.

But then, you were lucky to see any sun there from one year to the next. Especially in the north. Climate change wasn't helping. Everyone was talking about it now. In the UK it meant rain, those floods that swept cars down high streets and filled houses with raw sewage. Here it meant relentless sun, distant clouds building, a miasma of heat in the afternoons. She worried about skin cancer, but for years she'd lived in rehearsal rooms, concert halls, hotels. Now it was time to stretch out and to relax. Now it was time to forget. Did it matter, after all, at her age? She'd taken her last lover a long time ago.

In summer the days here were almost unbearable. China-white skies that deepened to blue as a brazen sun rose behind the mountains. Those late afternoon clouds piling themselves high in the heat, so tantalisingly. But it wouldn't rain. They couldn't let go, the moisture drifting away inland, dissipating into scorched air, falling over other mountains in Spain or Italy. She shifted on the deckchair and felt something against the small of her back. It was her mobile phone. She put it on the table. She'd lost the charger somewhere. She'd need to look for that.

There was a faint smell of burning foliage. It reminded her of childhood days when her grandfather used to make bonfires on his allotment. She laid her book across her chest to push back a strand of hair. A small brown bird hopped from the jasmine to the prickly pear and let out a cheep. C-natural. Deep orange. Like her swimsuit that seemed so new next to her skin. Colours that vibrated in harmonic sequence. She hadn't told anyone about that.

They sat her at the piano in the parlour of their gloomy little terraced house in Durham and she'd been able to play anything. A prodigy, except it was easy when every note, every key, every chord shimmered as an unmistakeable colour. Hearing music was *seeing* it. Each key had its own shade of the rainbow. They didn't need to know. Not at home or at school or at the Royal College where she'd studied violin on a scholarship. What she saw and felt inside was all hers.

Christina shifted in the deck chair and lifted her book to shield the sun. Her skin was wrinkled now, it fell slackened from her bones. She'd been tall, for a woman. She'd commanded attention: long auburn hair and a slender waist. Now the hair was white, twisted up on her head and held with a wooden pin. There were liver spots on the back of her hands, ridges in her fingernails that she didn't remember before.

She put the book down on the cast-iron table and took a sip of water. It had heated up and had a brackish taste. A swallow flickered past, then another. They were working shifts to feed their young. She half-closed her eyes so that the flowers in the garden merged into blotches. She waved her head slowly and let the colours flow into each other. Her violin was locked away in a temperature-controlled cupboard in the house behind. After retiring she'd sold all her instruments, except the Gagliano, her first love. She'd been tempted out to play at local concerts a few times, but had always regretted it. After all, her recordings were out there for anyone to find.

She thought of Hywel laid out in his best cream suit, that last argument in the car. How his coffin had slid into crematorium flames. He'd been returned to molecules, to the air. And she thought of all the others, their mouths hot at her breasts, devouring her, their hands slipping off her silk underwear after concerts, in hotel rooms that were the same as every other hotel room. The sheets sterile and smooth and anonymous. The mini-bar fridge humming. The lovemaking urgent and then suddenly emptied of meaning. That sense of compulsion drained, like music falling into silence.

She was dozing under her sun hat when the phone rang inside the house. She got up to answer it, slipping her feet into plastic flip-flops. Horrible things with garish flowers printed on them. After all these years she hardly knew a word of Portuguese or how to form a sentence. Hywel had been the linguist, the one who stood between her and all that foreignness. Christina had been able to come and go, and somehow things were always the same. He didn't ask questions and she didn't tell lies. It was not an *arrangement* exactly, not in the old-fashioned sense. There'd always been a sense of danger. Of him finding out things that he probably knew or suspected. She'd had two lives: one with the orchestra and one with Hywel. Now, here in this valley near the Spanish border, heat itself was a kind of dependable truth. How strange now to be drained of passion, even of her passion for music, which had never been abstract for her as they said music was, but a show of coloured light.

When she reached the phone, a voice harangued her. Probably trying to sell her something. Wine. A washing machine. Timeshare in some godforsaken ex-pat development along the coast. Christina put the receiver down and the bangles on her arm slid over her wrist. She would have preferred France to northern Portugal, but that had been Hywel's choice. Logistics. Management. He'd found this place. A couple of hours from Porto on the Minho river. A landscape of wooded hills, scoured hilltops and big rivers that flowed out of Spain. He liked borders, edges, places you could slip away from. There'd been some issue with the last job. Accounting irregularities, that had been misinterpreted. He'd done his best to sort things out, but he'd moved on in the end. Life being too short. And he always seemed to find something else.

Christina been able to devote herself to music and everything that had meant to her. He'd been content with what she brought home. That hadn't been inconsiderable. That hadn't been nothing. From a tight little terraced house in Durham to concert halls across Europe and beyond. Not many people could have been said to have made that move, to have had that level of *mobility*. If that was the word. Her life had been molten with music and through music. Sequence, harmony, rhythm. They were as real as the deckchair sliding under her thighs as she took up her book again.

The swallows had built their nest under the overhang in the porch. She'd locked that door to remind herself not to disturb them. They'd littered the tiles with spikes of grass and mud and white streaks of dung. The nest had taken shape gradually, the female building as the male kept watch. They crossed in the air now. There were three chicks in the nest, looking out with glum, anxious faces. Sometimes they chittered frantically, driving their parents on. Christina looked at the loose skin on the underside of her arms with astonishment.

Hywel had been the manager of the first orchestra she played in. A genius at logistics, at finance, at dealing with people. He didn't know a thing about music from the technical point of view, but that didn't mean he couldn't handle musicians or understand their whims and needs. He'd seen through her straight away. The brilliant young violinist who was just a provincial ingénue. He was from South Wales. A background he'd taken pains to erase. He'd lost the accent, but kept the easy charm, his Welsh name, the air of *culture*. He'd understood her at once, her insecurities, her need for attachment. After that first concert at the Hallé he'd asked her.

– What do you see then, when you play?

– See?

– Yes, during the Haydn especially, it's as if . . .

He was casting about for words, which was uncharacteristic.

– It's as if you're seeing a vision, like Joan of Arc.

She laughed, feeling herself on dangerous ground. Nobody knew what she saw.

The second movement had been a cascade of magenta, deepening and glowing.

- Joan of Arc? Really?

She allowed herself the throaty laugh that her mother had considered vulgar.

- I don't see anything, Hywel, just the music. What do you see?

- Me?

Hywel shot his cuffs and gave her an appreciative smile. He needed a shave, but that gave him a roguish look. He wore a tight Italian sports jacket, square cut at the back, no vent.

- I see an artist at full-stretch . . .

A cliché, of course, but the seduction had begun. And it went on, with Hywel paying court to her. Until a few weeks later they slept together. When they made love she came, and her orgasm had quivered from colour to colour. She'd loved him for that.

They moved to Portugal when she was already retired. Far too old for the circuit where looks meant as much as technique or interpretation. It wasn't always easy to believe you'd remember things, that your hands would know where to go when you stood up to play. And her hearing wasn't as sharp as it needed to be. Years of brass sections and timpani making it ring as she lay in bed after the concert. People thought only rock bands did that, but a Rachmaninoff or Beethoven symphony was just as punishing. Even the quartet had become difficult before she let go. Her own sound seemed somehow lost in the other instruments, even though the violin was there, vibrating right next to her ear.

They'd made the move to an easier life when Hywel landed a job with one of the British port wine companies, organising storage and exports, learning a new trade with the enthusiasm and application that distinguished him. It was fear, really, of course. Fear of not knowing things, of being caught out as a second-rate, grammar-school boy. He'd worked in Porto and commuted, arriving home late most evenings. She didn't know about that other business. Letters came from some legal firm and he tore them up for the bin.

He worked part-time so there was no real excuse to be late home. So, she knew he'd got himself one of those little tangle-haired Portuguese women to sleep with, stroking her belly as light filtered through the shutters onto the bed. Telling her his troubles. Fucking her gently because he'd always had that kind of emotional sleight of hand in pursuit of what he wanted. Offering his feelings but never really giving them. Smoothing her tantrums. Leaving a neat little stack of Euros on the bedside cabinet before putting on his watch. Christina had never asked, and he'd never told her. That was how they were. She could hardly complain. It hadn't been easy for him when she was away, living a different life.

He'd have loved the swallows. Just liked he loved the sour little apples that grew on the crooked tree overlooking the valley at the end of the garden. He'd have loved them because they were *theirs*, because he was still a peasant at heart.

It was almost mid-day. Christina went into the cool of the house to switch on the TV. A bluebottle was buzzing against the window. She flapped at it with a magazine. The English channels had stopped working. Something to do with the signal. Someone was supposed to have sorted that out. They needed a booster or something. She clicked the control and watched the Portuguese news station come up. There was a feature on the recent election, the formation of the new government. Well, as far as she could tell.

Then images of a burning forest. Planes scooping up water from an estuary to dump on the flames, bouncing away from the fire as the thermals lifted them and the water fell. That was all about eucalyptus trees. Hywel had explained that. They'd colonized the country and were the first to regenerate after the fires. Uncut bracken spread the flames. The farmers didn't need it for animal bedding any more. The land was slipping back to a wild state. Trees exploded like fireworks. The eucalyptus needed rooting out. Fires were burning along the Douro river, inland from Porto. There were desperate people trying to save their houses, refusing to leave, forming chains to beat at the undergrowth. It was sad. Dusky blue. She didn't *see* the colours exactly, but she experienced them. It was hard to explain.

That evening, a blue haze over the hillside. That smell again. Her grandfather taking down his bean canes and tipping the rainwater out. His purple-veined hands stacking plant pots and chopping old tomato plants into the compost. Pigeons wheeling over the allotment like tiny airborne petticoats. He'd been a miner, a coal cutter, working the machines at the face. Sometimes he took her to the Working Men's Club and once, when she was older, he'd persuaded her to play the piano there. It was out of tune. She'd tried a Liszt waltz, but the colliers had looked at her with incomprehension, staring over their pints. Years later, she realized that it wasn't the music they didn't understand. It was her. Christina closed the windows, glimpsing the swallows where they were using up the last light. She drew the curtains, slipping into bed. Her skin had burned a little in the shower under the hot water. She needed to be careful.

The next day she drove down to the supermarket and bought some things for the next few days. The village seemed eerily quiet. Just a couple of cars parked in the street. A tractor driven by a grey-haired woman with a dog chasing behind. It was hard to get fresh meat, but there was plenty of frozen chicken and fish, and there were always vegetables. That was something. *Bacalao* was plentiful. Salt cod. But she'd never cared for it. It took an age to prepare and by the time you were ready to eat it, you couldn't be bothered or felt nauseated. In the old days they'd soaked it in a stream and let the current take the salt away. The middle-aged man behind the counter nodded to her as she entered. The shop sold everything from food to kitchen utensils to underwear. Once she'd seem him demonstrating a bra to three old woman who'd gathered at the counter. No one else seemed to think that was funny.

She bought washing power, and a pair of ridiculously large oven gloves. She'd burnt the others on the gas ring. They'd proved remarkably flammable. Hywel would have enjoyed the irony of that, his eyebrows rising in mock alarm. But he hadn't been there, of course. She'd stood there with her hands burning. Fire was a kind of lust. The same colour as when sex started. She must have had nearly every conductor she'd worked with. Sometimes she hadn't taken no for an answer. Somehow it became necessary to the music. For hours bathed in the swirling colours, her fingers moving to Janáček or Arvo Part or Brahms. Then straddling the man who'd directed her performance, taking his cock in her hand, watching his face become helpless and silly under her. She packed the shopping into a canvas bag and headed for the car. The church glared, white as cuttlefish. She remembered she needed cash from the ATM.

The next day it was too hot for the garden. Christina stayed in the house, reading her novel. She toyed with the idea of phoning her sister, but in the end, she couldn't bear the platitudes. Delia had been a director in Social Services. She'd done well in her own way. It was so hot that she wanted to read Chekhov again, to lose herself in the snow of nineteenth century Russia. He'd been a man of passion, Chekhov, a man who understood what was bearable and what was unbearable to the soul. How she would have loved to have had such a challenge. But in the end, all the men she'd taken had caved in. And afterwards, that little death. That deep, dark blue moment of loss and emptiness that is sex without love. She knew that because of Hywel, because making love to him had been different. Afterwards she'd felt at rest. Sure, it lacked the danger of a breathless fuck in a hotel room. But there was time to lie together afterwards, to recoup, to feel their love as immediate and undying.

Later, she realized it was built on a silence that was merely a lack of lies. Lies might have helped her to ignore the curled hairs on his collar, the perfume of other women. The things you remembered after you'd forgotten them. She hadn't meant to grab the handbrake. She wasn't drunk, but on the edge. She was burning up. Deepest green. She'd become jealous with a suddenness that was astonishing. *You bastard. You slut-fucker! You absolute cunt!* The words had poured out of her. Out of nothing. Out of nowhere. After all, they'd come to terms with and accommodated and never mentioned their other lives. The feeling filled her up like hot liquid. The rocks on either side of the road hemming them in. Metal or tyres screeching. Then slowly spinning blue lights, the paramedics fitting a neck brace, lifting her.

Things can change in a moment. Then you have to live with them. They'd been at Jorge's bar listening to a fado singer. Hywel loved that kind of thing. The singer's cleavage showing through her flimsy top, the black lace shawl thrown off at a dramatic moment, the sorrowful eyes cast into the distance. Then vibrato. Melisma. Every cheap musical effect in the book to milk emotion. She hated it all. After a lifetime playing great music, music of complexity, music that was fastidious, she was supposed to listen to a whore singing in a cheap bar and show her appreciation. It stoked something in her. But what Hywel took to be musical affect was something else. Something neither of them recognized until it flared up in the car.

The phone rang and she realized that she'd dozed off again. The sun was like a set of blades unfolding around the house. Glittering. It was the same voice again. A recording. Exhorting her to do something or buy something. That language that sounded like Spanish with a Russian accent, its softly meshing syllables. Did they even have Jehovah's Witnesses in Portugal? She put the receiver back into the plastic holder that was screwed to the kitchen wall. It was slightly crooked and that had always annoyed her. Hywel getting slapdash in his old age. He'd never have made a mistake like that in his prime. One thing he was always brilliant at was appearances, after all.

Christina was thinking about her violin locked in its case, of the music manuscripts she filed in a special cabinet with sections for each composer. She listened for the birds as she went back to the garden, their iridescence. What she heard was the shriek of tyres, a sound so dark it had felt like a pulverisation of the deepest hues of the night. Of course, he was well over the limit, so there'd been no real fuss at the inquest. Just another ex-pat succumbing to the easy life. Except it wasn't easy. It wasn't even life. Without him, of all people, it seemed like nothing.

By late afternoon there were wispy clouds gathering. Christina took a pair of secateurs into the garden, dead-heading roses, composting the agapanthus that had gone over. Magnificent white and blue flowers heads. She'd never managed to get them to grow in the UK, but here they flourished with a kind of brash vulgarity. She cut back the montbretia and fuchsia where it was overgrowing the paths. By four o'clock a few spots had darkened the paving stones, but no rain came. She heard the drone of aircraft and there was that smell again that reminded her of home and childhood and loss. The loss of things she'd never valued. Driven out of her by those blank stares in the Working Men's Club. She'd let her fingers die on the keys.

She wasn't hungry tonight, though she knew she should eat. She sat with a gin and tonic, swirling the ice against a slice of lime, feeling the sting of juniper in her throat. Swifts appeared above the tree line, cutting the air as the sun retreated. But there was another very faint glow to the south, as if sunlight was being dabbed between the trees. When Christina woke in the night, she went to the window and pulled back the drapes and there it was, the hillside glowing like some depth of Hades. It reminded her of the slag heap that had burned beyond the pithead through her childhood.

In the morning the phone woke her.

– Christina! Sweet Jesus! Are you still there?

– Still here?

It was Delia, her voice shrill with anxiety.

- I've been watching the news.

Where was this going?

- Yes, so surely you've seen the fires?

- Oh yes, that.

There was a little silence swelling between them like a bubble of soap or blood.

- You're not worried. I mean now that Hywel's . . .

Delis caught herself in mid-sentence.

- Gone.

- Dead. Hywel's dead, Delia. Most people are.

She'd been told that wasn't true anymore, that the world contained more living people than those that had lived and died over millennia. God knows how they'd worked that out.

- Yes, I'm sorry, I wasn't trying to be tactful.

- You were.

- OK. I was. Is that so bad?

- It can be irritating.

Well, that wasn't really fair. Playing the diva with her own little sister.

- Anyway, all that's miles away and they're dealing with it.

- Are you sure, Christina?

- I'm sure. How's Nigel?

That was the signal to move on. But she remembered that last year people had died in the Parc Natural, down in the central region. They'd died in their cars trying to escape. Suffocating or waiting for the petrol tank to ignite. *Whoosh*, Hywel had said, *absolutely fucked!* Adding: *At least it'd be quick*. But it wouldn't be. Nothing that involved waiting to die was quick.

Delia rang off and Christina went to the window again, watching the swallows cross, thinking how like those little planes they were, scooping up water and frantically trying to put out the flames that were engulfing the forest. Delia had two daughters, Christina's nieces, who sent birthdays cards and Christmas cards with almost identically neat writing. But that was the extent of their relationship. They were both university researchers or something. Well, one of them was, she was sure, though she'd no idea what she was researching. Christina pressed her stomach to the cold enamel of the sink. Children had never been a possibility for her and Hywel. Though he might have been good with kids. Up to a point. The point where being comical and funny, the way he played at being an uncle, was no longer enough.

The day passed. She went to bed. She slept well. In the morning, she woke with a vague sense of resolution, dressed, went downstairs, reached for a set of keys. Her car was a stupid little Seat. An ancient tin can that used hardly any petrol, with a sticky gearbox and soft suspension. The sump caught on the track as she bumped home from the village. It was parked in the car port where Hywel's Opel used to stand. The car port was useless too and the sun had already made the inside of the car unbearable. She had one of those tinfoil things that you were supposed to put across the windscreen to keep the sun off. Or was it the rear window? It probably didn't matter because that was pretty useless too.

Christina turned the key in the ignition. The engine stuttered and stopped. She tried again and this time there was a rapid clicking. No more. When she checked the lights, she could see that she'd left them on the last time she used the car. She hadn't even needed them because that had been daytime. That trip to buy oven gloves. She slammed the door. Maybe it would pick up charge. Maybe she could push it to the edge of the driveway and bump-start it on the hill.

She went back into the house and poured a glass of water, standing at the sink to drink it. The bluebottle was back, crawling across the glass as if it owned the world. As if the future belonged to it. This time she was angry and too quick. She crushed it with a copy of *Vogue* and wiped the smear of blood and yellow matter away with a piece of tissue. Christina dropped the magazine in the bin. An aeroplane buzzed over the treeline, heading over the river. There were swifts high up, circling effortlessly. And there were the baby swallows lined up on the telephone wire. By day they'd taken to practising their swooping runs over the garden and at night they piled back into the nest, heads and tails overhanging. Waiting for their parents to feed them. A family.

The day passed. Morning, then afternoon. Heat rose to a crescendo then ebbed into blue shadows. Dusk settled and the hillsides to the south emitted a dull glow. She watched from the bedroom window as goblins of flame flickered in the underbrush, igniting the bracken and then dying back again. They'd been bombing it all day. She'd seen yellow diggers clearing fire-breaks through the trees. From where she stood, it looked like the inside of a hellish mouth. She'd grabbed the handbrake, Hywel shouting that she was a silly bitch, then the back end of the car was swinging round and smashing into those rocks that choked the road to a chicane. Maybe hell was what she deserved. She'd been wearing her seatbelt, but Hywel was half-pissed. He'd cracked his head on the metal pillar where it met the windscreen, which had shattered into snow. He died at the hospital of an intracranial haemorrhage, without waking up. He died on a ventilator with a tube down his throat. The consultant had explained – in perfect English, of course – just why they needed to switch off his life-support. They asked her about his organs then, and of course, she'd said yes. They'd been *harvested*. A fantastic euphemism he'd have laughed at. Hywel had been nothing if not generous with himself. Sometimes she still wanted him inside her.

Christina went to bed, closing the window to keep out the smoke that was blowing towards the house. But it seeped into the room. In the morning, she was woken by a slow cracking sound and there, at the edge of her garden, was the fire. A huge eucalyptus flamed like a totem, then fell in a crackling mass of sparks. She ran downstairs to the phone. Nothing. She could see where the tree had brought the line down. Her mobile was on a coffee table in the lounge, but she remembered she'd lost the charger and then forgotten to look for it. It was completely dead. Like the car.

Christina found her sandals. The good ones she could walk in. The fire was crackling towards her. Who ever thought it could move so fast? That it could be so utterly sure of itself? She could feel heat blowing from the flames, see how sparks chased each other into the undergrowth and glowed there. Fire had its own logic. It had its own colours that nothing could supplant. She saw what she saw and heard what she heard. Without music, the world was unadorned.

Christina went back inside and found a bottle of water in the fridge. Then she set off down the track towards the village, a scarf wrapped around her face, the fire on her right, the deep green of the mountain on her left, her feet catching on stones as she went. She turned to look back. The curtains of her house were burning up in rags of flame. The washing she'd left on the line was blazing. She thought of her violin. The glue melting, spruce, maple, ebony cracking apart. The horsehair bow curling and snapping. She remembered the smear of the bluebottle against glass. How easy that had been. Now her manuscripts burning, sailing away into the conflagration of the woods, their black flakes clotting like key signatures. Then ash. Slag. Remnants of their life smouldering.

Slut-fucker. That had felt good. And he'd deserved it. She wasn't afraid. But she was curious, feeling the heat against her back. Fear, after all, was facing an audience. Her smothered breath, people coughing, the conductor poised, the pianist flexing his hands, Hywel watching her from the edge of the stage, smiling in encouragement as the baton fell.

VIA URBANO

A BELGIAN, BORN near Ghent in the flatlands. An awkward teenager who collected postage stamps and listened to American blues on the radio. An only child whose father was a leatherworker, whose mother farmed lavender. But it was possible in those egalitarian days for a country boy to be educated at the Sorbonne, then in London, the first of his family. Married to an Italian, settled in Naples. A widower, now. A wanderer always. Sometimes I felt (I should say, feel) like a cosmopolitan citizen of the new Europe. At others, I'm a waif, a lost soul, a ghost with no language and no culture to call his own. Flotsam on the tide of time. Jetsam of a failing political age.

I met Beatrice at a diplomatic function when she was working for a children's charity and I'd got my first posting with a British NGO. She was taller than me, frail with finely chiselled lips, a floss of curly hair and golden skin that showed her blushes. Jade bangles chinked on her arms and a dimpled smile showed strong teeth. She was twirling a flute of prosecco, pretending to listen to an elderly man who had white sideburns and was leaning too close, to catch her quiet replies. *Beatrice*. Her mother was a Somali and her father Italian, a coffee trader from Bari in the East. They'd called their only daughter Beatrice. *Because of Dante*, she'd joked when I rescued her from the man, asking her if she'd heard from Natalie, taking her arm politely. There was no Natalie. But there was us from that night. *Inferno, Purgatorio, Paradiso*. Except our lives ran the other way.

She'd been named Beatrice, the traveller, but it was me who'd travelled and she who'd stayed put. I only met her father on a few occasions, but it was clear that he was the restless one, too. Full of stories of Africa and South America where he'd sourced his coffee. Full of distance and wistfulness and the kind of wry wisdom that meant you left people alone to get on with things. He never interfered between us, even though I was a foreigner with poor Italian at the time. I never really understood what he made of me, or his pious wife, Jamilah, Beatrice's mother. At times I felt like a mongrel who merely navigated the situations he landed in. Like my stay on the Via Urbano, which I'm coming to.

I'd stayed two nights with the sisters when I was passing through Rome, years before, just after my first contract finished at the UN. Now I found myself 'between jobs', as they say in English. The future looked a little hazy, but I'd saved some money and Rome seemed as good a place as any to regroup. I'd got some freelance work, but I hadn't really formed any plans. What had happened with Beatrice was too raw, was really too overwhelming to allow the future to present itself. So, I'd been living from day to day, without desire, head down, numbed, working for the consolations that work could bring. Living in a kind of suspension, like the lees in wine or particles of dust settling through the air so that things clarified, but always beyond me, always letting the light fall somewhere else and reside there.

I heard the sisters' story from an acquaintance, even before I met them. Well, it was a story of sorts. They'd grown up in a large flat on the Via Urbano and never married. They had a younger brother, but where he'd disappeared to, no one knew. Lisette and Sofia had grown up under the care of their parents who were Jewish, non-orthodox, and had been sheltered by friends during the Nazi occupation. They had an income from investments and provided everything for the girls – and for their son while they had the chance. The sisters had never married but the youngest sister, Sofia, had a son, Amadeo, hollow-eyed and delicate, who haunted the stairwells and the long gloomy corridor that led to the marble steps at the foot of the apartment. I knew his name meant 'God's love' in Italian. Acknowledgement that his life was a gift, I suppose. At the least, a consolation, like my work.

On the first floor lived two single gentlemen: a physician of some sort, and a lawyer who rode a bicycle in his three-piece suit with a leather dispatch case slung over his shoulder, his long grey hair streaming behind. No one knew who Amadeo's father was. There were stories about the missing brother. The kind of rumours that often surround a family living in isolation. Especially a Jewish family, whose very survival was suspicious to some. They meant nothing but spite. Even a city like Rome, with its deep sewers – its *cloaca maxima* – and imperial history can seem like a hamlet stewing with gossip. Especially a city like Rome, which like all capital cities was really just a group of villages, each sullenly insular.

After their parents died, the sisters had a dilemma. They were in their late thirties, and though they'd studied at university and Lisa did some private tutoring in English, they'd never held down jobs. They inherited a large upstairs apartment with half a dozen bedrooms – not forgetting the two apartments downstairs that were already rented out. The age of the internet – the age of information – had arrived, and

Rome was busy with overseas visitors, as it always had been. So, they decided to turn the apartment into high quality bed and breakfast accommodation, reserving bedrooms for themselves and Amadeo, and taking a couple of months off each winter to recoup their energy. They used a local laundry service and provided a simple breakfast. The first guests arrived from England, then the US, then Germany, and soon they had recommendations on their website and a good reputation. *Buona!* They could live, at least.

I'd passed through for a couple of nights all those years ago. Now I was returning indefinitely; for as long as I needed to, or for as long as I was wanted. If the promise of work held up, I'd find my own apartment. Eventually.

The Via Urbano itself ran roughly north-south from the central railway station to the Metro at Cavour. It was a busy street with many restaurants and artisan businesses that sold leather goods, scented candles, bicycles, jewellery and exclusive clothing for men and women. There were more basic premises hidden behind metal shutters: carpenters' shops or little firms that specialized in mending washing machines or computers. There was a musical academy on the upper floor of one building and you could hear the sound of piano scales or a junior jazz band practising, whilst, at certain times, the street seemed to fill up with young people carrying guitars. It was noisy at night until late, and in the mornings – except Sundays – the street woke early. But it was Rome and there was a sense of excitement this close to the Colosseum and the ancient ruins that were a magnet for visitors. For me, Rome had become an expensive vulgarity with its overbearing imperial architecture and its woeful transport system – the evidence of years of neglect or misappropriated funds – but there was an undeniable sense of energy surging there, even as it contemplated its own ruin and loss. And you could forget yourself a little.

I'd picked up some consultancy work for an NGO who were active in Libya, trying to deal with the refugee crisis: the Africans who were testing the anger of the sea and trying to get into Europe. Since I had to be in Rome for a few weeks, I dropped the sisters a line and booked a room. What it lacked in opportunity, adventure or sophistication would be compensated for by reliability: clean sheets, a smoke-free environment, hot water and wi-fi. All I really needed to survive. I could walk to the office each day and at night I could write up my notes and keep an eye out for other projects. Cheap it wasn't, but it was convenient, and I never had to talk to anyone.

I arrived on an evening of light drizzle with a wheeled suitcase and a shoulder bag. A large panelled mahogany door fronted the building. I pressed the security buzzer to announce my arrival. It was October and the streetlights were coming on, the street glistening, still thronged with tourists walking arm in arm, checking menus and prices at the eateries. There was no reply, but the lock clicked and I was able to push the door open. In front of me ran a long corridor with a dim window set to one side at the far end. I didn't bother with the electric light but walked down the corridor and up the stars. I passed the apartments of the two professional gentlemen on the first floor and was soon outside the door of the sisters' apartment. When I pushed it open, there was Sofia behind a desk in the lobby, peering at a computer screen. She wore a green cardigan and her glasses were pushed up into her dark untidy hair.

– Signor . . . ?

– Gérard. Antoine Gérard.

She typed something quickly and then looked up.

– Ah, yes, there you are!

Whether she meant on the screen or before her in the flesh was hard to say. She opened a drawer and took out a bunch of keys, showing me to my room, asking if I'd stayed with them before, then ignoring my answer.

The room was positively monastic, dominated by two narrow single beds and a huge dark wardrobe that might well have belonged to her parents. Lisette, elegant and a little febrile in a simple black dress, appeared in the corridor to welcome me and ask if everything was suitable. She'd tinted her hair a kind of ash blonde since I'd last seen her and pulled it into a bob. The women looked so different, but if you looked carefully, you could tell they were sisters. It was in the bones, what lay underneath the skin, beneath surface appearance. I shook hands and said the room was perfect, eyeing the tightly tucked up beds with some disappointment. Not that I was planning any kind of liaison. It's just that I like my own space. But it would do.

As I left the apartment to find my evening meal, I saw the boy Amadeo watching me with listless, pale eyes. He'd been a toddler when I last saw him, just babbling his first words. Now, I guessed he was about twelve years old. He was standing in the upper hallway, his hands hanging loose, his chest hollow, a tee shirt hanging from thin shoulders. I gave him a wave and an indescribable expression – somewhere between grief and anguish – flitted across his face. It was a look that followed me down the stairs and the long corridor into the street where I was about to find somewhere to eat. The rain had ceased, leaving the pavements a little greasy.

I used to love wine, but the older I get, the more it disagrees with me. At one time I could drink without thinking much about the day after. Now, if I have that extra glass I wake up feeling fine - if I sleep at all, that is - but by three in the afternoon I can feel a headache coming on, like a needle at my temples. The more committed I became to my work, the more stupid I felt nursing a hangover like a teenager. The wonderful thing about age is remembering that you might feel under the weather the day after and refuse that extra drink you'd just offered yourself. That's why, when I managed to find a table at a restaurant near Cavour, I chose to drink only mineral water with my meal. When you can afford good wine, maybe you don't need it.

By the time I got back to the house on Urbano, the flow of tourists was calming down. Most of them had gone home or were safely ensconced in restaurants, enjoying exorbitantly expensive food. Food that was an imitation of food, piled vertically on the plate, minimalist and bland. You had to cross the river to get anything decent. Or without going into debt. I'd got chatting to an American woman in the restaurant who sat at an adjoining table. She spoke some Italian - her grandparents were from Lombardy - and it gave me a chance to practise my English. She was at Harvard, in the final year of her PhD and studying the murals at the Bhorgese. Something about following a clue to the way Renaissance artists were thinking about the symbolism of the New World. But maybe some of that got lost in our slightly haphazard translation. Anyway, we had an entertaining conversation in which I felt able to tease her a little and that enabled us to exchange cards before I left. Stepping into the street, I half turned and saw the waiter bend over her as she looked after me. Strangers.

Passers-by who'd shared a few moments together and would probably never meet again.

At the house, I was able to let myself in with the key. I could hear choral music playing inside one of the downstairs flats, a saxophone adding melody. Jan Garbarek, the Norwegian jazz musician, had recorded something like that. I paused to listen and recognized the eerie melodic line. I had the CD somewhere, back home. It was weird hearing his saxophone swelling over the massed voices of the choir. Music I'd shared with Beatrice in the years before she fell ill. In those last stages of pain and morphine and confusion she'd found music unbearable. *It's too beautiful*, she said to me one day, *please, it's too beautiful*. Meaning too full of life and future as she lay dying with the scent of jasmine outside the open window, birdsong mingling with the music. For the rest of that summer she heard only the birds. And she died one day in autumn in the early evening with a song thrush repeating its cry, as if calling her back to life. But she'd let go, at last. I held her hands and stroked the soft skin above her knuckles where the canula was taped. I'd always secretly hated the scent of jasmine.

I opened the door to the apartments and fumbled with my key in the dark. Lisette appeared in her nightgown, disturbed by the noise.

– Why don't you use the light switch?

Sofia appeared beside her, still tying up her hair.

– Is everything alright, *signor*?

Her voice was sharp, but I swept it aside the way a swordsman parries a thrust.

– Yes, of course! Goodnight, goodnight!

Then I climbed between the tight sheets that made me feel

as if I was fastened to a stretcher, reading my English novel for a few minutes before sleep overwhelmed the sounds of the street. I was vaguely aware of some disturbance in the night, but I never fully surfaced, and I fell back into the grip of a dream I can't remember now.

The next day, I was woken by a call from the office, asking me to come into work at once. Apparently, I'd slept through an earthquake that had been felt by others in the city, making ornaments tremble and window panes shake. The epicentre was in the mountains north-east of Rome. Over a hundred people had died. The political fallout had begun, and it continued to land over the next weeks and months. Buildings that should have been seismically secure had proved otherwise. Work on schools and municipal buildings that local politicians had signed off, had never been carried out. Corrupt mayors, underhand officials and contractors. Bungs and backhanders. It was a huge mess and the NGO I was working for had been brought in. The immigration crisis went on hold.

At – let's call it village X – twenty-six people had been killed, including young children. The school had collapsed and many houses had been damaged or had fallen down. My company was working with the survivors, trying to coordinate services for children, providing counselling and support for bereaved families. Then the aftershocks came, adding to the fear and trauma. We spent two days on the phone trying to understand what was going on. Then I was asked to go north and liaise directly with groups who were busy on the ground with an improvised school and other projects.

In Italy, the emergency relief services are made up of volunteers. When disaster strikes trained personnel are released from their jobs and their firms compensated. In a country that has its chaotic side, this service has developed an *esprit de corps*, a pride in its work and its voluntary nature that even full-time professionals can't match. Unfortunately, the spirit of volunteering had spread to the rest of the population and people had just turned up at the earthquake site – even families with children who camped out there – hoping to be able to help in some way. But those people just became part of the problem, so it was important to get the message across to the wider population that they had to keep away. That would be part of my report, as well as looking at what was happening on the ground in terms of reconstruction, communications networks, what was helpful and what might not be. So, I was to make a visit to the epicentre of the quake.

I set off on a Tuesday morning, having spent Monday reading preliminary reports and making phone calls. I left the apartment casually dressed, with a pair of hiking boots, an overnight bag, just in case, and a few bottles of water. I took only a piece of fruit for breakfast, shook off Sofia's protestations, and closed the door of the apartment. There, below the first short flight of steps was Amadeo, staring through the window. It was covered in a heavy iron grille that looked onto the courtyard with its decrepit fig tree, the leaves grey with dust. He half-raised a hand at my greeting, as if fending me off. His eyes looked luminous in the faint light. I wondered why he wasn't at school. I'd arranged to have a hire car delivered and had to wait a few minutes before it arrived, hearing hesitant piano scales rise and fall from the rooms above, like a crippled lizard climbing a wall.

I loaded my bags into the boot of the car and slung a bottle of water onto the passenger seat. The car had satnav, but I'd brought a map. It was important to understand where

I was heading, not just to arrive. I had to drive east out of Rome, following its impossibly constricted traffic system. Then better roads to Tivoli and L'Aquila, then jinking north, heading into the National Park and through the mountains. The whole trip was about two and a half hours. Gradually, the roads narrowed and climbed higher on hairpin bends, only a steel barrier between the road and the wooded valley below. It was a hot day with guncotton clouds and I had the aircon in the little Fiat running, sipping water to stay hydrated. Close to the village there were diversion signs. Sections of the road had slipped into the valley. Then I saw the first damaged houses. Whole hamlets had been shaken to the ground. There were hens pecking at the rubble and stray cattle still wandering the fields. The newer houses looked intact at first glance, but a closer look showed them riven by huge cracks. There were caravans beside some of them where people had adopted temporary shelter to keep an eye on what was left of their property.

I drove on through a landscape that had been changed utterly and that might never be the same again. There were still empty villages left after the last quake. This time far too many people had died and the survivors wanted answers. I missed a diversion sign and came face to face with a steel barrier where two *carabinieri* were leaning against their motorbikes. They waved me away and I had to reverse for a hundred metres, sweating, my neck aching as I twisted in the seat. The road climbed again, coiling across the mountainside, little more than a metaled mule track with potholes and patches of loose gravel. Then I was at the village. The main road was closed and a new track had been improvised out of the rubble of demolished houses. There were police and relief vehicles parked bumper to bumper and a talc of dust filled the air. They were pulling down a house to my left. I watched the shattered walls collapse inwards as the digger nudged them. I was in a line of cars and we waited almost twenty minutes before a civilian waved us through.

The meeting was in a restaurant that had been commandeered as an operations centre, set beside an ornamental lake. It was lunchtime now and the place was heaving with *carabinieri*, soldiers, paramedics and relief workers in blue overalls. I met my contacts, Carlos and Stephanie and we talked over lunch. After that, Stephanie would take me on a tour of the village, or what was left of it. She was woman in her early thirties, tough and capable with a ponytail of grey-flecked hair. Carlos was younger, his arms and neck tattooed with Celtic symbols. He had a full beard and unruly hair, coppery gold. Both, in their own way, were strikingly handsome. The pasta was excellent, even in this improvised canteen. As we talked, the lake glinted like a slice of ice. I imagined it rippling under the seismic shock of the quake, then falling still again, its carp rising in rings of light.

I'd left my Dictaphone running through lunch to capture our conversation. Afterwards, I killed it to speak off the record. There were real problems under the surface of things. The mayor was in sole charge of the disaster operation for forty-eight hours after the quake had struck. The same official had been accused of not overseeing seismic protection work on the church steeple. It had fallen onto a house and the family had been crushed to death. Half the school had collapsed and half was intact. So there were questions about why that had happened. There were more questions about official records and receipts and responsibilities. It was possible, Carlos said, glancing covertly at Stephanie, that the mayor had been more concerned with covering his back than dealing with the crisis. The weirdest thing was the people who'd been drawn into the area. Some came to help, but others simply came to watch, blocking the roads and parking spaces. In either case they'd added to the logistical problems and this was something that had to be managed better in future.

After lunch I shook hands with Carlos and put on my boots to accompany Stephanie who took me on a tour of the area. The main street was still cordoned off, but beyond the barriers you could see the diggers busy with the debris around the collapsed church. The newer houses on the outskirts of the village appeared to be in good condition, including the new secondary school, but in fact they almost all had vertical cracks in them making them unsafe for occupation. Stephanie showed me the new timber school that was being built by carpenters from Liguria, soon to open. There was a children's play area, a tented village with its guy lines and walkways laid out like an army camp. Another tent served as a nursery where a group of specialist teachers and therapists were working with traumatised children. Children who'd lost siblings, parents, grandparents in a single moment of destruction. At the horizon the mountains glittered in the sun, quite unchanged. Yet here, everything had been transformed in an instant. What had existed as a dependable future was simply and inexorably and inexplicably wiped away.

I realized then, that the future was a place like any other. That our lives were stories and that a story that has no continuity or destination frustrates our very existence, frustrates even death, which is another story. Even Beatrice lying in that sick room with the sun making dust glitter in the air and that songbird calling made sense compared to all this, though at the time it had seemed meaningless and cruel.

Before we left, we shook hands with a group of aid workers. One of the men had helped carry bodies out of the collapsed building in the first hours of the recue. His eyes were tight against the light, his handshake hard and prolonged. As if he didn't want to let go. As we were children of a lost future who had wandered home somehow. The quake had struck at night and that had helped to reduce casualties. *Think of the school*, he said, *think of it! The children!* But darkness had also been stealthy and omnipotent, tipping the sleeping into death before they could even awake. A little girl with dark curly hair and violet eyes stared at us, gripping a guy line and leaning out from it, as children do, testing gravity, never taking her eyes from us. And all the time we spoke, children were playing beside us, their laughter falling and breaking like that of children anywhere. But it was a temporary thing, a departure from the memories that would haunt the rest of their lives.

I drove home as the sun was sinking behind the wooded hillsides in a huge conflagration. Driving into the light, driving into an unknown future that was, nevertheless, an expectation I could depend upon. I drove from the mountains towards the city and the gloomy suburbs that held the half-light of transition. I dropped the car at the garage and walked through the streets with my bag. The little curio shops that were shut during the day were opening for the evening and the workshops that repaired things or made furniture were closing for the night. The two cities' lives met and over-lapped and reached into each other. Then I was on Urbano, walking down towards the apartment, past the cycle shop and the leather goods shop and the shop that sold ceramics and expensive bric-a-brac. There were the piano scales again, as if the same pupil was still practising. *Not music*, Beatrice had said, *please, not music*.

When I pushed the heavy door open, the corridor seemed long and gloomy. There was a patch of light where it turned next to the window with the iron grille. And there was Amadeo, his face lit like a white plate, as if he'd never moved from where he'd been standing that morning. As if everything had somehow stood still, awaiting my return.

Lisette was at the desk when I made it to the upstairs corridor. She was peering at her computer screen, its light harsh against her skin.

– Welcome back, *signor*. Did you have a good day?

I put the bag down and stood my boots on top, fumbling for a key.

– Well, good enough. But it was sad. *Triste*.

She caught her lip in her teeth and looked directly at me, tucking her ash-blonde hair back from her face.

– Sad? Why sad?

– Oh, I was up north. In the earthquake zone in one of the villages.

She shook her head slowly.

– Yes, you know we felt the tremors. Even here in Rome! Everything shook, just for a few moments.

She paused and picked up a pen from the desk.

– It felt as if God was angry, you understand? As if we were being punished! For . . . *something* . . .

I pushed the door to my room open and glanced back at her. She seemed agitated, pale-faced in the dim light.

– Well, I don't know about God, but there's a lot of work to do . . .

I shrugged. Then the door was closing behind me and I was thinking about a shower and clean clothes and the report I had to write.

Hot water and clean towels can go a long way to restoring one's sense of self. Not self-worth, exactly, it's more a physical restoration. And in physical well-being maybe we find at least part of what used to be thought of as the soul. I was clean and the shower had made my skin-tight and refreshed. As I cleaned my teeth, I thought of the rows of tents up there in the mountain villages. Of the people whose futures had gone out on them like a light, whose stories had been interrupted. I heard Sofia calling Amadeo in for his evening meal, and when the coast was clear I slipped out into the warm night air, passing the solicitor with his leather satchel, as he wheeled his bicycle down the hallway. Outside the streets were busy with tourists and the sudden nightlife that breaks out in Rome, even in streets that seemed dark and abandoned by day. After a moment's hesitation, I set off towards Cavour.

When I got to the restaurant, the American woman was there in the window. She saw me and waved. I hesitated, then went in.

– May I join you?

She had ordered, but her food had not yet arrived. There was a bottle of white in an ice bucket by the table. Melanie called for another glass and I chose something quickly from the menu. She was wearing a cream cotton top that showed off her arms, a tasteful butterfly tattoo. As we clinked glasses it flexed on the tanned muscle.

– What a nice surprise!

She was laughing at me as if we'd really planned to meet all along.

– Yes, what a coincidence. How's the research going?

She wiped her lips on her linen napkin and there was a trace of lipstick.

– Oh, research! It's slow, you know . . . I think I'm getting there. You?

– I'm just back from the mountains. The earthquake . . .

But she was nodding, forestalling me, her hand on my sleeve.

– But you didn't say . . .

– I didn't know.

For a moment silence thickened against us. I wondered where she thought she was going. *I'm getting there*, she'd said, as if the future was another stop on the metro or a bend in the Tiber where it spooled through the city. I thought of the little girl leaning out from the guy rope with eyes of indigo silk. And of Amadeo, his moon face haunting that darkened corridor.

Our antipasto arrived and we fell silent, picking at slices of Parma ham, spearing olives and placing the stones in a circle. Beatrice had died in the autumn and that winter brought a flock of male blackbirds to the garden, driven there by snow and frost. They strutted on the lawn, at peace for now. But in the Spring, they'd drive each other from that territory. I looked up and Melanie was saying something about her work, about patterns of tessellation, and I was watching the skin of her face gleaming in the light. The way her tanned skin creased around her eyes when she laughed. The way that round American face seemed so full of innocence and enthusiasm. I thought then what a strange race they were, like water boatmen skating over the fragile meniscus of life. But that wasn't fair, and anyway, she was Italian by descent, and

I didn't believe in races. When I raised the wine bottle, she placed her hand over her glass.

– You finish it, I'll be drunk!

And she laughed that full-hearted laugh, as if she was living always in the moment. I poured the wine, watching it bubble in the glass and clarify, nestling the empty bottle into the ice. When I looked up I caught her eyes and they were a cool grey, the colour of mild steel. She lived over the river, just a few tram stops away. I knew I'd wake there, pulling net curtains from the view of a long street, watching the flicker of starlings above the rooftops, turning to where she would lie, still naked in the bed. Or pulling on a tee-shirt to make coffee. Fastening her sandals or deftly clipping her bra. Or appearing suddenly with pastries to nudge me awake, yanking open the shutters, laughing at my sleepiness.

I finished the wine, tilting the glass back to savour it, wondering whether I'd regret it in the morning, knowing that the boy would be there when I returned to the Via Urbano, loitering the long corridor where light fell through the iron bars of the window, and the fig tree filled the courtyard with shadows and fallen fruit.

MEIJERSDORP

T HE PEDALS FELT hot, my feet gritty with sweat. I checked my side mirrors and pulled into the outside lane, sliding past a battered backie loaded with sacks. A woman in a pink tracksuit sprawled across them. Then a horse-drawn buggy mounted on car wheels, the driver upright at the reins, the horse trotting smartly. A mini-bus taxi was hanging on my bumper. You don't fuck with those guys. I pulled over. The window washers sprayed water onto a scrim of dust, the wipers cutting two clear arcs. Sun polished the windscreen. The sound of the horse's hooves fell away. I passed a township improvised from planking and corrugated steel. A plait of smoke twisted from orange flames where some tyres were burning.

Meijersdorp. A name I'd found on the map. A name that didn't belong there. I wasn't really sure how to pronounce it. Maybe the 'j' was silent. But, if you could read a map, you could see it was there in a wide valley, surrounded by mountains on three sides. And all the names were wrong: if they weren't Dutch they were French or English, stamped onto that territory. *Language communicates and excommunicates*. Who said that? Probably Kamitha. She taught English, after all. Language is power, a means and an end. We should know, we'd slung enough of it at each other.

Meijersdorp. It looked out of the way, it looked like somewhere I needed to be, just for a couple of days. I'd hired a car to travel to work and had been planning to use it to get out of the city. But something had always cropped up. Then I'd got tired of Cape Town, of Observatory where I was living. Blanking its down-and-outs and drunks as I walked past. The white kids with their dreadlocks and skateboards. Addicts nesting in stained sleeping bags in the arcades, their eyes blank. The stink of piss in the subway that caught you by the throat in thirty-degree heat. The wheelie bins going out each Monday and people rummaging through them to salvage anything useful. I was tired of giving or not giving, tired of thinking about it as the car pulled up at traffic lights and their hands opened. I'd got weary of living behind a security fence, the white stare of Groote Schuur Hospital where Cecil Rhodes had his estate in the last century.

I wanted something that made more sense, something beyond the tattoo parlours and junk shops and hip bars. Something that was under the skin. To be honest, I didn't know what I wanted, just to be out of the city where it curled against Table Mountain. Lion's Head with its eyelash of trees, the waterfront cranes and container ships and tourist haunts. The old industrial zones: Mowbray and Salt River and Woodstock that reminded me of Manchester when I was a kid. I must have stood out a mile. A white guy fresh from the UK walking through the hustlers and African curios on Long Street, the roads seething with traffic. A Zimbabwean taxi driver said to me with a huge smile, No, *it can never stand still, my friend!* And I needed stillness. I thirsted for it, like the water the city was running out of.

The drought was another reason to pull clear for a few days. Before I ended up unwashed and queuing at a standpipe with a jerry can. Like they did every day in the townships. I was heading north, following the N1 towards Paarl. There were clouds puffing up from the sea, but they wouldn't last long. The highway passed close to Belville and the airport where I'd been working, then jinked north again. There wasn't much traffic at the weekend, just a few hitchers. All black people with bags and cases, making it home to their families. Twenty-odd years after Apartheid things could look just the same.

I'd picked an Asian guy up in Woodstock, a few days before. He was about sixty, trying to get to his wife in hospital. He told me she had colonic cancer. He'd been hit by a car and showed me an ugly scar on his shin. He told me he'd been mugged by three coloured guys. Then he asked my name and swung on it like a pump handle, asking me for money to get the bus when I dropped him off. I found 100 rand in my pocket. His bad luck stories ran into each other like tributaries. Did I believe him? Did it matter? After all, no one begged because they wanted to.

Before Paarl, I got lost. Road signs are not South Africa's strong point. No Satnav, but the sun was in the wrong place for too long. I swung the car round and managed to find the R101 over Du Toitskloof pass, a ribbon of road that hairpinned over the mountains and back down the other side. The alternative was a tunnel, but I wanted air and sky and altitude to wash me clean. The route was spectacular. The valleys parched by drought, the rock ancient and gnarled, as if iron mountains had rusted and flaked. There were pale-breasted buzzards on the telegraph posts and a sky that looked eternal. Those early clouds had burned away into wisps and wraiths. I swung the car into tight bends, braking hard on the descent, glad of the aircon.

The first French and Dutch settlers had dragged ox-carts

through these mountains, killing the locals as they went. Khoi herders and San nomads. They'd marked out farms, taking on the land. The Cape colony had been based on slavery and it showed in a population that mixed Europeans with Khoisan, Bantu with Cape Malay. Though they weren't really from Malaisia. There was every skin type, every shade of religion, every thorn of exclusion and cruelty buried in their history. But they were beautiful people. Polite. Quick to laugh when life let them. Which was a lot of the time. I wondered what they saw when they looked at me.

I dropped the car into low gear to top the final rise and there were two guys walking ahead of me. Small men with woollen hats and knapsacks, jerking their hands as they moved. Rapid, contained, purposeful. What was the middle of nowhere to me was somewhere to them. They were walking into the sun, their shadows bobbing behind. They didn't even glance at me. They looked as if they didn't need anything in the world except their own onward motion, that insistent stride. As if they'd walked out of ancient history and right into the future. I guessed they were brothers. I lost track of them in the side mirror as the road swerved through a stand of blue gum trees, their trunks pale where the bark had stripped. Even those trees were foreign. Australian eucalypts.

I lost my way in flatlands where the fields were burnt white and cattle gathered at dried out waterholes. Then found it again, driving up a broad valley with mountains to left and right. I had to slow for a group of baboons scattering in the road, the mothers carrying their babies on their backs, a big alpha male watching me from the verge. They were drawn to food waste dropped in the lay-bys. It was forbidden to feed them.

Now I was in wine country. It was after the harvest, the vines shrivelling and dying back. The vineyards looked like braids of hair, their dark shadows slashing the soil, the wheat fields in between shorn of their crop. I could have been driving through France, Burgundy or Bordeaux, except for the mountains backlit at the perimeter, hazy blue against the sun. The road went on, unswerving. Then a white stone marker at a T-junction, shaped like a Dutch gable, *Meijersdorp* etched on it in black lettering. I pulled up, checked behind, reversed a few metres, then swung right onto a long, dipping road. Five kilometres into town. A minibus pulled out and passed, the driver staring across at me. The town was really just a wide street with shops and houses buried in the foliage along the road. I'd got up at seven to the last of the muesli and a black coffee. Now I was hungry. I slowed to look for food.

I parked on the steep camber and went into the first pub I came across. One of those sports bars with craft beers and big-screen TVs. The locals were watching a rugby match. I got a cold beer and went down some steps to order steak and chips from the kitchen. The girl who took my order smiled at my accent. There was a sign offering free wi-fi. I'd packed my laptop and cables. South Africa was two hours ahead of the UK, so it was still too early on a Saturday to think of Skyping Kamitha and Sean. Sean was seven now. A curly-haired kid with Kamitha's big, dark eyes. He wouldn't say goodbye to me when I left. Africa, China, Vietnam. The more I travelled, the less of me came home. Kamitha said that, once, after making love, after too much wine.

There were seven or eight locals in there. All white guys and women, clustered at the bar, thickset and big-boned. A bearded guy was teasing his girlfriend, pretending to smash his beer bottle over her head. She didn't think it was all that funny. On the walls were photographs of a strongman in a leotard humping barrels at some local show back in the last century, or the one before that. Rugby shirts pinned in glass cases, tennis racquets, crossed hockey sticks. Comical notices, like the ones back home.

We don't serve women, you need to bring your own.

If you're drinking to forget, please pay before you leave.

Please don't ask for credit as a smack in the mouth may offend.

A coloured guy walked in wearing greasy blue overalls and a peaked cap, waving to the woman who'd served me, stopping to kiss another woman with streaked blond hair. He said something to the bearded guy, jerking his thumb outdoors. Then he was waving as he left. When the steak came it was an inch thick and running with blood. *We're all coloured*, someone said, *or you wouldn't be able to see us.* True. But colour, skin colour, was significant everywhere in South Africa. *Man, things are really fucked up here!* Akhona, the office secretary, told me. As if it was news, as if it was all a big joke. They told me her uncle had been shot at a demonstration and lost a leg and was still waiting for compensation. Other times, when parts or paperwork were late or went missing, I got the shrug. Meaning, WTF? Meaning, what can we do? Meaning, don't ask. And I didn't.

I gave the woman behind the bar a wave as I left, but she was counting a stack of rand and didn't glance up. The blonde woman gave me a hooded look. Like that buzzard on the telegraph pole. There was no shade on the street and my armpits felt rank. I thought about a shower. At the garage next to the bar two black men in baseball caps were working on a truck tyre while a big bearded guy in shorts and tee shirt watched them. There was something written on his chest in Afrikaans. *Ontspan!* I'd seen it before. He certainly looked relaxed, tugging his beard and grinning as the guys levered the tyre off the wheel. The car was unbearably hot. I wound down the window and reversed out, craning my neck. He turned to watch me drive away.

I'd booked a room in an old-style guesthouse. It'd been built as a teacher's hostel originally. I tried to navigate using the map I'd printed from the website. It got me lost. Driving in circles, past the white spire of the Dutch Reformed Church, then out to the low hills above the town. Beyond the old houses with Dutch gables and streets of modern bungalows was a settlement of utility houses with grey metal roofs. They were like the matchbox houses I'd seen in Soweto. Cheap housing built for black and coloured people. You rarely saw a white person on foot, but there *they* were, walking the streets with their shopping, trekking home from the KwikSpar or Pick n' Pay with bottles and carrier bags and sacks of potatoes on their heads.

I found Pieterse Street by chance. There was the guest house on the corner, white-painted, with a courtyard, a veranda, purple flowers on a trellis. At reception a handsome middle-aged woman greeted me and handed me some keys. It was cool inside the house, thick-walled and shady. There was a lot of South African Air Force memorabilia and photographs of the sea lashing a lighthouse. The dining room was fitted out in dark mahogany. All the furniture was heavy and old-fashioned. I dragged my bag up the stairs and found my room. It had twin beds, a rotary fan on the ceiling, an aircon unit, and a large en-suite bathroom. Considering there was a drought on, the toilet must have flushed away at least five gallons of water. It was cheap, it was homely. I'd be fine for two nights.

I washed my face with the block of olive-coloured soap. Kamitha would have liked that. She had her rustic side. There were enough towels for half a dozen people. I unpacked my laptop and found the wi-fi network. I tried to Skype with Kamitha. She picked up, but the screen pixilated. Her voice kept elongating and drifting away. I thought I saw Sean behind her and gave him a wave. But it was hopeless. They kept dissolving, wavering into a mosaic of needle-point light. I'd try again tomorrow, I said. Kamitha's reply was shredded.

I hung up a couple of shirts and sprayed on some sunscreen. Thinning hair, so I burned easily. I took my bush hat and set off to explore.

Heat boiled from pavements, reflecting off the walls of houses. There wasn't much to Meijersdorp: a garage, bars, restaurants, a craft shop, that big church, the supermarkets selling groceries and cheap liquor. I sat down on the stoep of a bar opposite the guesthouse and ordered fizzy water. There was a guy with five-day stubble and a ponytail hunched over his phone. A woman with crinkly auburn hair, slim and high-stepping, brought me my drink. I noticed a PA system at the end of the stoep, a poster behind me advertising an R&B band that night. The Blue Flames. I might catch some of that.

Ice cracked and jostled as I poured the water, like the way my computer screen had dissolved when I tried to make contact with Kamitha. The guy with the ponytail leaned back and took a swig of beer. He nodded to me and went back to whatever was happening on his phone. He'd perfected the art of being out of the moment. It was four o'clock and the mountains were with tinged with a mist of blue shadows. I tried to linger over my drink.

A Jeep with a torn hood pulled up at the bar. A woman got out to stretch. I guessed she was in her thirties. Cut-down jeans and sandals. She'd tied her hair back, sunglasses perched on her head. She was followed by four guys in Blue Flames tee-shirts, one with a baseball cap and tattoos, the others unshaven and tousle-headed. They greeted the guy with the ponytail, then were hugging the landlady, speaking in Afrikaans, laughing, rubbing each other's backs, lugging amplifiers and a drum kit to the little stage.

I went across the road to take a shower. The guesthouse was cool, its walls thick, blinds drawn against the sun. There was an insect trapped against the window. I flicked it away with the hand towel, then dragged the plastic curtain across the bath, mindful that I shouldn't waste water. When it arrived, it was hot and plentiful. I dropped the block of soap. It thudded into the bath and slalomed. The towels were huge and soft. I stood naked for a moment, then found slacks and a polo shirt. There was a technical paper I had to read. I could have done with sending off a few emails. Instead, I lay on my bed and dozed under the ceiling fan.

I woke an hour later, groping for my glasses and watch. It was just past seven. It was rare that I drank at lunchtime, especially in the heat. I hated that seedy feeling. I rinsed my face in cold water. It was dropping dark outside. The street lamps had come on, luring insects. I could hear a commotion at the street corner. Outside, there was a traffic cop and a group of young guys clustered around a white Mazda. They were laughing now.

I passed through them and up the street to a restaurant

I'd spotted earlier. It seemed quiet for a Saturday night. I sat outside, nodding to a family who looked like tourists. I got a glass of Shiraz, one of those raspy South African reds that was like drinking warm jam. Then I ordered a starter of salad leaves and some kind of chicken schnitzel for a main. It wasn't the best, but it was OK. I was tired of my own cooking, of eating out in bars and cafés. Of punctuating each day with meals. Of trying not to drink too much or too often.

I drank the wine slowly. A nebula of flies circled the candle on my table. The road was wide and dimly lit and people had gathered to talk. White people on the verandas of cafés and restaurants. Black and coloured people out on the street. I wondered what Kamitha was doing right now. And Sean. I missed him, the smell of him, his goofy smile when I pretended to pinch off his nose.

I drained the last of the wine and asked for the bill. The guy who brought it looked a bit like Sidney Poitier. Slim and handsome in an easy way. Gay, I guessed, but maybe that was just good manners and attentiveness, a faint look of wounded sensibility. I rose to leave and whacked my knuckle against the edge of the table. The taste of blood, salt, iron.

There were a few people on the veranda when I got back to where the band would be playing. Mainly white families out for the evening. The odd coloured person. The band members were sitting out front, near the stage, talking and smoking. I found a chair next to my grizzled friend with the ponytail. Next to him was a thickset guy with a white tuft of beard and slicked-back, thinning hair. He was smoking a joint and operating a little mixer desk. Chicago blues was pumping through the PA. Muddy Waters, Junior Wells, Little Walter, Sonny Boy Williamson, Slim Harpo. I knew them all.

I had a headache after the wine and the drive out of town, so I ordered more fizzy water. The guy with the ponytail leaned forward to shake my hand.

– Nils.

– Hi. I'm Andy.

– Cool. Where you from, Andy?

– The UK, the north.

– This is Chris.

The guy on the mixer took my hand in a firm grip.

– Welcome.

He offered me a toke. But I raised a hand and shook my head.

– I'm good, thanks.

That was cool, too. The spliff passed to Nils, then to the woman who'd driven the band. She'd put on an embroidered tunic over scarlet trousers. The band took to the stage.

The guy with the tattooed neck was the drummer, his eyes glaring from behind the kit. A tall square-shouldered guy played guitar. The thin, bearded one with grey curls blew blues harp. The bass player fronted the band, singing and playing. He had an English accent and a high, clear voice, that rose over percussive bass notes. They were good and tight, though they didn't deviate much from the R&B I'd heard back home. A staple of Chicago blues, a smattering of Dr Feelgood, the odd Ray Charles number. I was at home in the music, at least.

The songs began to blend together, one twelve-bar blues followed by another. Now the singer was announcing a new number, swaying back on his heels. Chris called for another round of tequilas. Only the guitarist and singer were drinking. They were flanked by the drummer, caged by his kit, by the harp player who was choosing a harmonica for the next song.

The night began to blur into its own special kind of heat: beer, dope, tequila and blues. A bright half-moon soared over the houses, a huge black thundercloud rising towards it. Lightning flickered across its top edge, where the moon streaked it with silver. The street was full of shadows and the shadows were full of people caught in the pulse of the music, the faint crackling of the far away storm.

A young guy came through the gate to sit next to Nils. A farmer, I guessed. Easy-going with short back and sides, shaking hands, making quips in Afrikaans, laughing, his suede boots propped up on a chair. He could have been there with his rifle at Spion Kop a hundred years ago. I couldn't shake off that image. Those lads from my home town. The way the sun had risen that morning, the Boers above, picking them off one by one. Those raked terraces on football grounds back home memorialising slaughter.

The band took a break, stretching and sauntering to their seats. Nils leaned forward, putting his hand on my arm, his speech slurred.

– Whaddya do, mate?

– Engineer. Hydraulics. You?

– I'm an artist.

– An artist? What do you work in?

He threw back his head and laughed a little theatrically.

– Paint. Ja!

He fumbled for his phone.

– I've got this commission right now. Working for a guy who owns a gallery. He didn't know what to do with the back wall. So . . . ja, look . . .

He opened the phone and scrolled to some black and white

murals he was making, each one about twelve-feet high. I recognized Chris, the guy on the mixer, then his high-stepping wife, then a woman with piled hair who smiled out at us.

– There's nine more. It's like the twelve apostles . . .

– They're beautiful.

What else to say? Nils jabbed his finger at the smiling woman.

– This is the woman I'm in love with. I'm damned if I know what to do about it.

He fingered his beer bottle and looked me in the eye. Remorseful. Resentful. It was hard to tell.

– I don't know why I told you that. I must be getting soft.

I patted his arm.

– It's fine. It's all fine.

He fired down the tequila that had just arrived, raising his glass to the band who were already back on stage, easing themselves through another R&B classic. The guitarist pulled off some flashy vibrato then stumbled over the opening of 'The Thrill is Gone'. Chris was grinning at me, pulling at his beard.

– Too fucking true!

The singer flashed him a V sign and the blond guy was leaning back from his suede boots, laughing his full-throated, Spion Kop laugh, showing neat white teeth.

Five shots of tequila didn't seem to affect the singer, but the guitarist was starting to repeat himself, a glazed look in his eye as he hunched over his Les Paul. The moon loomed behind a gauze of mist. Below it the dark cloud was rising, a show of lightning still flickering about its rim.

Black people had gathered in the street outside to listen, saving their entry fee. Or maybe they didn't feel welcome. They danced in and out of the cars that were gliding up the street. One couple held each other in a patch of light that dropped from a street lamp. She wore a red frock and dark pullover. He was dressed in a buttoned-up jacket and a tilted pork-pie hat. They weren't young. They were small and light-boned, skinny-looking, their eyes glinting in the electric light. They'd lived through their own non-existence and now they were here, alive, dancing, linking hands and jiving in the old-fashioned way, raising their arms, losing balance, staggering drunkenly as the paying guests cheered them. It seemed part contempt, part affection.

The cloud edged up to the moon, blotting it up, leaving only the flickering of the far-off electrical storm. The music pulsed and those dancers were somehow lost in each other or some deep memory. I thought of them sleeping and waking in those little houses, behind the town. They reminded me of my parents dancing at my sister's wedding, their feet turning on a remnant of time.

The moon was finally engulfed. The woman fell backwards into the man's arms and he led her away, hand in hand. The night ended with the audience singing along to Muddy Waters' 'I Got My Mojo Working', gloriously out of time. Chris was collecting money from the crowd. The people who'd been watching drifted off under the street lamps and into the shadows at the edge of town.

I slipped away as the audience were cheering, letting myself into the guesthouse with the security code I'd written on my hand. Low lighting helped me find my way upstairs. I drew the curtains, chose one of the twin beds and got in it. All night I was mithered by a mosquito. It had the knack of lying low until I was almost asleep, then whining close to my ear like a ricochet. I switched on the light and hunted for it.

No luck. I lay down again in the dark, pulling the sheet over, faint light coming under my door. There it was again, high-pitched, punishing me for leaving the window open behind net curtains and drapes.

I dozed off and woke up grateful that I hadn't drunk much the night before. I had a line of itchy bites down one arm. Breakfast in the shady dining room was scrambled eggs and fatty bacon, with pannankoeken with syrup on the side. The coffee was instant. It was bitter and strong and I had to add warm milk to take the edge off. Everything was slow and old-fashioned. Everything was as it had been and as it would and should be.

It was a clear day, still cool. Girls passed the window on their way to church, dressed in their Sunday frocks. It reminded me of home and the Baptist Sunday School when I was a kid.

I went to the car and drove up the valley to where the road petered out. It spread into tributaries, each one leading to a farm or a clutch of houses. There were vineyards and wine-workers' cottages, fields of stubble. Lanky horses with canvas blinkers. Stands of eucalyptus trees, their pale trunks peeling. Three white birds with long necks rose and flew up in a V formation. The farm workers' houses were tucked back from the road, bare and functional. An old man walking the highway raised his hand. He had a grey beard. An Old Testament prophet. I remembered the two men I'd seen climbing Du Toit's Kloof pass, moving relentlessly towards something.

I parked up where the road turned from public to private and got out. The air was still cool. There were fields of maize yet to be harvested. Below a banking that separated it from the road, a reservoir, its water sunk into an iris of cracked mud. The mountains reared in the early sun. White tongues of cloud were creeping down the passes like avalanches of snow. It was peaceful, almost unbearable. A version of Europe inscribed on Africa. All this set below mountains threaded by the footpaths of Khoi and San peoples who'd lived here since the first humans set out to find something beyond themselves.

The only way forward now would be on foot. I went back to the car and started the engine. A boy appeared from nowhere and made his way along the ridge above the reservoir. His dark skin glowed. He was wearing a tartan shawl and white shorts, ducking into the head-high field of maze. I thought of Sean, back in the UK. There in that glass and steel city. Then this boy, growing up here, remote from most things, except history, which was everywhere and everything. I watched him vanish into the tangle of all I could never understand.

One thing I had realized - sitting in bars, eating in cafés, pretending I was waiting for a friend, checking my phone as I nursed a beer - was that I'd never really belonged any-where. Places weren't home for me. They were just another reminder of how I didn't fit in. Even Kamitha was unreach-able. Unattainable. As if you could ever attain or even know another person. That mystery of proximity, love, *otherness*.

I thought of those two guys again, walking through the pass side by side, the mountains rearing, their arms jerking with each step. Now clouds were pouring towards me and evaporating at the same time. I had another three weeks to go, then home again. I could hack that, just about. A bird was moving above the maize, pulling itself on swooping wing beats. It came into the sun - some kind of egret - its legs trail-ing. Then I was driving back to Meijersdorp, light strobing

through poplars, licking koppies and wheat fields and vineyards that lay drenching in heat. I looked down and there was
still a streak of dried blood across my knuckle.

SAINT PETER

SHE LOOKED MID-THIRTIES. Small with brown hair, anxious eyes, sharp cheekbones. An Old English sheepdog tugging on its lead. A blond lad, about nine, at her side, clinging to the railings outside our new house, staring through the windows. I crossed the street, clutching a tape measure.

– Can I help you?

The dog took a sudden interest in me and growled. The woman tugged back on its choker and the boy turned to look, his hair spikey in the sun.

– Do yer live 'ere?

There was a hoarse edge to her voice. I stepped up to the front door and put the key in. The door jammed. I pushed and turned back to her.

– I'm about to.

She smiled. Her front teeth had been capped. Her skin was pale, not unhealthy, but with an ivory tint. She tossed her hair from her shoulder and pulled the dog back again. It cocked its leg and pissed against the low garden wall.

– I used ter live here. That's why we were looking.

– When was that?

The door screeched on plaster dust.

– When I were a kid. Until '96, when my dad died. I'm thirty-five now.

I pulled the Yale from the lock and dropped it into my pocket, remembering something I'd been told.

– You're Vince's daughter . . . Vince Harrison?

It wasn't really a question, more an exclamation that petered out on me. The boy leaned forward to peer through the windows. His voice had a high, manic edge.

– Did 'e die 'ere?'

His mother ignored him. He didn't. Even I knew that.

– No.

I tried to change the subject.

– Do you remember the house?

The boy was slouching away bored and the dog lifted a leg to scratch at its neck.

– Yes, pretty much . . . Leo, come 'ere!

She pulled on the chain and I realized she was speaking to the dog, not the boy. He spoke up now, wheedling.

– Mam!

– Hold on. I'm talking ter the man.

I don't know what made me say it. A sense of trespass, I suppose. Mine, of course.

– Would you like to look around?

She hesitated.

– I wud. But I'll have ter put dog in't car an' come back.

She leaned to tousle the dog's head, then held out her hand. A thin arm emerged from her baggy jumper. Her skin had faint white scratches on it. There was some writing tattooed on the underside in Gothic script.

– I'm Lizzie.

– Gavin. I'm pleased to meet you. What a coincidence!

I knew it wasn't of course. News travels fast in a Cumbrian village. Every post office and corner shop doubles as the information super-highway. Practically everyone must have known we were moving in. Well, that *someone* was, if not specifically

179

us. Someone from *off* as they used to say. We'd been off-comers and blow-ins everywhere we'd ever lived, Matt and me. And we'd been worse than that.

– I'll come back. Give us a minute? Connor, come on!

She disappeared up the street, walking with a slightly pin-toed gait, dragging the dog and the boy with her.

I pushed into the house. There was a smell of wet plaster and dust, mould and wallpaper paste. The hallway was almost blocked by a pasting table and cans of paint. Matt was finishing the rooms as I was stripping them. But he'd been called back to Manchester, lighting a new show at The Exchange, because there'd been a falling out over something or other. So, I just carried on, keeping track of emails and other stuff in the mornings and working on the house in the afternoons. We'd moved into one bedroom that wasn't too bad. The bathroom and kitchen were useable. We were still at the stage of filling skips as far as most other rooms were concerned.

I was just marking out the fireplace for the new lintel when there was a tap on the window and there was Lizzie's face clouded by dust that had gathered on the cobwebs. I gestured her to come in. She'd obviously left the dog and the boy somewhere. The door shrieked on the tiles and she was outside the room, watching me. She saw the question in my face.

– I've left 'im with 'is gran, me dad's mum. She still lives in't village.

I must have looked surprised.

– Din't yer know? Uncle Martin has that farm just over't river bridge. She lives wi' 'em.

I knew it: a Victorian farmhouse built in grey stone with a shitty farmyard and a barn full of rotting hay bales. Lizzie wandered into the kitchen, reaching out to touch the wall.

– It's not changed much. A family from Thirsk had it, then a couple from Broughton moved in, but they didn't last long.

Lizzie laughed, as if that was funny. The wallpaper was hanging off in strips and a curious look crossed her face.

– Is all this comin' off?

She was picking at a corner with a fingernail. I nodded, and she pulled at the edge of the paper. It had dried out and bellied away from the wall, so it tore easily. There was a drawing behind, under the residue of dried paste.

– What's that?

– It's me dad's instructions for mekkin' a cup o' tea.

And there it was, written onto the raw plaster before Vince had decorated. A long list of instruction with a drawing of a spoon and a cup and a tea bag. There was a magic wand to one side, sprinkling sugar. She took me upstairs to the small bedroom, our feet echoing on the treads. There, when she prized away the paper, was a drawing of a dragon snapping at a night sky full of stars and breathing fire.

– They're all over't place. Me dad did 'em when we moved in. He were doin' the place up and we were bored.

– He had a nice sense of humour.

– He had.

She pulled another strip of paper and there were two children staring up at a crescent moon with 'bedtime' written next to them. She gave me a sly look and grimaced.

– Sorry.

– It's OK – it's all got to come off anyway.

In the garden she peered up through the branches of the old Bramley. Then she moved her hands over the fork in the branches, as if she was remembering something. When we moved in, the grass was covered in brown windfalls that the birds or squirrels had gnawed at. Now it was just coming into leaf, creaking in the wind outside our window, renewing itself. We went back into the house and upstairs again. There was a roof space you could almost stand up in. Lizzie went up the ladder and peered inside. She came down, knocking dust from her cardigan, drifted back into the bedroom, pressing her face to the window.

– We used ter play in that tree. There were allus lots of apples. Me mum used to mek pies. But you couldn't give 'em away . . .

There was a short silence, her Doc Marten's scuffling in the dust.

– You've a job on!

– Yes, we'll get there . . .

Lizzie nodded.

– I'd better go.

She gestured towards where she'd left the car and her blue eyes were glittering with tears. She drew the cuff off her jumper across her nose and sniffed and was making her way downstairs when she looked back at me.

– I've heard you're two lads?

– That's right, me and Matt.

– Good luck wi' that!

I watched her walk away up the street, texting Matt to find out when he'd be home, then went back to knocking out the tiled fireplace that Vince had built. He seemed to have a knack for what was garish, what had probably been considered modern in its day. There was always a bit of shame in an old house and people couldn't wait to modernise. Boxing in the beams. Taking out the old fireplaces. Now we were turning that back on itself.

It was getting towards lunchtime. I made a sandwich and took it outside to sit on the rotting bench near the pond. There was an area of decking on the far side that reached over the field beyond. Sturdy-legged lambs were playing king of the castle where the land fell away to a little beck. The pond was pretty overgrown, but I'd seen newts and there were toads. I'd recognized their spawn amongst the weeds, like a tangle of ticker tape, as if the eggs had been printed. Yesterday, I'd peered through the window at six a.m. to see a heron rising from the decking, seeming to assemble its body and wings as it rose, a grey dawn spectre. I'd found an old garden spade in the shed that stank of soil and creosote and jammed it upright between the decking, hoping to keep it away.

I took my plate and cup and went back inside. All the houses in our row had been built onto each other at different periods, so interior walls were once exterior walls, deadening sound between the rooms. Our house was formed of two old cottages that had been knocked together and extended out the back. Vince had done quite a bit of the work. His signature was dressed stone and Tudor-style stained oak, but the effect was more suburban than rural. *Cottagey*, Pete, the joiner had said, when he dropped his tool bag to start work freeing up the sash windows. We'd laughed at that. It certainly covered a multitude of sins.

Matt and I met in Manchester in one of those night clubs that come and go around Canal Street. He'd just finished his college course and I'd got my first job as a GP in Timperley. I'd grown up in York but had trained in Manchester and stayed there. There was a big gay scene and it was easy to be out. I liked Mancunians, too, there was sharp sense of humour that gave them a bit of edge. Not like Scousers, more throwaway, somehow. Matt was from Failsworth, north of the city, towards Oldham. His grandfather had been a German POW from the East. Dresden. After the war, there'd been nothing to go home for. Matt had grey eyes and dark hair. He'd stood out, tanned from a trip to Naples he'd just made with a touring show, sipping beer from a tall glass, leaning against the bar in Levi's and Timberlands, somehow more at ease than I could ever be.

I'd got rid of the tiles. I had to crouch under the lintel where the wood-burner was going to go, spreading lime mortar on the wall. I'd mixed it myself from a recipe on the internet. There was something satisfying about finding the knowledge through Google and then making it up myself in a trug. It went on like butter mixed with sugar. My dad had been a maths teacher. My mum was a school nurse and that had been what sparked my interest in medicine. I dropped the trowel into the trug and stood back. Not bad. I had another three weeks to work on the house, then I started at a new practice in Kendal. It didn't do to work too close to home. People thought you could read them. Their bodies, I mean. The way a tree surgeon spots a diseased or dying tree. It was rubbish, of course, for the most part, but my job was never a good topic of conversation at social gatherings. Which were a long way off here. We didn't know a soul.

It was Wednesday and I wouldn't see Matt until Friday evening when he drove up from the gig. Long days and longer nights, when I woke with a jolt in the early hours to the musty smell of the house. When Pete the joiner had come into the kitchen, he'd paused and squinted, hamming it up.

- By 'eck, I can just see Vince now, leaning against that sink an' having a bit of a laugh. Reet theer!

He flung out a hand for dramatic effect. The little finger was amputated at the knuckle. He made it sound as if he'd seen a ghost. And if Vince was anything to me, he was a haunting. The electrician, the plasterer, the builders who screeded a new floor in the living room had all known him. They'd played football together, dated the same girls, got married and had kids around the same time. When Bunt Capstick was pasting wallpaper, he told how Vince and his wife, Jenn – *she were a reet nice lass an' all, bonny, like* – had got hold of one of the new VHS video cameras. She'd filmed Vince, *bare-arse naked except for a hard hat*, dancing to 'I Will Survive'. Some wag had got hold of the tape, put it in a *Star Wars* case and placed it with the other entertainment in the local Spar. *Vince din't give a bugger, he reckoned blokes could learn a thing or two from that video. I don't think Jenn were right suited, though.* And he chuckled, lining the wallpaper up, drawing the brush down to seal the joint. I wondered if he was the wag. Or if it was all just a bit more of Vince's improbable legend. *An urban myth*, Matt reckoned, *all bollocks*. Except it was a rural myth, I reminded him, so probably double bollocks.

From then on, I felt Vince was watching me as I worked. After all, he was a real builder and I was playing at it, pulling out his handiwork, getting my instructions from the web and carrying them out to the letter. *A reet fuckin' swot!* I could hear him saying it, like the lads at school, turning away to draw on the wall with a stub of pencil, dark-jawed, stocky and vigorous. *There's happen a bit of Italian in us, round 'ere*, Pete had said, hammering the door frame. *Some lasses came over before the war to work in't mill and stayed, they liked it that much.* And he winked at me as he drove in a nail.

Our neighbours on one side were a couple who had a house

in Spain and were rarely at home. They were decent enough in a bluff kind of way, though I don't think they were from Cumbria. *Nottingham way, 'a reckon*, Pete had said, as if it was Babylon. The guy on the other side was a plumber from Luton who'd made a few bob. The house was their holiday home. Every few weeks he came with his wife in a black BMW and they set about the garden in overalls and gloves, cutting the lawn and pruning back the leylandii hedge. They didn't speak much. Just a curt nod over the garden wall that was falling down and that we'd have to talk about some day. They weren't our type. And as Matt said, watching them pull away one Sunday evening, *I'm bloody sure we're not theirs.*

I washed my tools out and left them outside to try on an upside-down bucket. Then I showered and changed. We'd need to get a new gas boiler when we could afford one. Sometimes it sputtered out water the colour of weak tea. I ate in the local pub, which was just a hundred yards away and where I got some curious glances. But the food was OK and the beer was from a local micro-brewery. Matt would like that. He called me when I was eating, sounding tired, but it was hard to talk in there. The signal was crap for one thing. He sounded a bit bleak when he said goodnight.

When I walked home the sky was full of dark-edged clouds. We had no curtains and the moon kept me awake all night, looming through the windows. I thought of Lizzie, pulling back the wallpaper to find those childhood drawings. I thought of Vince who'd collapsed at a new build on the outskirts of the village lifting in a stone lintel. One moment alert to the world – the smell of wet mortar, the cold weight of sandstone – the next reeling into death. His arteries had been silting up all those months and years, his heart giving out with no warning. *Forty-two*, Pete said, *God save us. He were no age.* I fell asleep thinking about Vince, the way the news must have reached home and stopped everything. The way presence becomes absence. Things that should have been finished left unfinished. The way life becomes suddenly and irrevocably incomplete. When I woke early again and went to the window, there was the heron on the decking, staring into the water, the garden spade upright beside it.

Matt got back at about eight o'clock on Friday evening. I was in the kitchen lifting a lasagne out of the oven when I heard the door open. He dropped his bag in the hallway. And came through. When I hugged him, his body felt thin and hot against mine. I thought he looked tired.

– Tired? Fucked!

– As bad as that?

– Long week! Bloody endless hassle . . . real twat of a director.

He was already lifting the bottle of white wine out of the fridge and splashing it into glasses. It was dark outside and we looked like ghosts in the double glazing.

– Go and look in there.

I gestured to the lounge with my glass, trying to remember where I'd put the Parmesan. His voice came back all echoey.

– Hey, that looks pretty good.

The stove had been installed and I'd lit a fire with a few off-cuts that had been left over by the joiners.

– We'll need some logs.

– Yeah, yeah, but it's looking good. Nice to get rid of all that crap that thingymajig put in . . .

– Vince.

– Fucking Vince.

187

Matt tilted his glass up and looked round for the bottle. I tugged his hand.

- It's on the table. Come on, we can eat. We can move on to red.

The lasagne had stopped bubbling and there was a golden crust over it, burned brown at the edges. The wine was from the village shop, a little harsh, with that faint taste of tarnished metal. But it was our first home-cooked meal and it made the house feel like it belonged to us. Even if it was draughty and dusty. Even if one of the faces at the window had seemed like Vince looking in and not us looking out.

We were both really tired and Matt slept heavily. I woke up about two a.m. and couldn't get off again, thinking of Lizzie and Vince, their lives in the same house. I must have drifted off, but the sun woke us early. We'd drunk a bit too much wine and I had a mouth like a doormat. I got up to use the loo and splash water on my face and clean my teeth. When I got back to bed Matt was sprawled across the pillows. His neck always looked childishly vulnerable, the short hairs glistening. When I bent down to kiss it, he opened his eyes very slowly, as if he didn't really know where he was or as if he was checking something. He rolled over onto his back and managed a smile. His body was smooth, without a mark on it, except for a tiny brown mole under one nipple. I loved his earlobes. There was something perfect about them. I pretended to bite them and he pretended to push me away as I fell back into bed.

After breakfast we decided to clean up the rubbish in the yard and make a bonfire with some old timber and a plywood cupboard I'd taken out of an alcove in the living room. Matt cleared a space in the garden. I watched him working, his

body moving with economy, as if every action was antici-
pated beforehand. That was his training, I guess. He didn't
waste energy and he rarely wasted words. We piled up the
rubbish together but decided to light it in the evening when it
might be less annoying to the neighbours. As long as it didn't
rain.

In the afternoon we managed a walk down by the river that
ran through a little dell below the village, a basin of rough
grazing land that trapped the sun. There was a dead sheep in
a swampy bit where rushes grew and rusty water seeped out
of the earth. The river was lined with hawthorn and ash and
hazel, running over smooth rocks where the strata lay parallel
to the surface, streaked with foam. There was a little pebble
beach before the river widened into a pool. We saw fish rising
to the surface to gulp at flies. We found fragments of pottery
and pieces of weathered coal that had washed out of the old
mine workings upstream. A woman passed above us with a
golden retriever, but apart from that we didn't see a soul, even
on the way back through the woods where we usually ran into
a neighbour or two. People who smiled at us curiously.

We stopped for a pint in the pub, an eighteenth-century
coaching inn with a mounting block and low mullion windows.
It looked authentic from the outside, but the inside had been
modernised. It looked suspiciously like Vince's handiwork.
We stood at the bar, chatting to the landlord, who was as
new as we were. There were a few locals, if you can call the
nouveau riche local. They were from the gated community on
the hill that had been converted from a corn mill. Near that
was a field where there were acres of solar panels facing south
instead of sheep or cattle. The community wasn't actually
gated, but it was exclusive. Or they thought it was. We were

getting evils from them and from the other locals who played darts and dominoes in the snug.

– Fuck it, let's have another, just to spite 'em.

The landlord must have heard. He was tall, ginger and bearded, and looked tired around the eyes. He glanced at Matt and smiled, sardonically.

– They'll get used to you . . .

– They'll have to.

Matt took a swig of the beer and wiped his mouth and the back of his hand and looked over to where the guys in brogues and cloth caps were enjoying their own company. He mouthed something at the landlord, who nodded imperceptibly. I leaned closer.

– What did you say?

– What do you think?

I was a bit surprised, but I let it go. He was right after all. Dead right. They were probably just whatever he'd said they were.

That night we watched orange flames and sparks pour from the bonfire, smoke coiling away into the night, our faces pale at the kitchen window.

The house progressed slowly, but at least we were living with our own things around us now. We could sit at the end of the garden, watch magpies and jays darting between the hawthorns down in the valley. There were overgrown vegetable beds covered in old carpets to keep the weeds down. We pulled them all up and burned the carpets, filling the village with the stench of burning wool. The weather became warm and then wet and then warm again. Maybe it was a window of some kind because the pond filled with frogs. They clambered over each other on the lily pads. We found tadpoles.

Then newts, unhurried and calm, sculling through the depths. *Common newts*, Matt said. They were protected, like the bats that flitted through the dusk that summer. The baby frogs were cute, the way miniature things are.

Matt started with on a new production at the Everyman in Liverpool just as I began work at the Kendal practice. At weekends, I watched him working in the garden when I was in the kitchen, making coffee or preparing lunch. Sometimes it's hard ever to get over another person. He seemed so self-contained, so unreachable at times. Weeks passed and May-blossom appeared, making the trees look like girls in white frocks running across the meadows. It faded, then blew away in a single night of storms. In the garden pond the newts disappeared, taking to the land for winter. We saw the glimmer of goldfish that had survived the heron, then maiden flies and water boatmen, dragon flies shivering over the skin of water.

I thought about Vince all the time. Haunting the place. Haunting me. Plastering a wall in the house. Squinting at the roof. Gathering windfalls from the Bramley. It had a bumper crop that first year. We put them into carrier bags and hauled them to the village shop. Lizzie was right, you couldn't give them away. Sometimes I spoke to Vince in those empty rooms, imagining he was listening with that wry, cocky grin. I saw his mother in the street: thin, determined, walking past with her shopping bags, trying not to look at the house.

Sometimes Lizzie passed with the dog or child. Rarely both. People said she'd had a troubled time as a kid. Not just because of losing Vince. They hinted at other stuff too. I got the impression she'd gone under and then surfaced somehow. She had the look of the saved. Vince's drawings were still there under the wallpaper, waiting to be discovered again. The house was old, built in 1785, according to the inscription over the door. Generations of people had lived and died and been born there. We were just another couple who'd turn into the past, into other people's imaginings. I'd put our names under the wallpaper too, *Matt & Gavin*, on each side of a bird's wings. Sentimental, maybe. But I didn't tell Matt. He'd have told me I was a gormless twat, allowing himself that wicked grin.

I guess we weren't seen together that much in the village. There was a generation of retired folk who'd moved there. Baby-boomers with suntans and final-salary pensions. They'd done alright. They volunteered in the local shop and ran the Parish Council and local history society and organised the village hall and playing fields. When the refugee crisis started and people were arriving from the Middle East, they got involved in that too, bringing the children to the village, organising clothing and food hand-outs. They simply didn't care about me and Matt. They were too involved in extracting the final goodness from their own lives to bother about us. They did the things they felt they ought to care about and we were none of that business.

We got through spring and summer and winter and were approaching the spring again. We were gradually getting the house into shape. We took a loan out on a fitted kitchen and had a new front door built by a local carpenter. The heron started visiting again, early in the morning. One day when there was still dew on the grass, I saw it on the decking throwing one of our goldfish in the air and catching it. I told Matt about it, leaning over him in bed and laughing at the cheek of it. But he was asleep or somewhere else.

Things went on and we began to enjoy the rural life.

No street lights at night, so we could sit in the garden and drink whisky and watch shooting stars. Cattle and sheep at the bottom of the garden. A sparrow hawk scattering its kill. Buzzards gliding above the fields, watching for the slightest movement before they zoned in on whatever it was they'd seen below. The crows and curlews hated them, but they were beautiful, soaring in slow circles, the sun catching their wings. If there is another life, I'd like to come back as a bird, not as a human being. Not again.

It was April. A Tuesday. I was working a late shift and had the morning to myself. The phone rang as I was catching up on an article in the *BMJ*, stretched out on the settee with a highlighter pen and the stove going. Matt was away in Crewe finishing a job. A music festival this time. We'd quarrelled on Sunday night and he'd left without saying goodbye. *Never let the sun go down on your anger.* But we had. Something stupid that set in over dinner. I'd touched his arm and he'd snatched it away. I can't honestly say I remember what we argued about. We'd drunk a bottle of wine, maybe more. Sometimes his temper flared like that and he sulked, for no reason. Or no reason I'd take the blame for.

Now someone was clearing their throat down the line. I was saying, *I'm sorry he's not here,* misunderstanding. *I'm sorry.* But it wasn't *for* Matt it was *about* Matt. It was about picking up the phone one day and everything being utterly changed in the time it takes for someone to tell you that he's dead. That he'd died. That there'd been an accident with a lighting rig and he'd fallen, though by this time you're not really listening. You're watching the kettle coming to the boil. The way water vapour appears some distance from the spout, the way a random bumble bee bangs against the kitchen window.

Those things and the fact that you were expecting him home, waiting for him to come. Water coming to the boil, surging, then sinking away. A bee. Then ragged clouds softly torn and thrown against the window as rain begins. You know you'll remember those things, even though they mean nothing, just random sequences in time. And there's the voice on the end of the phone and you're saying, *Of course, of course,* as if good manners are everything. *Thank you.*

I stayed on in the house for a time. Telling myself, telling our friends over the phone, how people don't really die after all. When they're away you keep them alive in your memory. But then there's a funeral. A procession with the coffin tilting in the sun. Matt's brothers, his father crying at the graveside whilst his mother's face could have been a hologram. *She can't cry, you know,* his dad, said to me, *she can't cry.* As if crying could put an end to something. Then there are other things to remind you that he's not coming home. There's the empty bed and the pillow with hairs clinging to it. There are shirts, smelling of him, there are shoes you can't wear. Then shaving gear and deodorants and *possessions.* Matt's camera. Matt's car to get rid of. And you're terrified that when something goes another part of him goes, too. That the house where we'd hung wallpaper and put up curtains and fitted carpets will lose him, that all traces will be gone. People avoid you, which is fine, because that's what you want. Then there are those long, waking nights. Owls calling to each other across the valley. Fields glimmering with frost when you tug open the curtains, when the difference between the living and the dead is blurred by lack of sleep.

After six months I put the house on the market. I was fed up with the practice in Kendal for all the usual reasons.

Managing a budget wasn't my idea of being a GP, nor was the corporate image we were supposed to project and protect. *Do no harm.* That's what we'd signed up to. So much easier said than done.

I'd decided to do VSO, working in Zambia in a rural clinic. A friend I'd trained with, a Dutch woman, Elly, had written to me when she heard. She was sensible, pragmatic, uncluttered. *Come over, Gavin,* she'd written in an email. *Things fall into place here and make sense, I promise you.* I had no idea what that meant, really, or what it would be like. But there wasn't much to stay for. I'd be flying to London then on to Lusaka at the end of June.

The house sold to a couple of teachers who'd just got jobs at the local high school. No doubt they'd rip out the things Matt and I had put there for the life we never had together. When the future stops, something in you struggles with reality. So, I put a new future there. I put Zambia there. A poor country in Africa, where other people's problems would wash away my own. And I didn't really care what it would be like, because whatever it was like, it would be without Matt. I ached for him. I woke in utter disbelief. I despised myself for never knowing what I'd had. Except I think I did know, had known.

A few days before putting my things in storage there was a knock at the door. I'd been sorting through paperwork. Old letters and bills, invoices, estimates. Some of Matt's bank statements and technical planning documents. The stuff that builds up in the back of your life. I junked most of it and was tying off the bin bag when the knocker rapped. A could hear an animal scuffing and a low voice scolding it. There on the doorstep was Lizzie with the sheepdog, its chain wrapped around her hand.

– Lizzie?

– I took this, last time.

She flicked back a lock of hair and held out her hand.

– I'm sorry, I shouldn't have.

She held out one of those little souvenir spoons with a holy image worked into the handle.

– Saint Peter.

– Saint Peter?

– It were in't tree, in a little hole. I put it there when I were a kid. It were a secret, like.

– But it's fine.

– I shouldn't have.

She was close to tears. I didn't take the spoon. It was made of tarnished silver. Saint Peter looked like a pupa, shrouded in holy robes. I closed her fingers around it and pressed them.

– I won't be needing it, so don't worry.

Peter the fisherman, crucified upside down because he was unworthy. The patron saint of locksmiths who held the keys to heaven. Lizzie stepped back, the dog grizzling.

– Shut up!

She looked up from under the dark hair, suddenly fragile.

– I heard. I'm really sorry. I've forgotten your name . . .

And she was walking away, taking tight little pin-toed steps, the dog hastening at her side. She stepped aside to avoid a car, pulling the dog close. Then she was gone, and I went back into the house to finish packing my things. The sun was chasing cloud shadows across the fells beyond the bedroom window. I thought about Zambia. I thought about that magic wand sprinkling sugar, those children gazing at the stars. I thought about Vince watching me getting ready to leave for the last time.

OLIVIA

THE SUN AGAIN. An ancient god staring along the sickle moon of sand. Unforgiving. Exposing the flaws in human flesh. Scars, wrinkles, cellulite, the hanging breasts and jowls, the withering skin on jutting bone. Gulls raucous above the water's edge, the sun glaring on old and young alike, imprinting, mortalising.

I'm walking into the sea, feeling the stones pierce me underfoot, pale legs wavering through clear Mediterranean water. A creature left over from the past. An ancient crustacean. The cold lapping my balls, salting my anus. Turning me to bone.

Without glasses, longsighted, everything out of focus, everything uncertain. White hair on my chest, liver spots on my hands. My skin a wrinkled wash leather. Sun searing my temples, branding me.

I brace myself, sink into cold water and swim, feeling the drag of its fathoms of ice. Then it's suddenly warm against me, bearing me, buoying me. A mother's arms.

Clichés.

They are all that is left.

Clichés in the glare of sun on sea.

The glare of sea in sun.

The blinding glare of memory. The taste of salt, of excoriation in my mouth as I turn to scan the beach. Other bodies, brown and glazed. Lying in the sun or raising splinters of light from the sea with their arms. White shards of a shattered day. I lift my legs and the sea takes me to itself. Kicking like a baby, I swim out from the shore towards the line of the horizon. Breaststroke. Frog legs. The way my mother taught me in the chlorinated town baths. Sea and sky. Low hills. White houses and villas. Air and water and sun welding them in its shimmering vapour of heat.

I never thought I'd grow old like this.

Like what?

Alone.

When I turn on my back and scull, a woman waves from the shore. Slender from this distance. Dark haired. Stooping and rising as if she's laughing. *Olivia.* Waving from the past in a black swimsuit. Mocking me. And the boy, Issy's boy, running towards her in the sun, his tousled hair sparkling with sand.

The wash from a speedboat breaks over me, lifts me with the weight of the ocean, and they're gone into the blur of colours. Another day. Here where volcanic rock juts at the sea that laps at inlets and pebble beaches, the strip of sand that is raked each morning from disorder into order. It's another cliché to say you can't tidy the past.

Now I'm close to the rocks again, that place where the sea urchins spined my feet once and I wrapped them in a bloody towel. The sea choppy here, the breeze sculpting serifs of saltwater above everything that lies below: the gale-wrecked hulks, the vacant seashells, tiny shoals of fish that nibble at me like prey. My flesh white and wavering. The rock spewed molten from a volcano to cool and set in the hissing sea, seasoned with salt. Nothing to do now but turn and swim away. Short strokes. My hands scalpels, slicing. Seawater in my mouth and eyes and nose.

₰

Follow the coastline past the village and you'll find a series of rocky inlets with pebble beaches. The way into the water is steep, the flat stones slimy. But you can swim out into clear, clean water that has a sharp head-clearing quality early in the morning. The fifth inlet is sheltered by cliffs that fall away from the road as it climbs. It's a long cleft, a canyon of rock that you reach by following a tiny path down from the tarmac that arches over to the next bay. Down there is a shingle beach and deep water where you can swim naked, secluded from view.

I'd set off early from the apartment, planning to pick up a coffee and croissant on my way back. It was in quieter times and early in the season, so a calm hour to myself seemed almost certain. The sun was flinching from white-painted houses that thinned as the road slewed upwards. The sea, every colour of green. The port's fishing boats pulling away from the harbour, nets furled. They'd spend a day and a night at sea, bring back mackerel and hake, cod and tuna, sardines, marlin and other tiny fish that had names only in Catalan.

I stepped down the path, careful not to slip on the loose stones. Past prickly pears and yellow sea thrift until the inlet came into view. There on the beach – my beach – was a figure stretched out on the shingle. I caught the scent of French cigarettes. It was the time before American tobacco had become ubiquitous. A white and chestnut spaniel ran over the shingle towards me, barking. Yapping. The woman called it back and clipped a lead on it, shaking a tangle of dark bronze hair from her eyes.

– *Monsieur?*

It wasn't quite a question. More of a challenge.

- *Mademoiselle*.

She permitted herself a small laugh at that, putting a hand to her chest and bowing in self-mockery. The dog moved towards me wagging its tail and she jerked it back, holding the cigarette in her lips. She was wearing a black swimming costume with the straps pulled off her shoulders. Her skin was smooth and lightly tanned. And she was so obviously French and not Spanish. I gestured at the dog.

- *Pas de chiens sur la plage . . .*

- *Mais, ce n'est pas la plage, monsieur*.

Inexorable logic. She was moving her things to make room for me. A woven straw mat, a novel, a packet of Gauloises and a lighter, what looked like a skirt and blouse bundled together. I looked at the sea. I looked at the woman who sat staring across the water with shaded eyes, pulling on the cigarette, blowing smoke away from me. The dog had lain down in the shingle. I tried to steal a glance at the book she was reading, but it was covered by her clothes. I could have dropped my things and stepped into the sea and simply swum away from her, but something kept me standing awkwardly.

After a few minutes, the woman stood up. She was slim and moved with a kind of sleepy grace. She hadn't swum, so her costume was still dry. She began to slip into her skirt. Fully dressed she seemed much smaller. Slender, with that tangle of dark-flamed hair. I wanted to say something to her. To apologize. For what? But I didn't trust my French. She pulled the dog from its doze.

- Albert! Albert! *Dépêche-toi!*

Then turned to me with that mocking smile.

- Enjoy your swim, *monsieur*. I'm sorry to intrude.

I let her go in silence. She'd spotted my Englishness at a glance. I watched her step lightly up the path, slipping off my sandals and tee shirt, inching into the water. Feeling the stones shift underfoot, feeling the icy touch of the sea's depth, its mysteries of salt and death and decay. I lurched forward to take it in my arms, swimming out into the long echo chamber of rock that converged above me, leaving only a slit of blue sky. When I rolled over on my back to float there, I could have sworn that I could see the dog's tail bobbing at the edge of cliff where the prickly pears grew and swifts had begun to circle.

It was two days later when I saw the woman again. An overcast day with snatches of sun glittering against a restive sea. Wind blowing a grit of sand from the beach, the moped riders scarved. She was sitting in the Café L'Ancora, smoking a cigarette, a book propped against a shopping bag in front of her. Flip-flops shedding sand. A summer frock of sun-faded stripes. A little cleft in her chin I hadn't noticed before under the mass of hair. No dog. In fact, I never saw that dog again, as if she'd borrowed it or was doing a neighbour a favour. It had given me a particular impression of her as a slightly silly type of French woman. An outdated typology, no doubt. She saw me enter, watched me order my drink, then turned back to the book. Issy, the barman, saw me looking at her and seemed to shake his head almost imperceptibly, pursing his lip as he dried the glasses he was lining up on the bar.

I ordered a glass of lager and then hesitated about where I should sit. The woman looked up at me through that disorderly hair and gave me a bleak, intriguing smile, raising her eyebrows slightly and drawing in her cheeks. She moved the shopping bag to one side and gestured for me to join her.

She'd been drinking an expresso and signalled to Issy for another.

– *Mas café por favor.*

She turned to me as I sat down, a cardigan slung over the chair beside her, her bare shoulders gleaming.

– So?

I took a sip of the lager, already regretting it. I heard myself repeating her.

– So . . .

She put out her hand to shake mine.

– I'm Olivia. We met at the beach. At *your* beach.

The accent was tantalisingly familiar.

– Ah yes, the woman with the dog.

A faint smile seemed to flinch across her face, passing in a moment.

– Tony. Anthony.

– Tony Anthony?

– Either will do.

– I'll call you Tony. I'm sure your mother did.

I realized that she wasn't French at all. When we met at the beach she'd been faking it. Now there was a faint north-eastern tinge to her English.

– Where are you from, Olivia?

Her coffee arrived, brought by Issy's teenage son, Raphael, who gave me a cheeky, knowing smile. Olivia took the cup graciously, stirring the foam with her spoon and setting aside the cubes of sugar in the saucer she'd already used.

– Oh, I'm from everywhere, really? You?

– I'm from here at the moment.

– And before that?

– Before that, somewhere else.

If she could play that game, then so could I. She nudged me under the table with her knee. Permitting herself a little gasp of laughter.

– Don't get too mysterious, Tony, I might just . . .

She raised the cup to her lips and blew on it delicately.

– Might just?

– Lose interest.

And a gust of wind shook the café's furled blinds, making the sea glitter, stinging our eyes, as if a shoal of fish had just risen from a parable.

Olivia raised the coffee cup to her mouth, wincing slightly. She reached into a raffia shopping bag and slipped on a pair of sunglasses.

– That's hardly fair.

She gave me a full smile this time. Small, sharp, charmingly crooked teeth.

– I'm not trying to be enigmatic, believe me. The sun hurts my eyes on days like this.

– What kind of day would that be?

She was lighting a new cigarette, clicking the lighter and sucking the tobacco into a glowing red dot. She pulled a speck of something from her lip.

– Oh, days of change, days when the Tramuntana's getting up . . .

She shuddered a little. There were the puffs of dust on the mountain where a vehicle was rattled along the rutted road from the next village bringing Calor Gas or bread or fish. Soon it would be honking through the cobbled streets, drawing the women down from their houses and holiday apartments. I finished my beer and pushed my glass forward.

– Would you like another?

She had the cigarette balanced, tapping off the ash with one finger. Her fingernails were plain and the backs of her hands had faint freckles. English freckles.

– I'm good, thanks. It's early for me.

– And for me, *monsieur*!

And she added that little flourish of a French accent she'd used on the beach, this time throwing back her head with its tangle of hair to give a full-throated laugh. The sea flared up again under the wind and the shutters banged against the iron uprights of the café and Issy rolled up his eyes as if praying. He looked like a medieval saint in one of those icons, backlit by the glare that came through the glass partition behind the counter. I stood up to leave and Olivia transferred her attention to her own hands, spreading them out for examination. I noticed then that there were traces of dried paint under the nails and in the cuticles.

I'd come to the Catalan coast to write a book, bringing the portable typewriter I bought before I left home for university. To study English, of course. I got it from a little stationer's shop in my Lancashire home-town. It was second-hand and cost twelve pounds with a case and spare ribbon. I'd used the machine all the way through my degree course, From The Anglo-Saxon Chronicle to George Eliot. And now I'd brought it out to Spain. After university, I'd saved enough money from working shifts in a dye-works to stay here for a few months if I lived sparingly.

And I did. I lived frugally on bread and sardines and fruit from the greengrocer at the bottom of my street. But I wrote frugally too, so the book, the novel, I'd been planning as part of my escape into another life, wasn't happening. Each morning I'd try to write for an hour, then take a walk along the coastline, then go back to my tiny apartment to try again, rattling the keys and watching the black and red ribbon jump to my commands. It was the Sixties and maybe this was a typically Sixties or even Fifties thing to do. I always felt as if I'd been born out of time, but maybe we all do. Maybe we just don't know what other people really feel.

It was Thursday, which I remember because of the day after. I'd written for a couple of hours, actually generating a few pages of new text. After writing, I liked to walk and think about my characters. I always feel queasy when writers say that their characters take on a life of their own. My life is their life, after all. After walking I'd revise what I'd written, annotating the pages and placing them into the lid of a box that had originally held the blank sheets. That felt like a restoration, replacing what had been empty space with words, sentences, paragraphs. Pages of smudged black type with *q* and *d* and *o* filled in where the keys needed cleaning. I had an old toothbrush and a bottle of meths I used for that when I could be bothered. What eluded me, of course, was not characters, but a story.

That morning I ceased work and cut across the sandy beach in front of the esplanade where they'd mounted a couple of old bronze cannon in acknowledgement of Spain's imperial past. Which wasn't over yet with Franco still in power. *Il Caudillo.* You might hear a few whispered words of Catalan, but that was all in those days of repression. The Guardia Civil kept their ear to the ground and people hadn't forgotten how the civil war had torn up whole families. There was something bracing about trying to become free in a fascist state, if what Franco believed in was fascism. Whatever it was, it was close. And close to God and the priesthood too.

At the end of the beach the rocky coast began abruptly. A series of deep inlets with steep shingle beaches, the green sea shading to azure. There were a few dogwalkers, a few tourists in hire cars taking the coast road to the next town. I followed the path for a mile or so and then took a fork down to a little bay where you could sit against the cliff of pockmarked volcanic rock and get out of the wind. From there you looked back across the bay to the harbour with its fishing vessels, and beyond that to the white square tower of the village church.

I climbed down the path to the beach and there was a figure seated on a folding stool, busy with a sketchbook and watercolour palette. She wore a white headscarf. My feet slipped on the stones of the path and she looked up suddenly. It was Olivia, and even this far away I could read a facial expression that was different from her usual insouciance. This time she was vulnerable, caught in the open. I crunched across the pebbles towards her as casually as I could. She folded her arms. Then she was searching inside her straw shoulder bag for cigarettes. The sketchbook was wet and lay open on the stones. It was a minimalist working of the view ahead, executed in rapid brushstrokes. Yet there was also something formal about the brushwork, like those stylised Japanese paintings I'd seen by Hokusai.

Olivia blew out a long slow plume of smoke, as if already exasperated.

– Well, Tony, you get around.

I didn't answer her. The breeze was getting up and there were whitecaps rolling towards us. She'd captured that movement in the sketch.

– Well, it's a beautiful view, as you know.

I gestured towards the sketchbook.

- Well, you *do* know.

- Oh, I do know.

- Is this your thing?

I suppose I was being deliberately provocative. That uneasy look crossed her face again. Then she smiled awkwardly, as if caught out.

- Yes, I suppose it is.

She removed an imaginary speck of tobacco from her lip.

- Though I've never thought of it as a *thing*.

Olivia tilted her head.

- And your *thing*?

I crouched down to look closer at the painting.

- It's a lovely sketch!

She laughed cynically, drawing on the cigarette again, which I realized was just a prop, a way of keeping things and people away from her.

- No, I'm serious, it's got a real sense of energy, the force of the sea.

- Well, Tony, quite the art critic.

- Well, Olivia, I know what I like.

And this time her laugh was genuine. I noticed a smear of lipstick on her teeth. It seemed odd for a painter, a bohemian, to apply make-up.

- Carry on, I didn't mean to disturb you. I'm heading for the lighthouse.

- Very ... Virginia Woolf.

- Indeed!

Now I felt exposed. Had she heard or guessed something about me? The lighthouse was about half a mile away, a stubby white cone on a promontory of rock against which more than one ship had come to grief before it was built.

– Brave you. This wind's getting up.

It was whipping at the edge of the sea, fraying it like a garment. And I left her there. She receded as I trudged the shingle. I looked back just once to see her packing up her things and walking back towards the town, a tiny figure against the backdrop of mountains and the thickets of bamboo that grew in the inlet that trickled into the bay.

By the time I reached the lighthouse the wind had gained enough force to make walking uncomfortable. Salt spray lashed from the sea made the skin on my face feel tight as a mask. I turned and set off back where Olivia had gone before me, stepping lightly, the folding chair tucked under her arm, the bag slung. I imagined her ordering a coffee in the café, my little room darkening as the sun swung away from it, the desk piled with papers and the typewriter waiting there for my touch. An Olivetti. That name seemed ironic now.

The next time I saw Olivia was Friday, market day. She was picking through the fruit and vegetables in the square behind the library. She was wearing a blue gingham skirt and a white blouse with lace at the wrist and collar. She'd just picked up a bunch of parsley as I approached and was saying something to the man behind the counter. He was dark-faced, Moorish, a southern Spaniard from beyond Barcelona.

– *Gracias, señor, gracias.*

The man gave a little bow and she turned to find me at her elbow.

– Tony!

– Olivia. How are you?

She gave that tangential smile, as if she was smiling at someone or something else and dropped the parsley into the bag she kept her painting things in.

- I'm good, as far as I know. Just shopping for a few things.

We moved on together and then paused as she stopped at the cheese stall to buy manchego and goat's cheese.

We chatted as we moved through the stalls that sold cheap clothing and kitchen utensils, leather goods, agricultural tools and shoes and every kind of vegetable. Olivia felt at some peaches but put them down and shook her head at the woman imploring her attention. She told me that she'd rented a little apartment behind the church at the end of one of the steep streets that rose from the waterfront. Then, without warning, she paused and gave me a different kind of smile.

- Would you like to come to lunch?
- When?
- Today, you dope. Today. Right now, in fact.
- Can I bring anything?
- Sardines. And white wine - unless it's too early for you, Tony.

She gave me a wide-eyed look, as if white wine at lunch time might be the limit of my moral compass.

- OK. Sounds nice. What number is the house?
- It doesn't have a number. It has a blue door. Just behind the church up a few steps. I'm in the upstairs apartment. I'll leave my door open . . .

And she was turning away to buy courgettes and aubergines, her tousled hair gleaming in the sun, her sunglasses trailing from the gold chain around her neck.

I got the sardines from the little fishmonger next to the bodega. The girl serving me had bloody fingers and a smeared apron and a lop-sided smile as she dropped the fish onto the scales. There was a small marlin on the counter, sheathed in dulled silver. It had the most mournful eyes. But to her and her father it was money.

– *Te gustaría algo de eso?*

– *No, gracias.*

I shook my head when she pointed to it and went next door to the bodega. Usually I bought the cheapest unbranded wine by the litre, filling an empty bottle. But this time I found a bottle of chilled Pescador in the fridge that rumbled away in the back of the shop. It was Spain. Everything was cheap and somehow still amazing. The bodega also sold olives and I bought a tub of them soaking in oil with a sprig of thyme to season them. I was ready. Rushing had made me sweat and I felt a little self-conscious about the damp patches on my shirt as I made my way through the back streets towards the white glare of the church.

Back in those days there was still a sinful frisson in visiting a woman alone, especially in Franco's Spain. The old women in the village still dressed in black and peered out at me from under their shawls – *el inglés* – whilst the retired fishermen sat smoking at the seafront or knocking back pastis in the bars. I found the blue door and followed a flight of stairs that turned on itself to the first-floor apartment. The door was ajar, and I knocked firmly. Olivia answered my knock and for the first time gave me a smile that wasn't suffused in irony. She beckoned me in. I handed her the Pescador first and she wrapped it in wet newspaper and laid it in the sink. It was a single room with two doors off. I guessed one must be a bathroom and the other a bedroom. There was a dining table laid with salads in glazed terracotta bowls and another table strewn with drawing materials and sketch books. I saw the folding chair propped against a wall.

There was no kitchen as such, just a sink next to a Baby Belling gas cooker. Olivia had put a white apron over her shirt and tied back her hair in a loose chignon. She was drizzling olive oil over the salad.

– Are you hungry?

– Moderately.

– *Moderately*! Well, well, we mustn't over face you then!

The irony was back. I ignored her with a shrug. Which wasn't really ignoring her, I realized. She opened the wrapping of sardines and rinsed them in the sink, putting them in a colander to drain.

– Sit down, Tony, for God's sake.

I perched on one of the hard-back chairs at the table.

– Drink?

– Of?

She hadn't opened the wine. I noticed another bottle next to the Pescador, also wrapped in smudged newsprint.

– I've got some cava left from last night.

I wondered if that was some special occasion. Dinner with friends, maybe.

– What was last night?

– Thursday.

This time it was me who was laughing. She brought two cloudy tumblers and pulled the old cork she'd used to stopper the wine.

– Sorry, not very elegant, I know. I think it'll be OK.

– Cheers.

We clinked glasses. The cava was dry and nutty. It still had plenty of fizz. Maybe a tiny edge of oxidisation, which I was too polite to mention.

– Hmn . . . that's nice. Thank you!

Olivia put her nose in the wine and took an extravagant sniff at the bouquet. She wrinkled her nose slightly.

- You know, Tony, if you're not careful I'll start to think you've been very well brought up.

-You know, I just might have been.

- Well, I hope not.

She touched my arm and her touch was cool and electric. There was that sudden thickening of the atmosphere when desire begins to smoulder between two people. Almost unexpected, but not quite.

Olivia switched on the gas and lit it with a match, cursing softly as the flame caught at her fingers.

- Fuck!

I must have looked surprised.

- Well, I never said I was well brought up.

She chuckled and began to drop the sardines into the hot oil.

- Open the window, will you? We'll stink!

I pushed open the big window that overlooked the street. Flakes of paint and rust fell from my fingers. Olivia was shaking capers into the frying pan.

- Could you slice that baguette up, please?

And before we realized it, we were working together, setting out the table with everything we needed, chatting about the village, the coastline, what drew us to the sea. Other kinds of desire. We finished the rest of the cava and I opened the Pescador. White wine with a slight prickle. It was a perfect meal: local wine, fresh sardines, bread, salads and thin slices of manchego to finish off. I realized that Olivia had an unusual knack - that of being simple in nearly everything she did. Minimal. Like the painting I'd seen on the rocks the other day. She didn't say much either, didn't need to.

When we'd finished the food, she licked her fingers. She caught me watching her and smiled sleepily.

– I told you I wasn't well brought up.

Outside the noises of the streets had subsided. It was past two o'clock and the sun was brilliant against the sky and the white-painted houses. Olivia opened the windows wider and pulled the wooden shutters closed to keep out its prying blade. The room softened into shadows.

What happened next could be explained in many ways. Maybe it was the wine, maybe the pressure of an unexpected situation. I remember the feel of Olivia's naked body between the sheets that smelt faintly of the sardines we'd cooked. She was slight, with small breasts and quick hands, her hair loose against the pillows. She had a tattoo of a bee under her wrist-watch, back in those days when women didn't really have tattoos. She tried to arouse me, laying her head against me, stroking my chest. But it was useless. Or I was. If I was aroused it was at some deeper level that didn't translate into physical arousal.

There'd been woman at Perpignan, on my way through France. Older than me. We'd picked each other up in a bar. She was Dutch, on her way to Figueres to join some commune of hippy friends. It was quick, and, in its own way, it was satisfying. It had felt like a release from England and its stuffy conventions. She had short blonde hair and a neat little nose. We parted with a hug and a wave and we were done, free again, as if we'd turned the page on one story and started another. The rest of our lives were still out there and nothing to do with each other.

With Olivia it was different, it was awkward and appalling. I felt taken to the edge of some awful vacancy in myself.

– Don't worry, Tony.

She touched my shoulder.

– It happens, it happens all the time . . .

She reached round for her cigarettes and covered her breasts with the bedsheet, as if she was no longer available. She clicked the lighter and blew a long stream of smoke into the room that twisted in the sunlight as a draft caught it.

– You know, whatever you're writing must be taking it out of you.

She laughed. It was then I realized just how much she'd understood about me. And there was that faint trace of Sunderland or Gateshead in her accent again, as if we were still anchored.

There's a point in a story where it can go on to completion or where it sits obdurately refusing to progress, to complete itself, to find any kind of satisfactory peak or conclusion, where an epiphany remains stubbornly out of reach. The hardening kernel in an unripe fruit. You might expect me to say that my sexual failure with Olivia infected my relationship with my creative work. That being unable to make love meant that my writing stalled and I had to recognize that I'd never work creatively again. In fact, it had the opposite effect, if my writing was related in any way to what happened. I finished my novel by starting again. By tipping the box of typed papers into a skip that stank of fish and closing the lid on its decay. In two months, I had a fair draft. In six months, I had an agent and an advance. Within another year I'd brought out a modestly successful novel with a London publishing house that gained favourable reviews in the Sunday broadsheets.

I went on to write five more novels and two books of short stories. I did some reading tours at literary festivals in the UK, and in Canada where they liked my work. A few residencies at university campuses in the US and the UK. It was a slim living, but a living. It was a life's work, after all. Right now, I'm writing a memoir of my life as a literary exile, here on the Catalan coast at a turning point in history for my adopted country. Of course, the Caudillo features in that. Along with the monarchy. The installation of Juan Carlos. The return of democracy. The restoration of the Catalan language that revived the old street names. The rise of the European Union that is failing now. The wheel turning. There's a version of Olivia in there, the hint of an affair, brief and unsentimental. It's mainly fiction, but that line is blurred now. My aim is to find a translator and publish it in Catalan as well as in English.

I did see Olivia again, if you're wondering. I saw her on the beach and on her bicycle and at the market and in Issy's bar, just as before. Once I saw her in the little square below the church at night. She was knocking a tennis ball up against the wall under electric lights, wearing slacks and sneakers, practising her forehand and sliced backhand. There was a thin moon rising above the terracotta roof tiles of the town. She never saw me watching her. And we never slept together again, even though there were moments where I felt she was enticing me. Something always stopped me in the end. That laugh as we lay together and she lit a cigarette. Remembering my blush of shame in her cool, thick-walled room, the *atelier* where she seemed simultaneously to pity and mock me. She began to sell her watercolours from a market stall and, after a few years, set up an art shop on the seafront that sold pottery and paintings and artist's materials. She never married, and neither did I, though she had something of a reputation among the locals who admired and resented her as an independent woman. Some frisson of lust or envy. None of what they imagined was true, probably.

The last time I saw Olivia, I was in her shop looking for a gift to send to my agent to mark her fiftieth birthday. She was there with her perfect Spanish and easy French and wiry white hair, wrapping some bowls in tissue paper for a French customer.

- *Voilà, Monsieur!*

They were glazed earthenware with a pattern of concentric yellow whorls. She'd aged of course, we both had. Age being that most persistent of clichés. As I paid for my purchase, her blouse slipped up her arm and there was the bee tattooed on the white band of skin where her wristwatch should have been. She saw me looking at it and when she glanced at me, I had to look away. Then her hand was on my hand.

- We've been industrious, Tony, haven't we? In our own ways?

She paused.

- We could have been something, you know.

And there she was wearing that ironic smile that had drawn me to her and unmanned me in the end. *Industrious?* As if that meant everything. Or all that was left to us. I remembered that we knew almost nothing about each other. We knew the after, but not the before, its pages unread or waiting to be inscribed. When I left, neither of us said goodbye.

I'm towelling myself dry on the beach. Watching the children of English, French and German couples splashing into the water, shrieking with horror at the cold. There are clouds gathering behind the mountains, a faint halo around the sun, promising a storm later. Olivia died, of course. Issy, too, though his son, Rafe still runs the bar. His wife's been ill and he has acid reflux and an anxious look, balding and prematurely obese. Serving the tourists tapas because they expect it in Spain. Working long hours in summer, spending the winters somewhere warm.

I roll up my towel and slip my feet into espadrilles, rescuing my glasses from where I've placed them inside my hat. I think of a coffee at L'Ancora, maybe some lunch. Then an afternoon working on those memories. *Memoirs*. The scent of sardines cooking, an open sketchbook, that exhalation of smoke clouding the room when Olivia and I lay in bed together, unconsummated.

I remember that for a writer the worst things can be the best. How we learn to be satisfied with what life gives us, not what it offers. How the sea will still be there in the end, consuming flesh and bone and time. How the only things that matter are words, and maybe they don't matter much. How hopeless it is to chase fame when we have to die anyway. How we shouldn't have left it there, that day, because we could have been something. *Something*. The way courage failed me, or love. Whatever that is. The way irony lingers like a tide, taking away what it gives, and more. In the end. Everything.

WHITETHORN

THE HORSE DANCED. It pirouetted in the road, a blur of hooves and hide, a vortex of mane, tail, foam-flecked teeth. A chestnut horse, not quite fully grown. A stallion or gelding, its white blaze flickering, its head jerking. A line of traffic slowed up opposite Pablo's car. Steam drifted from under its bonnet and dissipated lazily. The sun was brazing a seam along the ridge above the valley. His wrist was numb. He unclipped his seatbelt, pushed the door open with a knee and shoulder.

The chestnut horse was still metamorphosing, rising from the churned verge, coiled from rope or turned from clay. Its hooves skittered, struck sparks from the road. Pablo reached back in the car to switch off the engine, one hand on the roof. A stink of petrol, horse shit, ammonia. The spores of dandelions floated by and stuck to him, making a fine mist in the air. A man in a white shirt had got out of his Volvo, leaving the engine running.

Then that braying sound. The sound of iron ingots dragged across concrete. The horse span on its shattered leg, still trying to rise, spattering the road with blood and dung. Then it fell in slow motion, its breath mingling with steam from the radiator; its hay-sweet smell mixed with the tang of antifreeze that ran green in the road. The horse coughed, then snorted in astonishment, clearing an airway. Dark blood from a punctured vein gushed from its nostrils.

The blood from its leg was brightest, the femoral artery

torn open. A loop of bluish intestine hung inside its flank. The road was littered with glossy turds. The horse staggered and sank and the road steamed. The brass fittings on its bridle glinted. Its head tilted against its neck and its eyes rolled backwards into white. The morning air was still crisp. Pablo watched and felt nothing. Everything seemed intense and slow. The hills were blazing now and there were deepening shadows. He was going to be late.

A woman with copper hair and jodhpurs was running behind the hedge. She appeared and disappeared through the foliage. When she dragged the gate open and saw everything her face was pale and tight with shock. The man in the white shirt inspected the backs of his hands. He took off his spectacles and cleaned them on the lap of his shirt. When he put them on again, they were smeared and dim. Then he was reaching for the mobile phone he wore in a pouch at his waist.

Pablo's ankle gave way. He leaned against the dented wing of his car. Now the horse was straining upwards, fighting the terrific force that tried to drag it from the light. And it knew. Somehow it knew about death and fought it there. Those who watched saw the horse crumple. They saw it drawn to the edge of the light to drink the dark, saw it dragging itself back from that terror on some attenuated thread. Its mouth was lost in foam and blood.

When the woman reached the horse it had sunk to its knees, sprawled on its butchered leg. She knelt in the road, cradling its head in her arms. Pablo was fumbling at his phone. But other people were already calling for help. His call wouldn't matter now, though he'd have to ring his father. Other things would have to happen first, he knew that.

The woman with copper hair was crying, pounding her

thigh where the jodhpurs pulled tight. Ghostly spores floated, jerking in air currents. More people got out of their cars, mesmerized. A woman in a yellow tee shirt was being sick. No one came to help Pablo. They were too stunned, too inward. They had remembered a distant fact: how some things happen in a moment, then everything is changed. A clegg landed on Pablo's arm and bit him. He snatched it away, watching the horse being dragged down towards the centre of the earth.

A hot air balloon was being launched from meadows near the river. The balloon was cobalt blue, an orb of canvas inflated by a spear of flame. It gave out a throaty exhalation as it rose, tilting slightly then drifting westwards. From the wicker basket suspended below the burner, its passengers saw the slate roofs of the village, the hall set into parkland, cars glinting on roads that made their way through patched fields. Beyond the village, the moors were deep brown, furrowed where streams began, scarred by peat diggings that had slumped under rain and frost.

The balloon passed over the village: a river, a church and pub, houses and outlying farms. They saw the chestnut horse lying awkwardly on the verge, cars slewed in the road, tiny figures standing by, the blue lights of police cars and an ambulance. Then they were too high and too far to see much: just the grey cube of a power station squatting at the horizon, the chain of stone villages that followed the river to the sea.

Pablo's day had started early, after the gig at JoJo's. That morning he'd been on the first flight from Schiphol to Manchester. His father called him on his mobile as he was boarding the plane. It was dawn and he was tired, light-headed from lack of sleep. His throat felt rough from the gig and a couple of late drinks with the band. The sun was beginning to crawl from the horizon, so the light was soft, peach coloured. His father's voice was thin, the signal breaking up. His father. That pang of familiarity, of guilt. Pablo's surprise that he'd mastered the new number. *I don't feel so good, son. Can you get over?* That's all he'd managed to say.

Pablo climbed the steps from the runway with his jacket slung over his arm. His knees felt stiff. Dawn light was tinged with red now, the air still cold, a faint scent of aviation fuel. A heron, its grey plumage fluffed out, was frozen at the edge of the runway. It could have been there for centuries, its eye needling the surface of a dyke. When he paused to look again, the bird was gone. He thought he glimpsed it beyond the airport terminal, sailing with slow wing beats towards the sun as if it had flown out of pre-history, conjured from all the other herons he'd watched taking off from the beck, steering down the valley.

He must have dozed off, his head resting against the plastic window. When he woke his mouth tasted sour. He pushed himself upright to squint through the porthole. Almost home. The Trafford Centre tilted as the plane banked over Manchester. Then a glimpse of green as hills turned under the plane's wing.

Pablo leaned back into the leather upholstery, rubbing at his stubbled cheeks. The woman next to him was reading a broadsheet. Huge and determined, she'd spread it out across her knees. She leaned against him, spilling over the armrest, pressing him back towards the window. Her pink suit made him feel faintly nauseous. He wondered whether she was Dutch or English. She didn't speak, staring at the newsprint, licking her fingers to turn a page.

He was tired from the gig, from another late night, from busking the set list. He'd been depping for Nat Copeland whose wife was ill. An old mate, Sol, had given Pablo a bell. *It's an easy one, Pab, it'd be good to see you.* He'd used Nat's Mesa Boogie, so gear wasn't an issue. It was an old Mark II with a sweet sustain. Everything was set up in the club, and the soundman was good, so that had been hassle free. But he was tired of travel and black coffee and other people. The undercarriage thudded. The woman started. He needed to get off the plane and on the move. The wheels touched down, juddered, slowed. Pablo was pressed back into his seat. He waited for the woman to gather up her things, then reached into the overhead locker for his holdall.

On the way to baggage reclaim, he had a quick wash in the Gents, splashing cold water on his face. A dark-haired man with a three-day stubble stared at him from the mirror. He'd got grey strands in his hair now. The bags under his eyes were blue and his eyes were bloodshot. His skin looked sallow and papery. He was fucked and the day was just starting.

Pablo set his watch to UK time then walked to the baggage carousel. He waited for his flight case to appear, avoiding the woman in the pink suit. A couple of kids shot past him and were dragged back by their mother, scolding them in a foreign language. They looked Indonesian, dark-skinned and slim. Beautiful kids. Their mother was plump and slow moving. She wore a gold nose stud and couldn't have been more than thirty.

There was some problem with luggage blocking the carousel. A woman in an orange robe was tugging at a huge suitcase, watched by three sleepy little boys. Her husband was trying to drag a metal box onto a trolley. One of the girls turned to watch Pablo, her eyes large and dark. Pablo winked at her and she turned away. The next moment she was staring at him again, giggling, wide-eyed, nudging her sister. Families were strange. Sometimes their closeness, their familiarity, was embarrassing. A kind of vulnerability. He was well out of it.

A low pulsing had begun in his temples. He'd need to take something. You had to play a few gigs to remember why you didn't play them anymore. Still, it was good to keep your hand in, keep up contacts, live on your wits a little. You could lose your chops really quickly and then your options ran out. Running a music shop or a studio was one thing; playing was another. He'd never really wanted to run a business, he'd just drifted into it because of Alec, because the chance was there. The gig had paid well this time – and money from playing music was the best kind. He'd always felt that, from the first time he'd been handed a tenner for a night in Clitheroe.

His scuffed aluminium flight case appeared. Pablo dragged it from the carousel. He'd packed his Strat, a tuner, a lead, some sheet music. He lugged it through customs. Then he was out of the terminal, heading for the bus to the shuttle park where he'd left his car. The air was sharper here, sky clearing to a burnished blue. When the bus arrived, three girls in culottes and crop tops jumped off, texting, lugging their bags, leaving the vehicle empty except for a woman in a black hijab, who dozed next to her husband, her head bumping against his shoulder. Pablo pulled his gear on board. They set off into scattered sunlight that bounced off concrete and glass buildings. He just had time to get to his flat and shower. Then he'd hit the road.

He'd sleep later. After a few pints in the local, watching his dad nurse a half all night. He'd sleep in his old bedroom, waking to pigeons calling from the woods behind the house. It wasn't their house, exactly, it was rented from the estate. But that didn't make it anyone else's, either. His father had been born in that village, his mother in the one that was flooded to make the reservoir. They'd met when she worked as a domestic at the hall. The bus paused at a barrier, then entered the shuttle park. Pablo had made a note of where he'd left the car and stowed it in his wallet. He rang the bell and the bus shuddered to a halt. The woman in the hijab woke up and her husband touched her cheek and said something that made her smile. The doors jerked and hissed open.

Pablo scanned the rows of cars for a silver Saab, long and low-slung. He dropped his guitar case and shoulder bag in the boot, fumbled the keys into the ignition, pulling the gear lever out of reverse. The engine started first time. His feet felt sweaty against the pedals. He let out the clutch and pulled away, pushing in his credit card to open the barrier, turning past the Shell garage towards the city, then gliding past rows of red-brick terraced houses and high-rise windows that gleamed in the sun. He thought of hot water, of breakfast. He thought of the road home.

The lift was out of order again. He collected his mail and dragged his gear up five flights of stairs with their stink of piss and cigarette smoke. There was a burnt-out scooter on the patch of grass outside, washing hanging from balconies, wheelie bins spilling their waste for gulls to fight over. He had a security door fitted to his apartment. Not that you could rely on that. Any flat left empty for long was likely to be taken over by squatters or dealers. Sometimes you had to shoulder through groups of lads on the landing, trying not to meet their eyes.

The flat smelled musty. He locked the guitar in a steel cabinet he'd got from an office clearance, bagged up some rubbish, dropped it into the chute with the junk mail and checked his answer phone. Nothing urgent. Nothing from the accountant. He left a message for Alec at the shop. *Hey, it's Pablo. It's 7:30 and I'm back and just touching base. Good gig. Catch you later. By the way, you should be there by now, you lazy bastard.* He half meant it. Then he'd managed a shower but hadn't had much to change into. He stuffed a couple of shirts, a pair of trainers and some jeans into a bag. Then he cut the mouldy bits from a loaf to make toast and fried some eggs that broke their yolks as they hit the hot oil. He couldn't remember if his father still owned an iron.

The drive to the village took an hour and a half, less if the traffic was sparse. He was on the road again in twenty minutes. He'd sleep later. In the house where he and Tim had grown up. Except that Tim hadn't. Pablo shook the sleep out of his head and re-focused. He let his eyes settle on the white lines as they zipped past the car. At this hour the roads were almost empty. The odd heavy goods vehicle, milk tankers heading for farms, a few motorcyclists screaming towards the Lakes. They passed insanely close, overtaking just before bends, engines howling, knees almost touching the road. Pablo changed down to leave the motorway just after Burnley. Huddled towns dotted with mills, hills pocked with old mine workings, blackened shale and sandstone walls, then hedges, fields of sheep and cattle. Even a herd of red deer where someone was raising venison. There were still empty farms and fields overgrown with thistles and buttercups, emptied by foot and mouth disease. He'd heard of a herd of water buffalo that had been put down. That was weird, water buffalo in Lancashire, where even the deer looked incongruous, grazing in a huddle behind barbed wire.

Pablo switched on the radio, but the aerial stammered on the rear wing until he gave up and turned it off. There were some lights out on the fascia, the rev counter had died, the window seals were turning green with moss. He nosed through another village where a boy in a Man City shirt was ramming newspapers into letterboxes. The road turned and dipped and rose towards the moor.

A spider had tied a thread of silk between the wing mirror and the body of the car. It trembled, gleaming as he drove. The Saab had a long bonnet and a wide windscreen. He'd bought it because of that, because he loved the bonnet mechanism, which slid forward as it opened. And the boot was flat loading. Great if he had to lug his amp to a gig, though not very often these days. He passed a posse of cyclists on racing machines, tightly clad in black and yellow Lycra, chatting as they pedalled, futuristic in their elongated helmets. They rode two abreast, trying to own the road.

Pablo felt the worn clutch lurch. He was tired, still buzzing a little from a late night and vodka, the adrenaline of playing live. The sax player had been good, but he knew it. A flash bastard, hogging the solos. Pablo exchanged a wry glance or two with Sol over his Zildjians. Young, something to prove. A real wanker, but at least he could play. Pablo had nothing to prove. He'd made his living from music one way and another since he'd jumped college, and that was more than you could say for most of the guys he'd started out with. Those that were still around.

Playing took you somewhere else. It blanked things out.

And that had worked at first. Then it hadn't been enough. He'd had a few years of hard drinking. Mad benders where he'd woken up with bloody knuckles and no idea why. Except his best friends stopped talking to him. One day he'd woken in the doorway of a Turkish takeaway in Tottenham. He'd puked over himself and broken a tooth. That had finally been enough. He'd cut the booze. Not altogether, but he didn't get pissed any more. Just nicely mellow. Like the tone he tried for when he played: warm, but with an edge. A little fire and danger. Pablo ran his tongue over the crowned tooth. Alec had been there for him with an idea when he needed it.

The road climbed steadily onto a rim of moorland. At the watershed it dropped down into another valley, dark green, funnelling out below him. It was the way home. It was the road he'd taken out of here twenty years ago. Now it ran back there, a smear of tar and gravel. Sun was just tipping the horizon, showing dust and dead insects on the windscreen. He pressed the washer arm. Worn wiper blades juddered on the scarred glass. The washer nozzles coughed up a few specks of foam. He'd have to get that sorted with the money from the gig. He'd signed for a wad of cash, even used his own name and address. He was getting too old to take on the taxman.

The trees were in spring foliage. The valley was bleak for most of the year, dun coloured or khaki. Then it was the most beautiful place on earth for ten days in May. Though sometimes it was June before the blossom appeared. Pablo's head felt as light as a paper ball. A wasp nest. The paracetamol hadn't helped. He was driving impatiently, almost losing it on a corner where loose gravel spilled into the road. He hit the brake and shifted down a gear. The bottle of mineral water shot off the passenger seat into the foot well. *Shit!* He stooped forward, catching his chin on the wheel, still unshaven. It was impossible to reach the fucking thing. He was drifting into the centre of the road, again. A motorcyclist flashed him a V sign in alarm.

Pablo angled his face into the rear-view mirror. There hadn't been time or inclination for a shave. He needed a haircut. His clothes still had that smell of stale beer and sweat. He'd have a soak at his dad's tub and change later. Then he'd take the old man to the pub for a pint. Then they could fall asleep together in armchairs as the television blared. They'd never talked much. Never needed to. And it wasn't much to ask once in a while.

The sun was behind him, the car chasing its own shadow, light taking on a harder edge. It'd been a dry spring. Blackthorn blossom had come early. Now hawthorn flowers were gushing from the trees. Whitethorn came after blackthorn and bore bright red berries instead of bitter sloes. He hadn't seen such heavy blossom since he was a kid. Days from his childhood had been like that, all sunlight and shadow. Chiaroscuro.

The blossom made bridal tunnels of the hedgerows, skeins of cream-coloured lace. White flowers picked out the thorn trees where they crouched on the fells. Even the lightning-struck stumps lying broken in fields had produced a show. All that bad luck: his mother had never allowed it into the house.

It was still only eight-thirty. His dad would have already been up for a couple of hours. Forty-odd years as a game-keeper had seen to that. He'd have the table set for his breakfast. Blue striped mugs and plates. A pot of tea that he'd keep going for an hour or so as he did his jobs. A lifetime working on the estate had left him rheumatic and slow on his feet. But he was pretty good for eighty-four.

Pablo changed gear and swung the car into a long bend. The village would be just the same: the pub, the post office and church, the old schoolhouse with its modern extension, the humped bridge at the river where they'd tried to tickle trout. The doors and windows of houses that belonged to the estate painted regulation white. A few pebble-dashed semis had grown on the outskirts. There was a new car park for tourists and The Lapwing Café where bikers gathered on Sundays. Pablo changed up for a straight run. A hen pheasant darted for cover. Faint mist rose from the tarmac. What little rain there had been that spring had come by night. Even in Manchester the soil had a baked, friable feeling. It smelled of the long summer just beginning.

Pablo made the window glide down. The blossom had a faint, almost erotic scent. He was a kid again, riding down a valley striped with light. The past was a dream he couldn't stop dreaming, waking with that suffocated feeling he'd had since he was ten.

Pablo pulled the car into a lay-by and scrabbled for the bottle of water. He felt desiccated. He needed coffee. He needed to wake up next to a woman. There'd be no one since Ellie. They'd lived together for nearly two years and then . . . it was hard to remember what had happened. And why was way too complicated. She'd moved out when he was in Majorca, playing in a nightclub in Palma. He'd wanted her to come out for a few weeks, but it was too late by then. She'd run into somebody else. Someone who'd stick around.

Pablo tossed the empty bottle to the back seat. A thin headache was mithering his right temple. He climbed out of the car and stood with the sun on his face, breaking a sprig of blossom from a thorn tree overhanging the wall. He'd taken his mother a bouquet one time. Wanting to please her. Tiny cream flowers with roseate centres. She'd almost panicked. *Not in the house, Philip. Never in the house!* But she'd loved those bunches of marsh marigolds he brought early in the year, the catkins from willow trees. They were dusted with pollen, the way her cheeks had grown soft with down as she grew older.

That was thirty years ago now. Maybe that was what the music drew upon when it was good. Memories. What was unresolved. You had to reach down to bring that back. Only it came out as a stream of notes. A musical phrase you hadn't found before. Slow vibrato. The nuance of a bent string searching for pitch. It came out as silence, the space between notes that the notes themselves were reaching for. The silence everything reaches for in the end.

Pablo yawned, glancing up at a kestrel hovering above the verge. It tilted its wings so they glowed rusty in the early light and then dipped away across fields. It became a speck and then invisible. He switched on the engine and pulled onto the road, taking the car into the long descent that ran to the village. His father would be shaving, brewing tea, cursing the tie he was trying to fit around his neck, swaying on his buggered legs. Leaning forwards, Pablo swept a dead bluebottle from the fascia. The rev counter flickered feebly at the start of its ascent. The exhaust puttered under him, almost blown, a thin integument of rusted steel. He hated cars. All cars, even this one. He'd need to get it sorted.

The front door hadn't been used in years. Pablo stared at it from the unlit hall that smelled of damp and distemper. Outside, the timber was cracked and purple clematis had grown across it. Inside, the cream paint had cracked into yellow scabs and lumps. The knock came again. He walked from the kitchen into the dark hallway.

– You'll have to go round the back.

– OK.

A woman's voice. His ankle was still sore and swollen. His own voice sounded thin, distant. It'd be one of the neighbours commiserating. He hardly knew them now. Or maybe his father took a paper. But the papergirl would know to leave it in the porch. And he doubted if his father had ever done any such thing. He went into the kitchen, moving cautiously. His shoulder and neck ached. Through the etched glass of the back door he saw a green shirt and a flash of copper.

He fumbled then wrenched the back door open where it stuck on the tiled floor. A woman with bright hair stood there. The hair was loose and frizzed out from her head in fine, unruly spirals. Her eyes were light blue, her nose straight with slightly flared nostrils. It was strong face and she was frowning.

Pablo saw the horse running across the field. The way light flickered in the valley. The way it flashed through trees or through the spokes of a bicycle wheel as he followed the road, followed Tim's striped tee shirt.

The woman wore Levi's and a green sweatshirt. She came two inches above his height. Not unusual. He was small, wiry and dark. It was why they'd nicknamed him Pablo. There was a dimple in her chin and freckles down her nose. When she moved her head the sun haloed her hair, a floss of light.

– Hello, I was . . .

Her eyes dropped. Pablo held himself awkwardly.

– My father's not here.

He shrugged as if it could explain something. She frowned slightly, trying to remember. Pablo started again.

- He died a few days ago. I'm Phil Beddowes, his son.

She looked at him is if he wasn't understanding something.

- Phil, that's right. I know. It's you I want. I'm sorry about your dad. I heard a couple of days ago. It must have been a shock. After everything else.

He swung the door open with his good hand and it squealed against the tiles.

- That's OK. It was a shock alright. Come in. But it's a mess, I'll warn you.

He hadn't been able to do much. There were piles of newspaper all around the room. Opened tins of meat for the cat. A dried-up saucer of milk that had evaporated in rings, like dust circling a planet. Dishes in the sink. The smell of old age. She stepped into the room, her hair brushing against him, a bush of fire, a sudden ionisation of the air.

- I could give you a hand if you like . . .

She gestured at his hand in the splint.

- No, no it's OK.

It wasn't OK. He'd got home from the hospital after the accident – after A&E, the unanswered calls and messages, after the ambulance had dropped him at the front gate – to find his father asleep in the chair. He was still cradling the telephone in his lap, wearing an old pullover with burn marks down the front where the sparks from his pipe had dropped when he fell asleep.

But he wasn't asleep. He'd called Pablo because of some premonition, remembering he was going to die. He didn't even look asleep. His head was thrown back and his mouth was open; his face was unshaven and grey, drained of blood;

his dentures protruded. Pablo had to prise the phone from his hand to ring the doctor. His father's hands were claws, cold and stiff. The fingernails were badly cut and dark, as if he'd bruised them. He'd had a series of mini-strokes the year before and was on tablets for blood pressure, when he bothered or remembered to take them. He had angina and carried a GTN spray. On the bureau was a tablet dispenser with compartments for each day of the week, untouched since Wednesday. He'd soiled himself and the room was sour as a rookery. He'd spent his life on the moor then died in an armchair. The cat had rubbed against Pablo's legs, mewing for food as he stood there, trying to decide what was best.

Pablo turned to the woman again. What was she saying? She smiled a little self-consciously. Her teeth were even and sharp. There were freckles in the dimple on her chin.

– I'm Anthea Lee. I'm sorry, I should have said. Do you remember me? I just came to . . .

She couldn't finish a sentence. He interrupted her, pointing to one of the kitchen chairs.

– I'm sorry, have a seat . . .

Anthea Lee? She was tucking herself in behind the pine table, crossing her legs, her feet in neat white pumps. He sat down opposite her. He saw the red horse leaping the gate, the halter tangling in the top rail.

– I've got you now. I'm sorry about the . . .

Another unfinished sentence. The horse's head jerking back in the woman's arms. The neat round hole in its forehead where it lay under the blanket on a green verge. Bad luck blossoming on every tree. She must have started a sentence, but he only caught the end of it.

– I'm sorry?

– . . . the horse. He was called Star. Not very original. The kids called him that. He was just two.

He. Like a person. The neat hole had been in a white whorl of hair. A white star sucking everything into itself.

– I'm sorry.

There must be something else to say. He thought of what she'd said. There were children. Dust glinted in the sunlight coming through the window. She was leaning forward. He eased the wrist support that was fastened with Velcro.

– Why?

– She looked away. Her face was blank.

– Why did I come to see you?

– Well, yes. No. Why did it . . .?

– What?

– Jump. The horse. *Star*.

That wasn't a question now, more a translation of what he'd been trying to say into something said.

– What made it do that?

– I don't know. It had never happened before. He was young. Maybe an insect stung him. I honestly don't know.

That clegg on his arm, its armour of silk gleaming as it pushed its proboscis under his skin to take a bellyful of blood. She was still speaking.

– You were lucky, you could have been killed. And then your father. I didn't know him really, but I saw him out and about on his bike. He seemed a nice old chap. He was the Keeper, wasn't he?

– Yes, his dad, too.

And yes, quiet. Worked for the estate all his life. Gamekeeper, mechanic, then odd jobs when he retired from looking after the birds.

234

Why was he telling her this? She'd know it better than him. He stared down at the kitchen table.

– Will there have to be an inquest?

– Don't think so. He had a few ailments. The doctor put it down as a stroke.

No inquest. Not like Tim. The inquiry opened, then adjourned. All those questions from the police. Then misadventure. Misadventure, as if . . .

– I'm sorry. And your mother, too . . . I knew her a bit. Just from going in the shop, the post office, you know, just bumping into her.

What did she know about his mother? That had been years ago. She'd been doing OK. She'd got a job in a shop selling knitting wool and had seemed settled there, getting up early every day to catch the bus. He'd been touring in Denmark with a little jazz-blues outfit, backing a Jamaican vocalist. Dorothy Gainsborough. Great voice with a huge range that rumbled at the bottom end and fell like tinkling glass at the top. He'd had to come back early for the funeral. That arsehole Ray Bostick had taken over and he'd made sure Pablo never got back in.

– Nothing to be sorry about. My mother was a long time ago.

– Yes, it was, I know. But we felt so sorry, after everything.

There was some kind of doubt in her eyes now. She pushed up the sleeves of her sweatshirt.

– I just wanted to say that if there's anything I can do, then I'm just in the village. And I wanted to tell you that it wasn't your fault, it was a chance in a million. Bad luck. It was very unlucky. And I'm so sorry you got hurt . . . and your car.

She let out a puff of air.

– It needed a service.

She smiled awkwardly, fiddling with her wristwatch.

– There was a bit of madness in him, Star. It happens sometimes. A bit of wild horse that can't be broken or bred out. We'd have had to get rid sooner or later. But it was sad for the kids.

He looked up, quizzing her.

– Two girls. Seven and nine. Amy and Sarah. They're at my mum's for a few days.

Seven and nine. He had to rouse himself then. Remember she was a real person through the haze of the dream.

– I could offer you some tea.

He corrected himself.

– Sorry. I mean would you like some tea? Might have to skip the milk.

The black and white cat came to the window and looked in, rubbing its cheeks against the glass.

– No, no thanks. I'm OK, honestly.

A little silence blew in between them. The cat jumped up and ran its arched spine against the window frame. Anthea smiled as if that was significant. Pablo felt a sudden spurt of anger. It was just a fucking cat. An animal.

– How badly were you hurt?

– Just bruises, a sprained wrist, I was lucky.

– You were unlucky, you mean.

Pablo shrugged again.

– I've got paracetamol. It'll be OK. I'm not even sure how it happened. I saw something moving in the field. All I remember is the horse appearing in the air. Then bits afterwards.

– What about the car?

– Written off.

She looked smitten, grimacing neatly.

– It's OK, it's insured. I'll get another. It's only a car . . .

He paused, shifting in the chair.

– It's funny, but I thought you'd be the one who was angry because I'd killed your horse.

– Not you. Not you. It was the vet who put him down. You only ran into him because he jumped out.

She put her hands together. Neat fingers. No wedding ring.

– I'd better get on . . .

She was standing up . . .

– . . . leave you in peace.

Get on? With what? With everything there was to do. To face, to sort out. None of which he'd really registered. And he'd felt nothing yet. Not relief. Not grief. Not anything really, except a kind of mild surprise.

– Shall I call back? I've got a couple of days. I could help out a bit.

– What about your husband. Wouldn't he mind?

Maybe that was overplaying it. She turned back to him, laughing quietly. A bitter little laugh that seemed out of keeping with her composure. Like the hair, unruly, when everything else was neat.

– You don't know me yet, do you?

But he did. He'd known her because she was burning back there in his memory.

– I was Anthea Kellett at junior school. We were in the same class. With Miss Henderson, remember? Nearly thirty years ago, mind.

– Anthea Kellett?

He was thirty-nine now, so they would have been ten years old.

– My parents had the village post office. We'd just arrived. You'd have thought I was a right stuck up little twerp.

He remembered that, too. A girl on a white pony passing him in the road with copper hair stuffed inside her riding hat.

– I married Billy Lee. I must have been mad. Remember Billy?

He had a scar below his left knee to remember Billy by, a little white moon. They'd called him Stacko. After the blues song. But he'd buried that, deep in the quiet and mess of the past. She was smiling at him again. That open freckled smile that he'd seen in the schoolroom thirty years back.

– I think I did it to annoy my parents.

She laughed, neat again.

– Bull's-eye!

He remembered the dark little shop and post office, which was a Spar now. Her mother briskly cheerful, her father who'd been in the RAF with his little white moustache, blazers and striped ties.

– How come I've never seen you around?

– We moved away after we got married. Billy got a job on an estate near Hexham. The girls were born up there. We came home when Billy's dad couldn't manage the farm, about two years ago.

She looked suddenly shy.

– You don't look much different, Phil. it's funny, I thought you might know me. You were nice to me. I remember. Your brother, Tim, I don't know . . . it was such a business, such a shame.

She was on her way through the door.

– Anyway, you don't want me going on like this. I kicked Billy out long ago. I should've had more sense than to marry him. He's not all bad. But about as sensitive as a brick, but you'll know that. I was bored, I suppose. And spoiled. He got worse after his accident.'

– What accident?

Pablo hadn't seen Billy in years.

– Caught his foot in a mower, haytiming. He was off work for months with not much to do but drink and moan about it. He has to wear a special boot. Being Billy, he thought it was someone else's fault, of course.

– Sounds grim.

– It was. I'd better go.

She shrugged and left, pulling the door a little so that it squealed against the tiles. Pablo sat in a band of sunlight, listened to her car starting up then going down the lane away from the house.

Billy Lee. Stacko. Thirty years ago they'd been friends at school. Thirty years was nothing. It was yesterday. The past was always there, always available. You carried it around somehow, like music. The way your fingers found it, stumbling, making sense of its scattered intervals. Pablo stood up and pushed the door to, dropping the rusted catch.

His father had planted damson and apple trees in the garden. There was a yew tree at the gateway that had always been there; an outhouse with kennels, a workbench and toilet. Then the cottage: two downstairs rooms with stone fireplaces, a small kitchen with a gas cooker and a broken range. The walls emulsioned white, stained yellow where damp had penetrated. A bathroom had been fitted in the Sixties, just before he'd been born, cut out from the largest bedroom with a studding partition, so you could hear everything. Nowadays, it was what the estate agents would call desirable. Unspoiled. But renting from the estate had always meant bodged jobs and penny-pinching. His father had retreated to one room that had a floral carpet trodden with food stains, twin armchairs and an almost-new TV. He'd never quite mastered the remote control and whenever Pablo rang him he cursed it to cut the volume, fingers fumbling on the tiny buttons.

Pablo started in the kitchen and moved outwards, throwing old newspapers, magazines, empty bottles, burst packets of soap powder, piles of used tea bags and other junk into black bin liners and stacking them next to the front gate. The porcelain sink was foul with grease and he cleaned it with a rusted scourer. There was no mains gas in the village and he had to get hot water from the immersion heater. The tank was mounted in the bathroom and rumbled through the floor as the water heated up.

The outhouse held his father's old bicycle, stepladders, deckchairs, a rusted push mower, tins of paint, spades, forks, trowels, plant pots, a sickle, a line of snares hanging from hooks, a tool chest, tins of screws and nails, an enamel pail, some coiled rope and a rotted dog leash. It was slow going with one hand and almost impossible to tie off the bags. His ankle had a dark blue bruise spreading outwards and yellowing.

Each morning he walked to the village shop for a newspaper and a few provisions to get him through the day. An Asian family had it now. The Patels. They'd had a restaurant in Mombasa and had decided to get out in the Eighties. Rajiv had arrived in Pablo's class in the 6th form. They were the first and only Asian family in the village. Though Rajiv always said they were African, just to wind up the locals. He'd got out too. Smart kid.

Pablo found a deckchair in the outhouse that hadn't rotted away. The grass on the lawn was knee-high and matted, but he cut a clumsy circle with the sickle, remembering the cigar-shaped sharpening stone that must be somewhere in the tool box. He'd find it when he had a minute and put an edge on the blade. In the afternoons he sat in the garden with the paper, knackered after his one-handed attempts to get things straight. He'd made arrangements for the funeral with the Co-op. So far, he hadn't had the heart to look through his father's papers, though he'd found a sheaf of photographs in an envelope showing the local snooker team in the Fifties. His father was a boy in a thick tweed jacket and tartan tie. His grandfather was there too, hair oiled back, a hand on his father's shoulder. There must have been more stuff like that. He was in no hurry. All in good time.

At night he sweated in a set of half-clean sheets in his old bedroom. His shoulder ached. He lay awake worrying about the flat, his gear. He ought to get Alec to call round and make sure everything was OK. When the insurance cheque came through he'd need a car. Right now, driving was out of the question and the bus service was next to useless. Alec would have to run things back in Manchester. And he needed to find the family address book to let people know what had happened. It was tucked underneath some magazines on the TV stand. Most of the names had a thick pencil line drawn through them.

He'd fallen asleep in the deckchair with the paper when he heard tyres on the gravel. It was a red VW. Anthea climbed out and walked towards him, freckled arms, hair blazing in the sun. Behind her, the blue-grey line of fells. Behind them, tall thunderheads puffing up. The hot air balloon was shrinking in the distance, the burner flaring, a breeze blowing away the sound of its breath.

Anthea glanced back at it. She smiled and held out a pair of rubber gloves.

– I'd love to try that.

She bit her lip.

– I've come to give you a hand, at last.

Pablo was struggling to rise one-handed from the chair. She took his wrist and helped him up, her fingers cool against his arm.

– How are the injuries?

He winced theatrically.

– I'm just a bit bruised. Chest and shoulder. Aches a bit when I laugh my head off.

– We'll have to be careful then.

She grinned, showing her sharp teeth. Pablo balanced on his ankle, wincing.

– Actually, I haven't had a laugh in years.

– I believe you. I'll be careful.

She was looking round at his handiwork. At least he'd got on with it. Made a start.

– How are the kids?

– The girls? They're OK, still upset, still at Mum's.

– Where's that?

– Clitheroe. My parents moved out when they sold the shop. Couldn't get a house in the village with the estate owning everything. We were always off-comers.

They were walking towards the house. Pablo paused in the doorway.

– We used to steal penny chews from your Mum when she wasn't watching.

– So did I . . .

He did remember her. She'd slipped back into a place. He wasn't ready to tell her. Not yet, because he had other questions. Things that might just as well be left alone.

They set about cleaning the kitchen, scouring surfaces, polishing the chipped sink. Anthea took the lead and Pablo helped as best he could. He found an ancient cylinder vacuum cleaner under the stairs and managed the carpets and rugs in the downstairs room one-handed. By the time he'd finished, she'd made a pot of tea. Somehow she got all the windows open and air began to flow through the house. Outside the sky had darkened with in-coming rain.

When she turned to bring the teapot to the table, he saw that she had a small blue tattoo on one shoulder. A single tulip, just below the neckline.

The damson tree was coming into bloom and the air smelled of rain and sap. His mother had loved damsons when he was a child. She stewed the fruit until the stones separated and rose, let them cool, serving them with Carnation milk. They'd always tasted like brass to Pablo, bitter and unforgiving. Like threepenny bits. But he'd loved their darkened crimson, the colour of his guitar.

When Anthea sat down, he noticed the neatness of her body, the fullness of her hips. She wore a gold stud in each ear and she'd pulled her hair back into a green band so that it was clear of her face. There was a spattering of freckles in the parting her breasts made before they dipped into the scoop of her tee shirt. Her eyes really were the blue of cornflowers. They gave her an air of innocence, of directness. She had a tiny gap between her front teeth and before she laughed her nostrils flared a little.

As a teenager, he'd been more interested in learning chords than going out with girls. He'd played his LPs again and again on his portable record player, riffling along on his first acoustic guitar with its hopeless action. John Mayall and early Fleetwood Mac albums. Then Lightnin' Hopkins and Freddie King. His dad had bought the guitar one market day, brought it home in the Land Rover. He'd never said why, what had prompted him, but Pablo's future had turned on it.

Anthea came the next day for a couple of hours, then the day after that. They worked quietly together, brushing past each other, getting together to lift the settee or a chest of drawers to clean behind. On the third day they made tea and drank it in the garden without sitting down. A line of teasels was spearing through against the wall. Anthea traced their leaves with her fingers. There was something ugly about them, malevolent.

After the tea they made a start on his father's bedroom. They worked without speaking for the most part. It was oddly intimate. Here, where his parents had slept and made love, where he and Tim had been conceived. There was surprisingly little in there. A few jackets in the wardrobe, shirts, neatly-folded underwear, striped pyjamas under the pillow. Anthea stripped the bed and carried everything to the washing machine in the kitchen. Pablo heard her fumbling around for washing powder and then the slam and rumble as she switched it on. His mother's stuff had been cleaned out long ago. Now this.

Anthea came behind him to look at the clothes. He could smell hot skin, a faint musk of sweat.

– They could go to Age Concern in town.

He nodded.

- I guess so.

- I could take them next time I'm in. Unless . . .

- No, that'd be great. That's kind of you.

His face was abstracted, as if he'd been carried away by a thought. She dropped her voice.

- I'm sorry, I don't mean to rush you.

- It's OK. You're not.

Anthea backed away. Had he sounded annoyed? Pablo wandered into his old room to lean on the window ledge where the paint was flaking. A few spots of rain had hit the flawed glass and were beginning to darken the dust on the track outside. She came behind him, leaning close to push at the rusted catch so that the window creaked open, so that her hair touched him. Her breast was soft for a second against his arm.

- It's going to rain.

Her voice was husky.

- Yes, guess so.

He could feel his heart pumping, that lopsided rhythm warning him.

- I didn't mean to sound cross.

His mouth was suddenly feathery.

- It's OK. I know.

Her eyes gazed directly on his, blue against peat dark. She touched his arm, tugging almost imperceptibly. He kissed her faintly on the temple, then on her throat, then on the tattoo, his mouth against her freckled skin. She steered him away from the window and pushed him gently onto the bed. For a long time they lay there not moving. There was peace, the weight of their bodies against each other; then his hand was across her waist and they were kissing again. Anthea winced and laughed as the Velcro of his splint caught on her skin.

– Ouch!

She undid it carefully, kissing his hand as he flexed it. She kicked off her shoes and they thudded to the boards.

– I don't have long. I'd better help you.

Pablo nodded, sitting up. When he was naked, she dragged the tee shirt over her head, unfastening her bra, stepping out of her underwear which was white with tiny blue flowers embroidered on the fabric. She pulled off her hair band and slipped it onto her wrist. Her hair burned like brass as she straddled him on the bed, easing her tongue gently into his mouth.

His body was thin and covered in dark hair. She nuzzled into his chest, allowing her fingers to trail up his thighs. He craned his head to her belly, pushing his tongue into her navel, then up over her belly and over each nipple. A little gasp shivered from her lips and was sucked back as he touched her.

Afterwards, they lay listening to the rain, to the washing machine rumbling in the kitchen below. She lay in the crook of his arm, her hair loose across the pillow, across his chest. There was a diagonal bruise there, blue and yellow, where the seat belt had stopped him. She bent over him to kiss it.

– Pablo.

She was whispering, almost to herself.

– Pablo. That was it, wasn't it?

Her breath was warm against his chest. She sat up to look into his face.

– That's what they called you, wasn't it?

– They still do.

246

Anthea lay down again, stroking his wrist, his arm.

– Do you remember me now?

– I always did. Couldn't quite place you at first, that's all.

Was that a lie? Maybe he hadn't wanted to place her.

– Do you still play the guitar?'

He wondered how she knew that. They'd gone to different secondary schools. Maybe she'd seen him in one of the high-school bands, knocking out Chicago blues through shagged-out gear. Rajiv had played bass for a while until he became more interested in girls than music.

– Yep. I still play. It's what I do.

– That's great. I wish I'd been good at something. Anything, I mean. I'd like to see you play.

– Then you should have been in Amsterdam last weekend.

That was a strange thought, because if she'd been there, none of this would or could have happened like it had. He hunched back against the pillows, raising himself awkwardly in the bed so that he could see her face.

– You were there weren't you? When Tim died? That's what I remember.

– It was a long time ago.

– But it happened. Time doesn't change that. Nothing changes it.

She bit her lip, didn't reply, but leaned over to kiss his forehead. They listened to rain striking against the window, to jackdaws clambering on the roof and their own breath in the moistened air. Then the washing machine began to spin, throbbing against the flag floor beneath. She'd have to go soon. Back to her mother, back to the kids. He wondered if she had a job. He hadn't asked, hadn't even thought to ask. He still hadn't had the courage to look behind his brother's bedroom door. And now she was using his old name. Now she was above him again, her hair touching his face, allowing her nipples to graze his chest. Whispering. *Pablo, Pablo. I always loved that name.*

Afterwards they dressed and went downstairs and loaded the boot of her car with bin bags and she drove away with his father's clothes and shoes. They'd end up being picked over by strangers. Maybe he thought about these things too much. She'd never answered his question about Tim. But that could wait. Other things were more important than the past right now. He picked up the phone to call Alec.

The latch on Tim's door was stiff. Inside, it could have been 1976. The bed still made, the sheets tightly folded. A pair of Superman slippers lay under the bed. A shelf with Tim's books, a deal table, a chair, a patchwork rug. A half-built glider hanging from the ceiling. They were going to finish that together. Pablo went to the window to look into the damson tree. The curtains had faded and the metal catches were rusted tight.

It had been the year of the long drought. Their father had bought them second-hand bikes and restored them over the winter, putting in new wheel bearings, fitting tyres and brake blocks, cleaning up the frames. They'd come down on Christmas Day to find them propped up in the hallway. He'd been a bit jealous that Tim got his at the same time, that he hadn't had to wait until he was ten. Their dad had lifted the bikes and spun the wheels so they could listen to the bearings. He'd made them learn to ride properly, taking their Cycling Proficiency Test at school before he'd let them out on the roads. Tim had taken his twice, but they'd got there in the end and that summer the whole valley would be theirs, with nothing much in the way of traffic other than the odd tractor or hay bailer to worry about.

That day they'd packed sandwiches in their rucksacks and set off for the reservoir. It lay crammed into the valley like amalgam in a tooth. Saturday morning and it hadn't rained for weeks. They set off in shorts and tee shirts, the radio playing from the kitchen. 'Going up the Country'. Canned Heat. Their mother calling at the doorway for them to be careful.

The valley had been flooded in the Thirties and the church moved, stone by stone, to a new site. It was said that all the bodies had been dug up from the churchyard and moved with it before the flooding could go ahead. Under that pane of water were houses, a post office, the village pub. The Fylde Water Board had bought up the houses and farms one by one. All flooded to send drinking water to Manchester. Conifers had been planted along the flanks by the Forestry Commission, regimented lines of larch and fir. They'd pretended it was Canada, imagined that China lay beyond the notch of the next valley, if they could only keep traveling into that grey-blue horizon.

That day, their father had left for work early and the house was peaceful. Sometimes he took Pablo with him to feed the pheasants, set traps for feral mink that preyed on the young, or check on the young grouse before the shooting season. That day they'd been free to cycle down through the scent of conifer woods, Tim in the lead, his spokes flashing, until they glimpsed the reservoir through the trees. It had been a dry spring and the water level was the lowest they'd ever seen. Hose pipes were banned, car washing forbidden. Not that they had a car, just the old estate Land Rover. All around the reservoir was a bleached rim of stones where the water level had fallen. They'd heard that the tip of the old school steeple and the chimneys of some of the houses had re-appeared. But all that turned out to be a lie.

They'd cycled into the sun where it flickered through the trees, Tim ahead in his striped tee shirt and baseball cap, the sun glancing against his legs, turning now and then to make sure that Pablo was still there. Still behind him, still looking after him.

Pablo lunched on sardines and toast then fetched the worm-eaten stepladders from the outhouse and dragged them up-stairs. He steadied them on the landing and climbed them, pushing up the loft hatch. Sunlight was filtered by the grime on the skylight. There was a stink of soot. Piled in there were a couple of cane-hooped trunks, some broken lampshades, a pudding-basin crash helmet that had belonged to his father when he had a moped. Pablo pulled himself awkwardly through the hatch. Some old door panels had been placed across the joists to make a platform. The lime torching had fallen from the underneath of the slates and lay everywhere. There was a dead bat cobwebbed to one of the oak beams.

There was his first guitar in a cheap tartan zip-bag. A plywood acoustic from Woolworth's with a slotted headstock and chrome tailpiece. Good for firewood, but his parents had kept it. It was amazing he'd learnt to finger chords on that. Pablo laid it back against the crumbling wall. He opened the lid of a cardboard box and found it full of his school exercise books. Tim's would be at the bottom, though they stopped in 1976. Pablo tasted a spurt of bile as he stooped under the eaves. He wasn't ready for any of this. There were other things to do and Anthea had promised to lend him her car.

Pablo borrowed the Volkswagen the next morning, waving at the two blonde girls who watched him from the kitchen window, wondering if they knew who he was. Maybe Anthea would have explained about the horse, about the car. The rest they couldn't know. But the fact he'd turned up at her house would have half the village talking.

His left arm and shoulder felt stiff as he drove. He didn't intend to be away long. He needed a few clothes. Maybe his little acoustic to practise on. He had a series of gigs in September at a club in Birmingham. Before that, a few hours in the studio. They'd got a new mixer desk to set up. He needed to straighten a few things out with Alec, take some time to himself now.

Pablo checked the mailbox in the foyer. All junk. The lock was stiff as he entered the flat, stepping into a smell like old oranges. There was a line of pigeons on the balcony railings, staring in. They took off, a handful of paper scattering. Pablo emptied his answerphone, packed some more clothes, found a dark suit, brought his guitars to the car. When he locked the door, it felt oddly final.

Early afternoon, he dropped into the shop to store his gear. Alec was setting up a drum kit. A grey ponytail, spotless trainers. Alec was solid. They'd helped each other out over the years: Alec's divorce, Pablo's break up with Ellie. He was tightening the snare drum to a stand.

– It's your old man, you've got to take some time.

Pablo punched him on the shoulder.

– Cheers, just don't mess everything up, eh?

Alec picked up a cymbal and turned it on one finger.

– Go on, fuck off, Pab. I hope everything goes OK.

Pablo found his work diary and phone, cancelling everything for the next two weeks. By then the funeral would be over and he'd have got his head around the other stuff. The studio was at the back of the shop and he spent a couple of hours testing new gear. The digital stuff was amazing, but they still had some old analogue gear – a Watkins copycat, a Vox AC 30, a WEM Dominator – because even young bands wanted those classic sounds. Retro sounds. He spent an hour on the accounts, checked out a new line of amplifiers and ordered a couple for display, then went out for a curry.

By eight o'clock he was on his way out of the city. He took the motorway to Clitheroe, then went on back roads. It was a close evening. A yellow moon burned above the hedgerows. Most of the hawthorn blossom had fallen and there were stands of cow parsley and meadowsweet in the headlights. He was tempted to idle, to stop for a pint. To spend an hour with strangers at a bar, lose himself in thought. But he pressed on. He thought about the village, about home, about Anthea. It had been so long since he felt close to a woman without wanting to run away. He'd been running for a long time. He tried not to think about the other stuff. The complications. They'd come soon enough.

The roads were almost deserted. People sat outside village pubs to catch the last of the evening light. The road narrowed and climbed. Pablo changed gear and gunned the engine. He was about a mile from the village when a set of headlights appeared behind him. They drove up close, backed away, came close again. In the rear mirror Pablo saw a set of chromed bull bars. He couldn't see the driver. He slowed down for a bend and the headlights flashed on and off three times. A few yards on, he pulled into a layby and the Range Rover drew up behind. He wound down the window and waited with the engine idling. He heard boots slur on the road. A figure came towards him in the side mirror, blackened by the headlights behind.

– Anthea?

It was a man's voice. Familiar.

– Anth?

Pablo wound down the window and turned his head.

– No. Obviously not. Sorry.

– Eh?

– I'm not Anthea.

It was Billy. Stacko. It made sense, somehow.

– It's her fucking car, pal.

He decided to lie, just for the hell of it.

– Yep, she sold it me.

– Sold it? Bollocks! And who the fuck might you be?

Billy had been there that day. Billy and Carl, both. When Tim died in the water.

– C'mon Stacko, you're losing it

The man's hands came up onto the roof of the car as he peered closer.

– Fuck me!

There was a pause, the big man in his baseball cap hunkering down.

– Pablo? Well, well! Pablo . . .

Anthea above him, her nipples against his chest. He could smell drink on Billy's breath. He stood up so his face was shadowed from the light.

– Oh aye, heard you were back. Heard about your dad. Shame.

Then he was laughing softly.

- Heard you ran into Anthea's horse, too, you stupid twat. She loved that horse. You always were a fucking disaster.

Pablo stayed silent. He thought about the heft of the wheel brace, but it'd be locked in the boot. The engine panted quietly.

- Did she, Billy? News travels fast, eh? Anything else you need to tell me that I already know?'

- Now don't get fucking smart, Pablo, I thought you were our Anthea, that's all.

- Yeah. Best not to, eh?

- What's that?

- Think, Billy. Best not to. Doesn't really suit you.

Pablo slipped the clutch, put the car into gear and pulled away. He saw Billy silhouetted against the lights of his vehicle, unmoving.

The Range Rover pulled out behind him, but this time it kept its distance. Billy and Carl and Anthea. They'd all been there. He couldn't remember why. Pablo pulled into his driveway and switched off the engine. The headlights faded, dropping the house into darkness apart from a smear of moonlight on the windows. His key grated in the lock. Then he was dragging his bags into that smell of bleach, mildew and damp.

The funeral was held on a Wednesday. A day that started with sunshine and turned to drizzle, then sunshine again, so that the headstones steamed in the churchyard. Someone had planted daffodils on Tim's grave. They looked like dabs of butter when the sun touched them. The service was held in the church, then a short ceremony at the crematorium. The undertaker handed him his father's things - wristwatch, dentures, wedding ring. He'd need to go back for the ashes.

Two of his aunts were there, an uncle, a couple of distant cousins, a few villagers turning up at the church to pay their respects. The vicar in his white surplice leading in the coffin; the formalities of the service; platitudes about a full life and the high esteem in which he'd been held. His father had never been a churchgoer. Weddings and funerals, that was all. He kept a black tie in a drawer like all old men.

Pablo had arranged for a small buffet in the pub, so he had a few drinks afterwards, standing with his back to the fireplace in his suit, talking to people he hardly remembered, who he'd probably never see again. They were taking away the remains of the sandwiches when Carl turned up, his big hands raw from farm work. His hair looked as if he'd cut it himself, his face broken-veined, hook-nosed and hard-set. He looked like his father. They'd bumped into each other now and again over the years.

– Pab. I'm sorry about your dad. Grand feller. Old school. It's a shame.

– Carl. Good to see you.

They shook hands.

– Drink?

They stood awkwardly with a pint each.

– Thanks for coming, Carl. I don't know many people here now.

Carl looked at him from under the tousled hair.

– Least I could do. They're pretty horrible dos, these.

They let that remark drop into silence.

– Are you still playing 't guitar for a living, like?

Pablo ordered a couple more on the slate from Millie, the landlady. She was married to Walter, a tight-fisted sod who took a delight in strict closing times and adherence to the law.

- On and off. Mainly studio stuff these days. Producing.

- Oh aye?

Pablo took another pull on the pint.

- Yeah, just keeping my hand in. I've got a share in a music shop and a studio, now.

- In Manchester?

He made it sound like Los Angeles.

- Yeah, it's handy enough.

- Globe-trotting get too much, eh?

Carl laughed and dipped his mouth to his pint. He'd lost a couple of side teeth since Pablo had seen him last. But that'd be a fair few years ago. Longer than it seemed.

- How's the farm?

Carl brightened.

- Oh, not bad. We've had us moments as you know. Got culled wi' foot an' mouth. Restocked. That were a bad job, but we're o'er it now. Started a pedigree herd.

He pulled on the pint, licking foam from his upper lip.

- Limousins. They can be awk'ud buggers, but I've tekken to 'em - more'n they've tekken to me any road!

Millie was hovering, leaning her fleshy arms on the bar.

- I'm in the farmhouse now, Mum and Dad are in a bunga-low. So they've retired at last. That last do finished 'em. Bein' culled. The spring went out o' me dad, like.

- Oh well.

Pablo wished he hadn't said that. It sounded feeble. He tried again.

- It's been weird going through things.

Carl put his face into the pint glass.

- I'll bet.

256

- My mum never changed Tim's room, you know. I don't know what to do with it. All his things are there. It's a time warp.

Carl was putting his arms into his coat.

- You should come up and see us before you go off on your travels again.

Except there was no *us*. It was just Carl running things. Carl who, like Pablo, had never married or had children.

- OK, I'll take you up on that. I'd like to see the place again. What's a good time?

- Oh, I'm nearly allus there. Any time'll do. It'd be good to see you. Like I said, I'm sorry about your dad. Hope you get sorted. Let me know if I can help wi' owt.

They left it at that. Pablo didn't mention Billy or Anthea.

The guests finished their drinks, made last visits to the loo, took their coats from the row of hooks below the stuffed fox in its glass case. Pablo refused a lift from a neighbour. He needed some air.

The rain had cleared earlier and the sun was raising mist from the road. Then rain came again. Pablo walked the mile home through drizzle, the hedgerows and ditches thick with garlic mustard, its musky scent. Then the stink of something dead. When he passed Anthea's house he saw the Range Rover in the drive. When he got home, the house seemed to have sunk into its overgrown garden, the unkempt trees.

Anthea was waiting for him in the living room, perched on the settee, knees together, reading an out of date newspaper. She'd let herself in with the key Pablo had lent her. He hadn't expected that.

- Hi. How did it go?

- Oh, OK. How come you're here?

– It's OK. Billy's with the girls. I told him I had to pick up some shopping. I put the car round the back. He can't be in two places at once and he promised to watch telly with them. It's none of his business anyhow.

Pablo laughed.

– Well, he seemed interested enough the other night.

Anthea rose to kiss him, loosened his father's tie, brushing rain from his lapels.

– What does he care? He's been with enough other women. That was the problem.

She straightened his tie.

– You look nice, dressed up. I'm sorry I couldn't be there.

She ducked her head against his chest.

Pablo slipped out of his damp jacket. It was chilly in the room without a fire. Even on a warm day the thick walls kept the heat at bay. Anthea was smiling at him, dropping the shawl from her shoulders, pulling him close. When they kissed, her mouth was soft, familiar. His fingers brushed her nipples through the cotton of her blouse.

The bath took ages to fill, the water discoloured from ancient plumbing – lead pipes and a dented copper cylinder the estate plumbers had reclaimed from somewhere. There were streaks of green on the enamel. The only soap he could find was a packet of Wright's coal tar that his father had bought in bulk. He lay in the hot water, letting the steam float past him, allowing the day to replay in his head. The funeral. The curtains at the crematorium parting. His father slipping away in the oak coffin. Carl, Billy, Anthea.

He was drying himself when he heard tyres on gravel. He tied the towel around his waist and waited. It couldn't be

Anthea. She'd be with the children now. Pablo switched off the bathroom light and went to the front bedroom, bare feet creaking on warped boards. The double bed was stripped. Twin wardrobes tilted towards each other on the ramshackle floor. Pablo moved to the window and looked down. He couldn't see a car at first. Then he caught the glint of green paintwork beyond the beech hedge.

Billy was at the edge of the little orchard his father had planted, standing under the damson tree, staring at the house from under his cap. He'd always been the biggest of them and he'd filled out over the years. He was wearing a camouflage jacket, cargo pants, yellow work boots. From what Anthea had said he worked as a contractor, fencing, walling, harvesting. That gave him lots of time in his own company. Time to turn things over in his mind where they'd get bigger.

Billy stood for a long time. It was dark in the garden, no lights from the house, a blade of moon sliding between clouds. Pablo stared down from the window. Billy cupped his hands and a flame lit his face under the peaked cap. Then he turned away, dragging his foot. He paused to take one last look, breathing smoke, as if he knew Pablo was watching. A door slammed. The Range Rover lit up, then started up, its wheels turning on loose gravel. Pablo sank onto his parents' bed and let the towel fall.

The next day Pablo sat down at the kitchen table with a piece of paper and a pencil. He'd found the rent book safely stored in the oak desk and up to date. They'd gone to the estate office with their mother as kids, a stuffy little room with brown lino and a storage heater on full belt. The woman behind the desk had given them wine gums. They must have bought the place twice over since his grandfather's day. When he was eighteen all he'd wanted was to be elsewhere. Getting those bicycles had been the first taste of freedom.

It had been early in the year, but already blazing hot. They'd stopped for Tip Tops at the village shop. Holding them to their cheeks then tearing open the plastic sheaths with their teeth, sucking the column of frozen blackcurrant juice until it whitened to ice. It was so hot, pine cones were cracking on the trees beside the road. The woods were tinder dry. Up on the moor the heather was already burning where their father was at work. Swifts were slicing up the sky.

So hot, their legs burned and the tar on the road was melting. Their bicycle tyres made a sticky swishing sound. Pablo following the print of Tim's wheels – a zip mark in the melting tar. Tiny stone chippings stuck to their tyres. The backs of their knees were wet and their plimsolls had that gritty feel of sweat between the toes.

Wood pigeons were calling, desire bubbling in their throats. A sound they didn't understand. Tim's Dennis the Menace tee shirt made him look like a wasp hunched over the handlebars as he cycled ahead, freewheeling downhill, changing gear as the road rose to the plantation. A milk tanker approached them and they pulled into the verge, dismounting, straddling the crossbars to let it pass. The driver gave them a friendly wave. He'd admitted them to the adult world, the highway and its code.

On days like this, buzzards drifted over the valley, spiralling on upturned wings like huge moths. Today the sky was empty except for swifts, an airliner heading south. It was weird the way the contrail began just after the plane, so that there was a space between. That was because the gases had to cool before condensing. He'd learned that in science. Things had a reason now. Things could be explained if you knew the right person or knew where to look.

Pablo's forearms scorched as he rode. The breeze in his hair dried the sweat on his forehead. His feet were on fire against the pedals, the road's ribbon of hot tar unfurling. Stone walls burned white in the sun. The valley funnelled them towards the lowest point of the reservoir. It appeared through the trees, a sheet of gleaming wind-beaten lead.

They were supposed to be meeting up with Carl and Billy, but someone else was there as well. Pablo looked down at his new wristwatch, freewheeling to read the time. It was twelve-twenty. That had stuck, somehow, luminous green hands against plain numerals. They had lots of time. They had sandwiches and Coke and an apple each in the rucksacks that bumped against their backs. They had the whole day. Forever.

Sometimes he thought he remembered flames. But the fires on the moor were too far away for that. The bit that mattered, the bit where things were happening, had gone missing, though he remembered the ambulance, the huge weight of fear and dread. He remembered Tim in the water, his white skin, his dark blue underpants. How thin he was. The feeling that something had happened that could never be changed. Suddenly knowing what love was, how deep and irretrievable.

When the knock came, the piece of paper was still blank. He'd made a list of nothing and he hadn't heard the car draw up on the driveway. A heavy knock, three raps. It wasn't Anthea, it wasn't Billy, who he'd been half expecting. It was Carl in blue overalls and flat cap, his wellingtons slurried in cow shit.

– Carl!

- Pab, I can't come in.

Carl gestured towards his boots.

- What's up?

- Bloody hell, Pablo, you know what.

- Such as?

- Stacko came round this mornin'.

- I bet that was a laugh.

- It's not funny Pablo. He were upset.

- About?

- About you. About Anth.

Carl turned the cap round in his hands.

- He's not daft, Pablo, he knows you're going with her. Half the bloody village knows you're shagging her. You didn't waste much time, either.

- And . . . ?

Carl put his hand to the doorjamb, leaning in.

- We're old mates, me and Billy. What was I supposed to say?

Pablo stared past Carl's shoulder. The yew tree shuffled.

- Do you think it's any of his business?

- Maybe not. They're divorced, but there's still the girls and he still cares about Anth. There's other stuff, too, you know there is. You can't carry on just as you like in a village like this. It's not Manchester where no fucker knows anyone.

Other stuff? Carl was putting his cap on and pulling at the peak.

- Anyway, you need to be careful, that's all, or it'll end in a bloody mess.

Billy silhouetted in the headlights, dragging his boot back to the car. *You always were a fucking disaster.*

- OK. Thanks Carl. I am careful. I will be.

- I think you'd better be wi' this one. I'll see you for that drink sometime . . .

He turned to leave.

- . . . and don't be a silly bastard.

When the Land Rover pulled away, Pablo was still looking down the driveway. But he wasn't thinking about what Carl had been saying.

Carl and Billy and Anthea. They'd had all been there, but he couldn't remember why. He couldn't remember if they'd all arranged to meet. He couldn't remember much except Tim in the water and the ambulance. That glimpse of red hair, which must have been Anthea, what drew them there. Though none of them understood.

Pablo's wrist had healed. He was able to practise, running through scales each morning on the little acoustic guitar he'd brought from the flat. Scales were beautiful in their logic, the way they cycled back to their source. The way chords were built, stepping off into new places and harmonies. What started off as a simple progression becoming almost infinitely complicated. Then the way practise became improvisation, spontaneity. It wasn't that practise made perfect, but it allowed you to take risks. Then to play with other musicians, inside the music, alert to the pulse of the moment.

The girls were back at school and Anthea had some time off. She came over most days to help with the house, to make love in the back bedroom. Pablo liked to trace his tongue over her freckles where her breasts divided. She'd laugh and roll over on the bed, so that sun fired her hair. He remembered Tim's back wheel blurring, that slight wobble as the tyre passed between the brake blocks. The sun had flickered through the trees as they rode.

Anthea put her fingers against his neck, feeling for his pulse.

– Still there?'

Pablo opened his eyes.

– I'd like to see you play.

– I'm not in a regular band.

– You said. But you played in Amsterdam?

– Depping.

She jabbed him with her finger.

– *Deputising*. Standing in for someone else.

– I'd still like to see you.

– There'll be a time. I've got a few of gigs coming soon with an outfit I used to play with.

Pablo rolled over onto his back and stared at the ceiling. When he spoke, his voice had thickened.

– How old were you in 1976?

– When?

– 1976.

– You know how old. I was eleven. I'm a few months older than you.

That made Tim the youngest, him next. Her armpits smelled faintly spicey.

– I need to know what happened. What were you doing at the reservoir?

Faint dust particles glittered as she sat up. She pulled a pillow behind her and leaned back, drawing the sheet over her lower body, folding her arms.

– That was a long time ago.

– I know. But . . .

She smoothed the sheet under her hand.

– We went there all the time. Me and Billy and Carl were already there when you and Tim turned up. We had a den, remember?

– What kind of day was it?

– It was hot. Sunny. Much hotter than usual. The water level was right down. They said you could see the school steeple, but you couldn't.

Anthea swung her legs over the side of the bed.

– I'd best get going.

She fastened her bra, pulling it into her flesh under the tulip tattoo where freckles clustered.

– I need to know what happened.

– You know what happened. Tim went into the water and got into trouble. Billy went after him, but it was no use. You know that.

Did he? Tim had always been the best swimmer. He'd been fearless in the water, like a frog, jumping into the deep end at the swimming baths. Putting Pablo to shame.

– I remember that. I don't remember why.

Her head emerged through the top of her tee shirt. She dragged hair from her face.

– Why what?

– What he was doing in the water. Nobody else went in.

– Apart from Billy.

– OK. Apart from Billy.

Anthea was slipping on her sandals and Pablo watched her from the bed.

– What were you doing?

– What was I doing?

– With Carl and Billy?

– Playing. We were just kids, remember? What else was there to do round here? Just . . . playing, larking around, the usual stuff. Carl had some cigarettes.

She shrugged and stood to go.

– It was nearly thirty years ago.

– But why Tim? I don't remember.

She didn't answer but looked back from the doorway.

– I'm sorry, Pablo.

She tightened the belt on her jeans.

– I'll see you tomorrow, if you like. But I've got some things to do first. So, afternoon?

Pablo let her go without answering. Tim was struggling, too far out. Carl had thrown the cigarettes away, as if they might get into trouble for it. They'd disintegrated in the water. And Billy never got to Tim. He'd disappeared under that grey surface, joining the ghosts in the village below.

Pablo had ridden for help. A man had phoned the police and ambulance. *You shouldn't have been playing in the water. What were you doing?* He kept saying it as if Pablo hadn't realized. He'd put Pablo's bicycle in the back of his van and they'd driven back to the reservoir, the scone his wife had given Pablo crumbling in his hand, the weight of dread pressing air from his chest.

It was a police diver who pulled Tim out in the end. Someone had got a message to his father and he was running down the path. Then the frogmen bobbing up and down in wetsuits and goggles. A commotion, then voices shouting. His father crouching down near the water until they were lifting him to the shore. He'd never forgotten the look on his father's face, as if something had sheared away inside him.

They kept asking him: *Why Tim? Why was he in the water?* And Pablo couldn't answer them. Couldn't answer them then and couldn't answer them now.

Pablo carried a stack of old egg boxes to the bin. He switched on the kettle, listening to its snare-drum rattle. He could smell Anthea's sweat on his fingers. He brushed some woodlice from the windowsill. He had to decide what to do with the house.

It was a fine day, with black-headed gulls hanging over the village. His father had always said that they meant rain. Pablo walked to village stores and bought a loaf and a newspaper. When he pushed into the street he almost collided with Billy.

– Now then.

– Hello Billy.

– Pablo, we meet again!

Billy grinned. He had good teeth, strong and white. He stood in his work gear. Boots and army fatigues, a blue baseball cap. He knuckled the stubble on his cheek, handsome in a careless way.

– Seems like it, Billy. How're things? Busy?

– Oh aye, they're busy alright, Pablo, allus busy in my line of work.

– That's good, then.

Pablo made to move past him.

– I hear you're keeping the cottage on.

That was quick.

– Well, I paid the rent, that's all. Is that OK?

Billy looked down at the back of one hand. There was a fresh scratch running across the knuckles.

– So you're staying around?

– I don't know. I've still got a lot to sort out.

Billy waited as one of the old ladies in the village went past, nodding courteously, then leaned in to where Pablo stood, tapping the rolled newspaper against his leg.

– You always were a rum cunt, Pablo.

– What's that supposed to mean?

But Billy was turning away now, pushing the shop door open to buy cigarettes.

– It means owt you want, Pablo. Things allus did wi' you.

Then the door was clanging shut, the little bell jingling. Pablo walked home slowly. Billy went past towing a trailer full of fencing stakes. There was a collie yapping from an old coat in the back of the trailer.

Pablo called Alec as he walked. He could hear someone thumping away on a bass guitar in the background. Alec reminded him that he was supposed to be working in the studio next week. He had six days to get back to Manchester.

His father's grey and white cat was back, brushing against his legs, mewing for food. He pushed it away. He was going to have to start throwing things out. He called Anthea.

– Are you busy tomorrow?'

– Not especially. Just in the morning. Got to be in work. She worked as a receptionist in a medical centre.

– Could you give me a hand? I've ordered a skip.

– You're moving out?

– Dunno. Just paid the rent. Whatever I do, some stuff's got to go.

– OK. I'll see you around half-two?

– That'd be great. Most of it's sorted. It shouldn't take long.

Pablo sat for an hour with the guitar, tuning it to open

E, practising bottleneck. His left hand still felt stiff from the sprain. He remembered the Woolworth's guitar up in the eaves. There was a lot of other stuff up there. School books, off-cuts of carpet and lino, an old folding bed they'd used whenever relatives came to stay. His mother never let anyone use Tim's room. Towards the end she'd begun to sit in there. Then Pablo's father had come home from work and found her in Tim's bed, her clothes folded on a chair, empty bottles of pills laid out neatly with a glass of water.

Pablo spent the afternoon dropping stuff from the roof space down onto the landing below. The chimney had a crick in it, so a hatch had been fitted to sweep above the constriction. The village lay under a ridge and its chimneys sulked in damp weather, laying hanks of smoke over the rooftops. Now everything had a thin layer of soot. He could hear jackdaws on the roof as he worked, a greenish light falling through the skylight.

By four, he'd pretty much emptied the space. He swung down into the box room, filthy with dust, and piled up the rolls of carpet, old travel trunks, exercise books and other debris. There was no point in doing any more until the skip came. He built a bonfire in the garden and burned the school books, stuff he didn't want to be retrieved. Then an old axe haft, a spade handle, some off-cuts of skirting board to stoke the blaze. The flames licked at them like a cat's tongue. Black pages curled and drifted. Afterwards he stank of smoke, like those days on the moor when his father was burning off the heather. He went to Tim's room and took down the glider, then put it back where it had hung for thirty years.

Pablo ran the bath and took a long soak. The smell of fire reminded him of the village on winter days when the rooks rose from the churchyard and smoke coiled over the roofs. He changed into his last clean shirt and jeans, then put his filthy clothes in the washing machine, crumbling congealed powder into the soap drawer. Then he lifted the ring-pull from a can of beer and sat in the ruined deck chair to read the newspaper.

That night Pablo was woken by moonlight shining through the curtains he'd forgotten to close. He woke thinking of the river meadow where they'd played cricket in the old days. There were still the remains of a pavilion and an old iron roller, though the strip was long overgrown and the team was a parade of ghosts in the black and white photographs in the pub.

The moon moved from view, but its light was bright. He heard a noise from the garden. It sounded like someone on the path. Then there was a crash of paint tins he'd piled against the outhouse and a soft curse. He moved to his parents' bedroom to get a better view. He stood for a long time before he saw the outline of someone in the shadows of the building. Whoever it was wore a peaked cap and was watching the house.

In the morning Pablo went to the outhouse and pulled out his father's old pushbike. It had a rusted chain cover and a sunken leather saddle. The gears were stiff and the chain dry. Pablo found some oil. He pumped up the tyres and they held firm. Then he found his father's bicycle clips, fastened up his jeans and took the road out of the village. He hadn't ridden a bike for years. It was a strange sensation, following the hedgerows, changing gear for the hills, rising in the saddle, just as he had when Tim was riding ahead, the sun milled into a thousand shards of light by his spokes. He had to dismount at that first hill with its hairpin bend, just as they had back then, pushing their bikes to the summit, then following the road down to the water.

The hot air balloon was there again, drifting over the valley. Some trees had been felled and there were new saplings in white plastic sheaths. Alder and silver birch had taken over where the ground was boggy. It had been a new frontier when they'd cycled down it that day. And he remembered that the others were already there when they arrived. This morning, the ride took him forty minutes. It'd seemed longer back then. But then memory stretched some things and compressed others. He'd read about that, how time does and doesn't exist. Music was like that, measured by beats and missing beats, by sound and silence.

He laid the bike against a wall in a layby and hung the clips over the handlebars. Then he walked through a mulch of mud and reeds to the same gate that led down through trees to the water. Black-headed gulls circled the woods. The tapping of a woodpecker came from deeper in the trees. Then the scent of pine and larch cones, layers of soft conifer needles decaying underfoot on the path that curved down to the little beach. Season upon season sank underfoot. If you dug deep enough there'd be the detritus of that summer in '76. The past crumbling through your fingers.

He'd never been back, not once. He'd got close to it a few times when he was a teenager, roaming the woods with Carl, but somehow they'd always turned away. Turned back. The beach was smaller than he remembered. Grey water lapped at the pebbles. An orange cartridge case bobbed. A beer bottle. The water must have been much lower back then. A moorhen was circling in the reeds, anxious for its mate. He remembered the tidemark on the beach, a scum of leaves and twigs. Right now, the water was high, lapping at his shoes. There was a red and white lifebelt hung above a warning notice. Useless. Tim was too far out by then, too far to throw the belt. Carl had tried and it bobbed uselessly a few yards from the shore.

Pablo sat on a fallen tree and stared at the water. The woodpecker drilled again, a rapid, dry hammering. A wood pigeon blundered above him. He watched a tree creeper working around the bole of a fir, its curved beak tapping for grubs. There was Tim's face, blue at the lips. He'd left his glasses on the bank on top of his clothes. His father had folded the glasses and pocketed them, picking up the tee shirt when they'd taken Tim away. It looked tiny.

Then all those nights awake in his bedroom with the voices below, his mother weeping, his father's blurred tones. They'd never blamed him, however much they'd wanted to. There'd been times when he wished they had.

When Pablo got back to the bike there were tyre marks next to it where someone had pulled up then driven away, a fresh cigarette butt trodden into the grass. He turned the bike round and rode back down towards home, remembering how he'd sat next to his father in the Land Rover, frozen. Knowing the enormity of what had happened and that it couldn't be changed.

He pumped hard on the pedals, hearing the whirr of the chain, the hiss of the blue balloon with its spike of flame as it drifted back towards the estate. He'd be a speck to them, insignificant, moving down the lanes towards the village they could see and he couldn't.

Back at the cottage he rang Alec to check on things in Manchester. *All good. Sound. No sweat.* He rang off and took stock. He'd almost finished clearing the house and putting things in order. He needed to give Anthea her car back and buy something else now that his was written off. Then he'd have to work out when to let the lease on the cottage lapse. When to let that go. He couldn't decide now. That was to do with the future. What happened next. Or what might happen. He needed to talk to Anthea. He remembered the horse rearing at the windscreen, the way she'd held its head as it lay dying in the road. That glimpse of copper hair through the hedge as she ran towards it.

Pablo made lunch from bits and pieces left over in the fridge, toasting some old bread. He'd need to shop again if he was going to hang on a bit longer. He spent an hour with the guitar, playing over some familiar changes, then tuning it for slide. He loved that ring of glass over steel strings, the way a slight movement of the wrist made them sing. He tried a version of 'Fixin' to Die', humming over its sliding chords. All music was about death or love in the end. Tension and resolution. Making love. Fixing to die.

At two-o'clock he walked onto her driveway. She appeared at the kitchen window first, dressed in a lumberjack shirt that might have been Billy's. Then she came through the door, smiling, showing the little gap in her teeth. It was funny how she was always able to do that. To smile, whatever she was feeling.

– Hi. Are you OK?
– Yep. Don't I look it?
She frowned.
– You don't usually come to the house.
– Come on. I'll drive.
He opened the driver's door.

- Where are we going?

- It's a surprise . . .

- I'd better put some decent shoes one. Hang on.

She was wearing leather flip-flops. A few minutes later she reappeared wearing trainers, locking the kitchen door, a shoulder bag slung. Pablo kissed her. She was all warm skin and freckles and hair that smelled of lemon shampoo.

- Hey! Everyone can see.

She was more than half serious, pushing his arm.

- It can't always be a secret.

Anthea pulled the seat belt across and locked it.

- Meaning?

- You know what I mean.

Pablo started the engine and drove down the valley, back to the reservoir. And then she knew. She knew where they were going and she sat in silence, twisting the strap of her bag. For a moment, as he pulled into the layby and locked on the handbrake, he thought she was going to cry. Instead, she was whispering. OK, OK.

They walked the tangled path through the trees, catching their feet on old brambles, Anthea trailing him through the scent of larch. Her shoulder touched against him as they got to the water's edge and she stumbled. Silver birches and alder. Pools of standing water. Pablo picked up a flat stone and skimmed it, watching it skip seven times before sinking.

- This is the spot.

Her hand was stroking his arm.

- Pablo.

He didn't answer, taking up another stone that died in the water.

- Pablo?

- You know I've got to ask you. You know that's why we're here.

She laid her cardigan on the trunk of a tree and sat down, brushing something from her knees. There were doves cooing softly behind them, music sobbing in their throats.

Night was settling when Pablo got back to the cottage. He pushed the door where it scraped on the tiles. They'd never got into the habit of locking up here. It'd never occurred to them that they had anything to steal or that anyone would think they had. The house had that faint musty scent, a smell of damp plaster and mould, the tang of soot from the chimney.

Now there was another scent. He left the door ajar and moved softly. The living room lay down a short corridor. It wasn't totally dark outside, so a faint light came in through the window that looked out upon the yard. He reached the living room door and waited. His breathing had quickened. He could feel his heart rising against his ribs. His hand found the light switch and eased it on. There was no one there. But there were three cigarette filters in the hearth.

Pablo paused again to listen. The floors in the house creaked under the slightest weight. It was silent except for the croak of a bird beyond the garden, a crow or heron roosting for the night. Pablo snapped the light on in the kitchen. Nothing. Just the sink of unwashed pots he'd left. He closed the front door, lifting it on its worn hinges. Then he took the two-pound weight from his mother's kitchen scales and moved upstairs, step by step. The weight in his hand was cold, deadly. Pablo went through the bedrooms, one by one. His guitar was missing.

He'd bought it in Denver on California St. It was hand-made, small bodied with a deep waist, a slotted headstock, abalone inlays and a biting tone. He'd lived for a time on the east side of town, not far from Union Station. Sometimes he and his Mexican neighbours jammed over a few beers on the steps outside. There was a girl who sang. Henriquetta. You couldn't place a value on that, on an instrument. His parents' bedroom was undisturbed as far as he could see, the bathroom just as he'd left it: towels scattered, toothpaste leaking, curtains blowing into the room.

He found the guitar in Tim's room, laid out on the bed. Someone had put their foot through the soundboard. The strings had done the rest, dragging the splintered wood into itself. It was wreck, a breakage of wood and steel and rasping bronze wire. Pablo sat on the bed and took the shattered pieces in his hands. It was beyond repair. It was senseless. Except there was sense here. There was purpose and logic. Whoever had done it had wanted to destroy, not steal, wound not kill. Whoever had done this had known where to hurt him. They'd known Tim because they'd carried the guitar to his room and stamped it to splinters there. Then those three cigarette ends left in the grate downstairs. Whoever did this had been there, that day.

Pablo took the guitar downstairs and wrapped it in a bin liner. Billy had always had that numb quality, that instinct to damage or destroy. Pablo's mother had bought him a new fountain pen when he started secondary school, a Waterman with a black barrel and gold top. Billy had taken it and put the top in his mouth. When Pablo had protested, he'd bitten down, flattening the metal, laughing. Pablo had tried to straighten it out and then he'd lied to his mother to protect

Billy. Like kids do, covering for each other. He remembered that look on Billy's face. That perverse delight in spoiling something.

Pablo was wearing his leather jacket. He zipped it up. It'd do. He could go back and borrow the car, but that was too much hassle. He'd drunk too much to drive. Fuck it. He'd walk.

The village was silent. Just a few lights on in upstairs rooms, the pub still lit as they cleared up. Pablo took a left over the bridge, climbing the southern flank of the valley. The moon was gliding behind ragged clouds and his eyes adjusted, picking out the dying blossom on the hawthorn, stands of mustard garlic and cow parsley. Two miles down the road he turned left again at a crossroads. Half a mile down that road a right turn took him up the track to Laithwaite Farm.

Limestone gleamed underfoot, scarred where overloaded trailers had touched down. He hadn't been here since he was a kid. The last time had been when his dad had something to deliver to Billy's father from the estate. They'd stood around awkwardly. Billy had left school by then and Pablo was in the sixth form. They were on separate paths. His father had never had much time for Billy's dad. *Rough farmers*, he called them. Not surprising when you looked at the land. Billy didn't keep much stock now.

The ground was marshy, spiked with rushes. There was just enough moonlight to follow the track. Pablo could see the lights of the farmhouse ahead. Billy still ran some sheep. Rough Fell and Blue Faced Leicesters. He had a small herd of Dexters for beef. They'd kept a couple of horses when Anthea lived with him. But they were long gone. The farm was set back into the hill, a low whitewashed building with a barn at one end. The outbuildings were newer: a steel shed for wintering cattle and storage for tractors and combines. The usual stink of cow shit and silage. A kennel with a chained collie inside. It was an old dog, nearly done. It came out to look at Pablo but didn't bark, shaking the chain incuriously, cocking its leg against the wall. It didn't seem like Billy to keep on an old dog, nearly blind.

He stepped into the yard and faced the house. Billy's Range Rover was parked there. He went past the dog to put his hand on the bonnet. The engine was still warm. Pablo knocked on the door, three raps. A light came on in the passageway. Then slurring footsteps on a flag floor. When Billy opened up, Pablo could hear the television. Billy looked past him to the dog, a flicker of annoyance passing over his face. Then that wide, easy grin. He didn't seem surprised to see him.

In the morning Pablo woke to unbearable light. A blade was hacking at his temples, a hot wire pulsing. He ran a bath, swallowed some aspirin, fried some rashers, dropped an egg into the hot fat. He made a pot of tea and drank it, cup by cup, feeling the tannin coat his teeth. He hadn't drunk whisky in years. He drank a long glass of water, cleaned his teeth, then walked to Anthea's, tapping on the window and pointing to the car. She passed the keys through the kitchen window. His face must have told a story, because she didn't ask.

Pablo drove out of the village. He was probably still over the limit, but fuck it. He drove three miles over moorland. Lapwings were rising and diving, a cluster of rocks was silhouetted on the horizon, the house hidden in the fold of a higher valley. When he reached the farm gate, he got out, opened it, drove through then closed it behind himself.

There was an uncut meadow, yellow with buttercups. Half
a dozen Texels grazed the field next to the house. The tractor
was in the yard, a bale of hay speared on its lifting spike. The
dogs at the gate set up a clamour as Pablo got out. No answer
at the house when he knocked or when he opened the door to
call. There were blebs of resin pushing through on the paintwork, a split bin bag spilling beer cans in the yard. When he
pushed his face against the window there was no movement,
just a settee scattered with coats in the living room, a gun
cabinet, a sink full of pots in the kitchen.

Pablo found Carl in the bottom pasture with a lamb
trapped between his knees. He was slipping an elastic ring
over its tail. He pushed the lamb away and it ran back bewil-
deredly to its mother.

– Pab!

His cap was pulled low, his face hard to read. He spat onto
the grass.

Pablo watched the lamb tugging furiously at its mother's
teat.

– I've been expecting you. I thought you might pay a visit.

– Like you did?

A fighter jet was streaking across the valley towards them,
tugging the sound of ripping sky in its wake.

– I'm sorry about the guitar.

Pablo waited, watching glossy grass bend away from them.

– I'll pay for it.

– You couldn't.

– It's not hand-to-mouth, you know.

– It's not the money that matters, Carl, it was a one-off.

– You're a fucking one-off.

– Meaning?

279

- You wouldn't listen, Pab. I tried. You just didn't get it. I'd had a few drinks. I only came round to talk, found the house empty, like ... thought you'd be at Anth's. I waited and fucking waited, then I just lost it.

Carl's hands, big and raw, hanging out of the blue overalls.

- Was it because of Anthea?

Carl turned the elasticator over as if inspecting it. He pulled his cap off and stuffed it in his overalls pocket, glancing at the sky where the sun was trying get out.

- It was because of everything, Pab. Because you wouldn't leave things well alone.

- I've talked to Billy.

- You're lucky he didn't fuckin' belt you. He'd have had cause.

- He told me you used to help my dad, when I wasn't around.

- It wasn't just me, Billy too. After your mother ...

- Why didn't I know this stuff?

Carl laughed, showing gappy side teeth.

- You couldn't wait to get away, that's why. We didn't even blame you, but you were no bloody use to anyone. Couldn't see the wood for the fucking trees.

- I'm sorry if I've made a mess of things with Anthea. I didn't mean to.

- That was never anything to make a mess of. I thought there might have been one time, that's all. I s'pose I was hoping. It's not just that, it's everything else. Come here ...

Carl took his arm and walked him to the high point in the meadow. They could see down the valley to the grey tip of the reservoir. Whitethorn blossom was wasting from the trees in the fields and beside the road.

- I don't know what this is to you, Pab, but this is my life. It's all there is. It's blood, sweat and fucking misery at times. But on days like this I want for nothing.

Carl wiped a finger across his eyebrow.

- Well, nowt but company.

The ragged calling of lambs came to them from the pasture.

- You come back and you're like a ghost. Poking about, knowing nowt. Nothing's ever been enough for you. You couldn't see we tried to look out for you, especially Billy. But you treated him like a twat.

Scraps of wool blew across the grass from moulting sheep. They weren't worth shearing any more.

- Did I dare him, Carl?

Silence. The harsh calling of mothers to their straying lambs.

- Did I dare him?

- Who? Tim?

- Who else?

Carl bit a piece of rough skin from his cuticle, brushed his fingers against his unshaven chin.

- Aye, you dared him. You were showing off to Anthea. She were well ahead of hersel' back then. Billy, me, you. Like a deck o' fuckin' cards.

Carl laughed again, a cynical spurt of breath.

- You dared him, and Billy tried to stop him. Then he went in after him.

- That's what you remember?

- It's what happened, Pab. But we never said a word. None of us. It were keeping quiet that fucked everything up. Mebbe we shouldn't have. Mebbe you should've had to live with it instead of us.

He touched Pablo on the arm. They'd kept quiet and shouldered the silence. For his sake. For his parents' sake.

– Jesus, Carl.

He was dashing the tears from his face. Watching the sun cast cloud shadows across the valley. Two buzzards circling high up, stray specks against the blue.

– You were a kid, Pablo. It's what kids are like. We were all to blame. Or maybe none of us were to blame.

Pablo thought about the horse that day. About the flash of copper hair behind the hedge. The horse dying there in the road. He felt Carl's arm across his shoulder, but pulled away. He nodded at him, the way you nod at an acquaintance.

– Thanks, Carl. That's something I needed to know. I have to get on with it now.

And he was walking back to the car, hearing the air fill with the cries of lambs. He passed a sheep feeding on her knees, another limping away from the hay Carl had put down. He drove down the track too fast, feeling the exhaust catch on the gravel, seeing the tip of the reservoir curl like a ram's horn, then disappear. When he got back to the cottage, a yellow skip had appeared in the driveway.

Pablo went to the window, watching a half moon sail behind clouds. He sat in Tim's room under the half-built glider that hung from the ceiling. He waited for birdsong, which came at four-thirty with the repeating call of a song thrush. He watched the first herons silhouetted against the sunrise, flying east to work the little becks that fed the river. At eight o'clock he left the house to buy bread and a tube of glue. He left the bread untouched on the kitchen table. The next time he noticed it the crust had been nibbled by mice. They left their droppings on the wood his mother had scrubbed and bleached.

He took down the glider from Tim's ceiling and slid a cardboard box out from under the bed. The balsa wood struts, tissue paper cladding and scalpel were there, just as he remembered. Even the front wheels on their wire frame, that still needed fixing. The plane had a three-foot wingspan and it took him half a day to complete the tail section, cutting the wood to shape and gluing it into place. When he'd finished it, he covered it in paper, doped it and hung it back up to dry. It'd need another coat. The dope smelt like pear drops.

On the evening of the third day there was a knock on the door. When he opened it, Anthea was there, her hair tied back, wearing the same green tee shirt she'd worn that first time.

– Pablo?

He couldn't answer and she took his face in her hands.

– Oh, Pablo.

He felt her arms around his neck.

– It wasn't your fault, Pablo, it really wasn't your fault.

And he felt the first sobs heave into his chest like rocks.

– I stink.

She smiled then, touching his chest.

– You do.

When he began to cry, she soothed him with her kisses, wiping his face with her hand, pulling him close.

Anthea ran a bath and helped him to undress. His body was thin. She traced his ribs with her fingers. The hot water closed around him and he wanted to sink under it. His heels squeaked against the enamel as he soaped himself. When he was clean and dry, Anthea led him to the bed. He was floating above his life, above his own self. Floating above the blossom-laden valley, her hands pressing lightly against him. He fell asleep almost at once, his head nested into the curve of her belly.

When Pablo woke, it was dark except for a glimmer of moonlight at the window. The landing light was on and he could hear Anthea downstairs clinking cups. Then she emerged with two mugs of tea and sat on the bed. They didn't speak, but cupped heat in their hands, breathed steam, drank bitter black tea.

– I had to throw the milk away.

Pablo didn't answer. He traced the silver bangle on her arm. He tugged at it, feeling that little shrug of resistance.

– Where are the girls?

– My mum's got them. It was all getting too complicated.

– With Billy? Carl?

She frowned.

– With you. With everyone.

Somehow she'd been the flame that drew them all together.

– You can't blame yourself, Pablo. We were children. All of us. Children do things . . . they explore . . . they don't really know what they're doing. Maybe Tim had his own reasons . . .

– He was just a kid. He looked up to me. I betrayed him, didn't I?

– He wasn't afraid. I remember that. Even when Billy tried to stop him.

– Why didn't I try? Why did I dare him?

– It wasn't just you. It was the game. It was a stupid forfeit, that's all. No one imagined it could go wrong . . .

She was blushing under her freckles, looking away to where

the branches of the damson tree darkened the window.

– That's what kids do, explore . . . don't blame me.

– I'm not.

Show. Then touch. Touch or swim. They'd all done it in the shelter of the trees. All except Tim. He'd thought it was stupid. But he took the forfeit anyway.

– It killed my mother, one way or another.

– Don't you think you've suffered enough for it? However it happened?

– You mean by forgetting? By burying it all? By blaming everyone else?'

She smiled and touched her hair to his face.

– Yes, because you weren't able to be free. None of us were.

When he'd touched a guitar in the early days, that feeling had melted through him as he played. Something guiding his fingers. *Duende*, the Spanish called that. Playing with passion, without thinking. But it meant more than that. It meant a dark thing, a diabolic inspiration. Robert Johnson at the crossroads, making his pact with the devil, fingertips against strings, pulling and bending, flattening and sharpening, those molten blue notes sliding between minor and major. Between sadness, hope, redemption. *Suffering*, the blues players would have said. You suffer to play and that's the deal.

When he woke Anthea was gone. Pablo dressed slowly, feeling under the bed for his shoes. He took his father's bike and cycled down the valley in the moonlight, the glider slung across his back. He stopped at the layby, leaning the bicycle. He took the plane and carried it through the gate, down the path to the little beach. There was the reservoir. Under it houses and farms, walls, chimneys, slates and roof beams falling slowly to rubble. The same water poured purified from taps and standpipes in the city.

Pablo laid the plane at the water's edge. There was a glimmer of dawn. Sun and moon rising and falling as counterweights. Waterfowl were calling. He thought he could make out their shapes on the reservoir, creasing its black foil. He took a run with the plane and hurled out over the lake, expecting it to nose-dive. Instead it began a curling ascent that took it back towards the land, just clearing the stunted birches, then back out over the water, gaining height. It appeared, then faded in the moonlight as its wings tilted, rising towards the faint apparition of hills. Then it was gone.

Chilled air seemed to hum with coming light. A pair of ducks took off in panic, wing tips scuffing the water as they fled. The moon was taken by a drift of cloud, black with silvered edges soldered to the sky. A barn owl called across the lake and another replied. Call and answer, the source of all music. Pablo watched a low planet, a pendant above the wooded ridge of the valley. It would also hang above the city that was rooted by concrete and steel to the curve of the earth, seething with electric light, riven by roads and railways, monumental with the anonymity he'd come to need.

Pablo walked at the water's edge in the scent of larch trees, feeling his boots press into leaf mould and sour mud. He'd been forgiven all along and not known it. He sat for a long time hearing birds awaken the valley. He remembered the horse plunging and falling as its life left it, eyes wild with inner-surging darkness. That was an age ago now, like the flare of copper hair behind hedgerows. He rose stiffly and walked to where he'd left the bicycle. The owl broke from the trees, flying with kissing wing tips. He rode home as the sun strengthened, tinning the hill ridge with molten light.

When Pablo reached the village, the hot air balloon was rising from the fields beside the river. It swayed, collapsing, inflating, righting itself with hoarse exhalations. Then tilting above a needle of flame, drifting over the glittering spillage of the reservoir, above its own drowned reflection. The passengers saw their double rise towards them from an underwater realm, its drenched fire ceasing, then flaring again. The balloon hung undecided in crosswinds. It rose engorged with heat above meadows, moorland, mown hayfields, the green sorrow of the valley. Then it seemed to flee its own shadow, veering towards the wide hush of the sea.

ACKNOWLEDGEMENTS

'WHITETHORN' WAS PUBLISHED in Long Fiction (USA) in 2017; 'Emporium' was runner-up in the Short Fiction competition, 2018, and was published in *Short Fiction in Theory and Practice*; 'Via Urbano' and 'Like Fado' appeared in *Eunoia Review* (Singapore); 'Shoo' appeared in *Dreamcatcher*.

Thanks to Petra McNulty for her close and enthusiastic reading of these stories and for spotting my tics, typos and infelicities.

This book has been typeset by SALT PUBLISHING LIMITED using Neacademia, a font designed by Sergei Egorov for the Rosetta Type Foundry in the Czech Republic. It is manufactured using Creamy 70gsm, a Forest Stewardship Council™ certified paper from Stora Enso's Anjala Mill in Finland. It was printed and bound by Clays Limited in Bungay, Suffolk, Great Britain.

LONDON
GREAT BRITAIN
MMXX